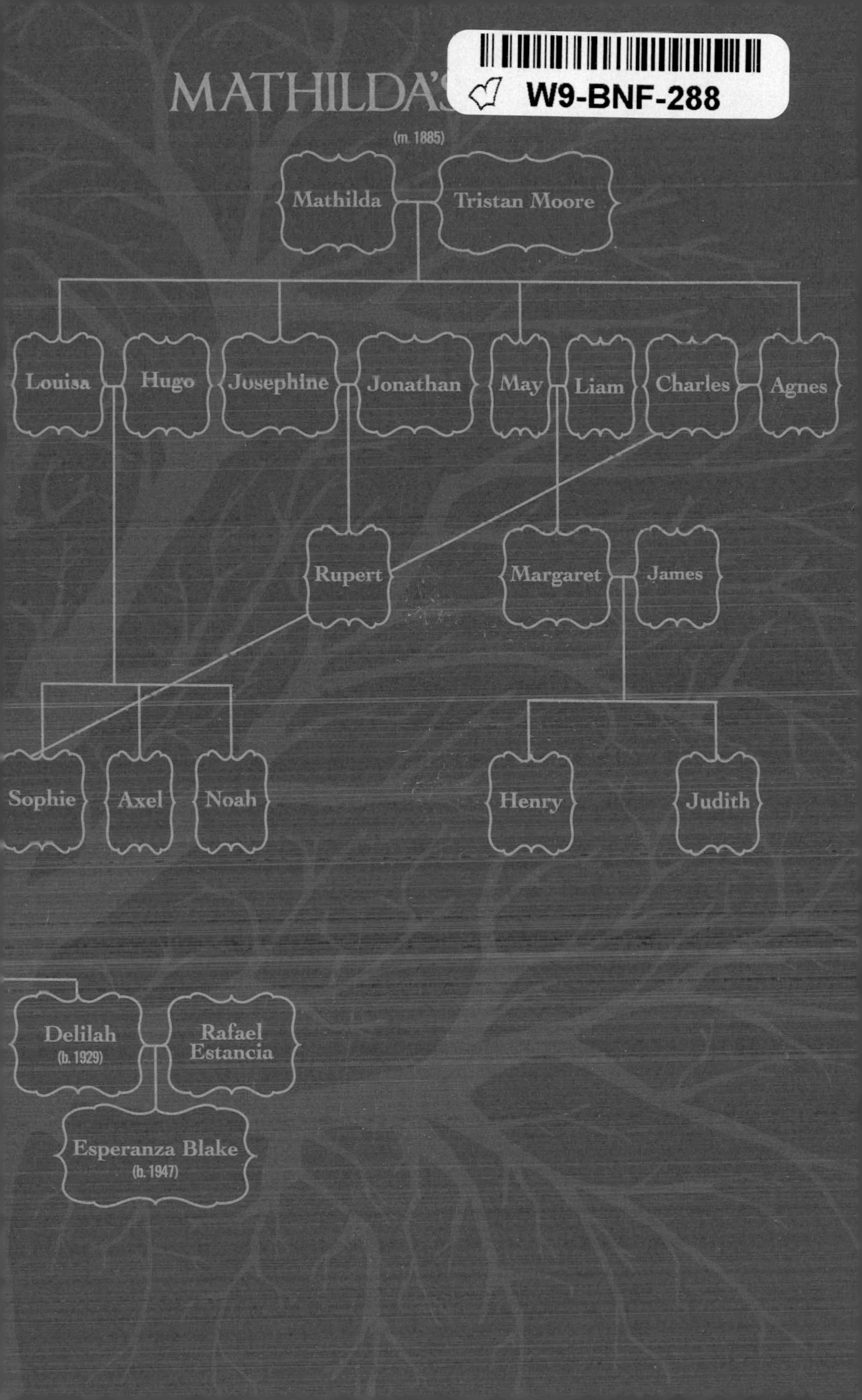
MATHILDA'S
(m. 1885)
Mathilda
Tristan Moore
Louisa
Hugo
Josephine
Jonathan
May
Liam
Charles
Agnes
Rupert
Margaret
James
Sophie
Axel
Noah
Henry
Judith
Delilah
(b. 1929)
Rafael
Estancia
Esperanza Blake
(b. 1947)

FRACTURED PATH

A MIRROR NOVEL

J. C. CERVANTES

HYPERION
Los Angeles New York

For Tom Holland (Yes, you, Spider-Man)
Because JSC said so

First Edition, July 2022
10 9 8 7 6 5 4 3 2 1
FAC-004510-22154

Printed in the United States of America

This book is set in Century Gothic Pro, Citrus Gothic,
Cochin, New Old English/Monotype
Designed by Marci Senders

Library of Congress Cataloging-in-Publication Data
Names: Cervantes, Jennifer, author.
Title: Fractured path / by J. C. Cervantes.
Description: First edition. • Los Angeles ; New York : Hyperion, 2022. • Series: The mirror ; 3 • Audience: Ages 14–18. • Audience: Grades 10–12. • Summary: In San Francisco in 1965, eighteen-year-old Blake Estancia searches the city for magical relics tied to her family's curse, reclaiming her dormant abilities along the way and barely managing to keep a step ahead of a murderous secret society.
Identifiers: LCCN 2021019095 (print) • LCCN 2021019096 (ebook) • ISBN 9781368046404 (hardcover) • ISBN 9781368046411 (trade paperback) • ISBN 9781368075497 (ebk)
Subjects: CYAC: Blessing and cursing—Fiction. • Magic—Fiction. • Ability—Fiction. • Art—Fiction. • Secret societies—Fiction. • Racially mixed people—Fiction. • San Francisco (Calif.)—History—20th century—Fiction. • LCGFT: Novels.
Classification: LCC PZ7.C3198 Fr 2022 (print) • LCC PZ7.C3198 (ebook) • DDC [Fic]—dc23
LC record available at https://lccn.loc.gov/2021019095
LC ebook record available at https://lccn.loc.gov/2021019096

Reinforced binding

Visit www.hyperionteens.com

"While the beasts of prey,

come from caverns deep,

viewed the maid asleep."

—William Blake

Other books in THE MIRROR quartet:

Broken Wish by Julie C. Dao

Shattered Midnight by Dhonielle Clayton

Splintered Magic by L. L. McKinney

TUESDAY, MARCH 9, 1965
SAN FRANCISCO

The rain was a soft pattering outside the classroom window. A smooth, rhythmic dance so unlike the movement of Blake's rebellious paintbrush hovering over the canvas.

The other Mission High students sat in front of their easels, painting and creating. Some were pensive and focused; others were gabbing with their neighbors. Blake, on the other hand, was bleary-eyed and entirely unfocused. She had managed only four hours of sleep last night. Again.

She blamed her sleeplessness on the strange recurrent dream she'd been having for the last couple of weeks. A dream that was hell-bent on consuming her sleep. Maybe her sanity.

Mr. Brown walked around the lively classroom, stopping at each student's desk to offer suggestions, words of encouragement, things like *Excellent layering* or *What does this represent?*

He wore a thick wool sweater with plain gray slacks that were an inch too long. The teacher was young, private, and forever distracted unless he was talking about art.

His hands were clasped behind his back while an overly zealous operatic tune emanated from the little record player in the corner. And while Blake questioned his choice of music, this was her favorite place to be, with its woody aroma of charcoal pencils, the intoxicating scent of oil paint on overused palettes, and the pungent smell of brush cleaner. To her, this classroom smelled of dreams and possibilities.

In the gray afternoon light, Blake stared at her half-finished painting of a girl sleeping in the same willow tree she herself had been dreaming about. She tapped her paintbrush across the palm of her hand as if she could loosen the bristles and force them into creative servitude.

Mr. Brown lifted the needle off the record and clapped his hands loudly to get everyone's attention. "Okay, class, I think we need some quiet, contemplative, centering time."

A few groans rose up from the students. Blake, however, was more than happy to fall under the spell of one of her teacher's meditations, close her tired eyes, and crash.

The rain fell steadily as Mr. Brown flicked off the lights, making the room a cool gray oasis. "Fold your arms on the tables and put your heads down." His voice was soothing, velvety.

Blake relaxed, inhaled, exhaled. Her eyelids grew heavier with every breath. Her limbs weightless.

"Now imagine a calm, quiet, peaceful place," Mr. Brown went on. "Let yourself go."

"Where to?" some smart aleck asked, but Blake was already drifting.

She began to imagine a stroll along the bay when...

A shadowy darkness unfolds.

Mist rises.

The willow stands tall, its branches heavy with the weight of untold secrets. With a resounding crack, the dark trunk splits down the middle...

To reveal a moonlit scene of weeping trees draped across a stately brick home.

An imposing iron gate adorned with the name "Deveraux" creaks open slowly, as if a phantom is urging Blake inside.

On top of one of the gate's spires floats a pale blue heart, transparent as glass. At its center is a drawing of a single brown eye, half-closed eyelid, long lashes. One inch lower, Blake thinks, and the iron will shatter the heart. Another appears on a different spire. And another. Large flakes of snow begin to tumble from the sky, and then a woman's voice comes from inside the house, muffled and distant.

Blake's limbs are heavy. An unseen force is pinning her in place, forcing her to see the heart, forcing her to listen to the whispering wind.

Look. See. Remember.

"Blake?"

Startled by her teacher's voice, Blake shot up, banging her knee on the table. A chorus of laughter rose as the guy next to her, Bruce, said, "Sleeping Beauty not getting enough rest?"

She threw him a glare before Mr. Brown quirked a brow and said, "Seems you're wanted in the office."

Half-awake, Blake rose, adjusted her cardigan, and smoothed her dark hair with all the dignity she could muster.

She took the pink slip from Mr. Brown and headed into the corridor, where she found Olivia, the sixth-period monitor. And her best friend.

"You won't believe what I just heard," Olivia squealed.

Blake, still a little light-headed from her sadly short-lived nap, said, "You called me out of class for gossip?"

"Well, yeah," Olivia said nonchalantly, leading Blake down the hall and out of Mr. Brown's sight. "Because it involves you."

"Me? What did I do?"

Olivia tucked a lock of shiny blond hair behind her ear and rolled her wide-set, curious eyes. She had been Blake's first friend when Blake moved to San Francisco to live with her aunt Remi (her mom's twin sister) and her uncle Cole after her parents' deaths ten years ago. Their friendship was cemented in second grade over snails. Willie Johnson had planted one in Blake's peanut-butter-and-jelly sandwich. Olivia had been the one to save her from the impending doom of crunch and slime. Blake had been the one to clean the poor sticky snail before setting it free on a lush piece of lawn outside. The two girls were inseparable after that.

"You didn't do anything, but—" Olivia stopped, leaned closer. "You know Carl, the fink from PE? Well, he's friends with Richie, and Richie is going to—or at least he *wants* to—ask you to the prom!"

Richie Bannister. The boy with sharp blue eyes and a Beach Boys grin. The truth was that Blake hardly knew him—she had only sort of admired him from the bleachers above the baseball diamond and in-between-class locker stops for the last several months. He was quiet, barely speaking a few hellos, a couple of heys, and a single apology for knocking into her accidentally in the hall.

"Richie?" Blake tried to make room for a plausible explanation. "He doesn't even talk to me. Why would he want—"

"Because you're Blake Estancia. That's why. You're beautiful and talented and mysterious. Boys love mystery."

Blake disagreed with her friend's assessment. She was not mysterious. She was just busy. Still, her heartbeats grew into hard, anxious thumps. "Liv, please tell me you didn't arrange this." It would be just like Olivia to play matchmaker, and the thought of that was both endearing and humiliating.

Olivia released an annoyed sigh. "Of course not." Then she grabbed Blake's hands and smiled. "I thought you'd be happy."

Happy. Terrified. Stunned. Was there a difference?

"I just wasn't expecting . . ." Blake inhaled slowly. "Just give me a minute to absorb it. And you're sure?" Her heart started to race again. "We can trust Carl the fink?"

Liv rolled her eyes. "You think I would even mention it if I wasn't sure?"

Prom.

Blake knew it was a rite of passage, but she had given it little thought. She had been completely consumed by her art since she had applied, at Mr. Brown's urging, for the most competitive internship in the city, with the amazing artist T. K. Grayson. He had been a child prodigy, had been compared to Picasso by the time he was fifteen, had shown his work in premier galleries all over the world by the time he was twenty. Had married and divorced two actresses and three models by the time he was fifty. Not exactly a role model, but getting the opportunity to learn from his artistic brilliance, to be his student, sort of overrode all that.

"Richie would definitely make for a nice prom picture," Blake joked. "But it's only March. The prom is two months away. There's still spring break, exams..."

The internship.

"Maybe he's an early planner. Or maybe he wants to clear the field."

A tingle of excitement ran up Blake's legs. "And you?"

"What about me?"

"Who are you planning on taking?" Blake knew Olivia would have her choice of who to go with.

"I'm keeping my options open. I'm kind of scared that Dean is going to ask me."

"Big, burly football Dean?"

"The one and only."

"Well, he *has* liked you since ninth grade, and he's really nice and—"

"Nice is such a drag. And speaking of." She reached into her pants pocket and pulled out a half-used pencil with teeth marks and a ChapStick. She glanced over her shoulder, then handed Blake the items. "Can you do your thing with these?"

"Who do they belong to?"

"A couple of guys I'm trying to choose between. I figured you might get a glimpse—good or bad—and it would help me decide. So how about it?" She gave Blake a coy smile. "Use your magic for your best friend?"

Magic . . . ha. Blake wouldn't exactly call what she could do *that*. Magic was the thing that always felt out of reach.

When she was a child, she had wanted to possess her mother's power. She would climb her backyard tree, raise her hands like a little sorceress, and try to call the magic to her. To make it bend the branches, incinerate the leaves, blow a gust of wind. Blake's longing grew to a size she couldn't contain—year after year it stretched and pulled, tearing apart her ribs and clawing up her throat. But her mother's magic never came.

And even though magic ran in both sides of her family, the greatest powers seemed to have been held by Blake's grandmother Zora, a woman she knew only through stories. According to Remi, Zora had the astonishing ability to create any disguise she desired and move things with her mind. And then there was her extraordinary music and how she could use it to channel her powers. That was useful magic. Significant magic, which changed the world and your place in it.

Sadly, Blake had *barely-there* magic. The rules were simple: She could sense things when she touched objects—a flash of the sea, or a single note of music, or the taste of lavender tea, or the fleeting feeling of regret. Nothing more. But the true power was in the object's memories, not in Blake. If the object chose to speak to her through any one of her five senses, she could get a small sense of its history, which could be interesting, sure . . . just not earth-shattering.

Blake's inheritance occupied an in-between space—not as powerful as her mother's and grandmother's telekinesis, but not as slight as her aunt Remi's ability, which consisted of sending a waft of air to anyone anywhere in the world. The truth was, Blake was just a bits-and-pieces girl.

"Nothing on the ChapStick," she said, handing it back to Olivia. "And the chewed-up pencil? I saw a puddle of blood."

Liv's eyes went wide with terror. "Seriously?"

Blake laughed. "No, but it sounds more interesting than the soda fizzing I heard."

"Well, that's not at all helpful." Olivia sighed.

"I better get back."

Olivia inched closer, studying Blake's face. "Hold on. . . . You look terrible."

"What happened to beautiful and mysterious?"

Ignoring Blake's attempt at humor, Olivia said, "Beautiful and mysterious but with serious bags. What's the deal?"

"Just some weird dreams lately," she admitted.

"About what?"

Blake thought about the dream she had just had in class, with the spinning heart and an eye at its center.

"Just weird symbols and a tree and stuff."

Olivia pressed her lips into a thin line. "Jung says that dreams are the psyche's way of trying to communicate important stuff, so we should try to interpret them."

"Fine, but right now my psyche better get back to class." Blake started to turn, when Olivia caught her arm.

"I bet I could help you interpret them."

Blake was about to argue.

"Look," Olivia said, "you'd be helping me. I'm supposed to find a research project—"

"Liv. I am not going to be your project. And really," Blake urged, "they're nothing."

Blake headed back to the art room, where everyone was back to work on their freestyle projects. Thirty minutes later, Blake set her unfinished painting in her cubby and packed up her supplies as the bell rang.

"Blake, can you hang back a minute?" Mr. Brown asked.

Shouldering her book bag, she waited for the other students to file out before she headed to Mr. Brown's desk. Maybe he had some kind of technical advice. Maybe he wanted to check in and learn why she had been so distracted today. But instead he handed her an envelope.

The paper was crisp, cool against Blake's fingertips. And then came the image of a shiny white floor just as Mr. Brown said four magical words:

"You got the interview."

Blake was too excited to breathe.

Too excited to notice everyone swarming in the halls, laughing, talking, and shoulder-bumping. Life was bustling all around her, and yet all she could hear was *You got the interview,* and all she could see was her future—getting into the college of her choice, studying art like a real artist. And it had to be a sign that her interview was scheduled for her eighteenth birthday. Finally something *good* would happen this time of year.

Blake had already decided that if she got this far, she would keep it to herself. Mr. Brown had helped her select her best piece as part of the process and had told her that a hundred kids from all over the city had earned the same honor, so Blake wasn't out of the woods yet. She didn't want to tell Olivia, or her aunt and uncle, until she had *real* news to celebrate. Though with her interview scheduled three days from now, she wondered if playing it close to the chest was a good plan after all. She might explode. Or die of nervousness.

It was Tuesday, which meant that Olivia was staying after school for her Psychology Club meeting and Blake was walking home alone—in the storm. She would have called her aunt, but the family only had one car and Cole took it to work at the university most days. If she hadn't been delayed by Mr. Brown, she could have caught a lift from someone. But most everyone had cleared campus. Now she stood at one of the double doors near the front of the school, silently begging the rain to go away.

She was adjusting her book bag on her shoulder when an envelope fell out—not the crisp one that held her future in its cream-colored folds, but another, thinner and a bit more crumpled, although it was clearly addressed with care. Blake snatched it from the floor and traced her fingers along the edge. She tapped her foot impatiently. *If only I had the power to control the weather.*

Just then Blake felt the familiar kiss of two short breezes, warm and pleasant. A message from Remi—her aunt's slight magic. They had developed a code years ago: One breath was to say *I'm thinking about you* or *I love you.* Two breaths meant *Call me,* and three breaths meant *Come home.* Remi's ability didn't extend beyond that; sometimes Blake found herself wishing that she'd insisted they learn Morse code.

Blake was trying to formulate a plan when she heard, "Hey."

She spun around to find Richie, blue-eyed, Beach Boy Richie, standing there in a white T-shirt and jeans, looking so casually attractive it hurt.

"Hey," Blake managed. *Oh God, is he going to ask me to the prom now?* Blake wanted to stop time—she hadn't even thought about what she might say if Richie approached her, and now she felt ambushed. Unprepared. Answerless.

Rubbing the back of his neck, Richie said, "So, um... I was wondering..."

Blake's heart stopped beating. *Yes? No? Can I think about it?*

"Do you live far?"

Oh.

"Over on Oakwood," Blake said.

Richie's eyes darted down the steps and into the road. Then back to Blake. "I could give you a lift... if you want."

Blake opened her mouth to agree, but what came out was "It's only a mile." *Wait! No! I didn't mean that. I meant, yes. Yes, I want a ride.*

Richie narrowed his eyes and watched Blake silently, like he was trying to figure her out. Or maybe he had changed his mind. "That's a long way in this rain."

Blake was nodding. *Why am I nodding? God, he must think I'm a weirdo.* "Okay," she managed, trying so hard to sound indifferent. "Sure."

"I'll bring the car around."

Blake waited anxiously, wondering how the day had turned from exhausting to surprising-slash-amazing so quickly. First the interview and now Richie. She was *definitely* going to explode.

Just then a blue VW Beetle pulled up along the curb. Initially, Blake thought maybe Richie would get out, open the door for her, but he merely waved to her. With her book bag in hand, she ran down the steps and jumped inside the car.

Roy Orbison's "Pretty Woman" was playing on the radio. She was glad for the music because she didn't think she could sit in silence for an entire mile.

"I love this song," Blake said, trying to make conversation.

"He's not as good as the Fab Four."

"Yeah, I like the Beatles, too."

Richie said nothing, just kept his eyes on the road in front of him. The windshield wipers dragged slowly with a groan.

Blake's hopes started to drag, too. *Why did he offer me a ride if he isn't even going to talk to me?* Maybe it was habit, or maybe she just wanted a glimpse into Richie's life, but when he turned to check the left lane, Blake snatched a single silver key that was lying in the open ashtray. Gripping it in her closed palm, she took a deep breath, trying to focus. Nothing. *Hmmm.*

Suddenly the rain halted, and before Orbison had finished crooning, Richie turned down the volume. "You said Oakwood Street?"

"Yeah, hook a right up here and then another right."

Richie drove past multilevel Victorian homes with delicate embellishments that always reminded Blake of dollhouses. Most had been converted into duplexes and smaller-size apartments, but she always imagined the families who must have occupied the beauties before they were split up.

"So, you're an artist," Richie said as he cruised slower than the speed limit.

Blake's cheeks warmed. She didn't feel like an artist, more like an artist-in-waiting. "I want to be."

"What do you paint?"

"How did you know I'm a painter?"

"My buddy Bruce—he's in your art class."

Bruce, the guy everyone knew was only taking art to meet girls. The one who had called her Sleeping Beauty. "Right. Um . . . I paint people. Places . . . stuff that's interesting."

Richie turned onto Oakwood Street.

"It's over there on the left," Blake said, pointing to the Italianate home, wondering how she was going to put the key back in the ashtray without his noticing. In the same moment she felt what could only be described as wet mud inside her shoes. There and gone, like always.

Mud? Really?

Richie cruised up to the house, a dressed-up box with a gently sloping roof, deep overhanging eaves supported by decorative corbels, and windows shaped like ghosts: tall, slim, and rounded on top.

The engine idled. Richie's fingers tapped the white steering wheel.

"Well, thanks for the ride," Blake said, setting the key on her seat surreptitiously.

As she turned to open the door, Richie blurted, "Do you have a date for the prom?"

Not exactly an ask, she thought. If she said no, she might look unappealing. If she said yes, Richie for sure wouldn't ask her.

"Do you?" she countered with a hint of annoyance.

Surprise flashed across Richie's blue eyes. Then, for the first time in the last twenty minutes, he smiled. "I will if you say yes."

Blake tried to still her thundering heart and breathe without it looking like she was practically sucking wind. But she knew that the second she gave her answer he would hear the tremble in her voice. She opened the door. "What's the question?"

Richie hesitated, inhaled slowly. Nodded like he finally got it. "Will you go to the prom with me?"

There was a beat, a moment when Blake wanted to be cool, to not show her ridiculous enthusiasm for a boy she barely knew. But her mouth and heart betrayed her with a resounding, way-too-enthusiastic . . .

"Yes."

Just saying the word sent her pulse skyrocketing. And she was already hopping out of the car as Richie said, "Right on. Um . . . see you tomorrow."

Blake nodded, shut the door, and turned toward the house.

A part of her wanted to look back, to watch him drive away, but her feet kept moving, dancing up the stairs to her house.

As soon as she stepped inside, she set down her book bag on the stairs, hooted, and did a little twirl.

Olivia is going to freak out! After she shouts, Told you so.

I'm going to the prom with Richie Bannister, AND I have an interview with a premier artist. Life is practically perfect.

The sound of music drifted from the backyard, interrupting Blake's solo celebration. She followed the beat through the house. The old Victorian always made her feel like she had wandered into an ancient book in which magic and wonder ruled the ordinary. Chandeliers with ornate medallions adorned the ceilings. A fancy wrought-iron staircase wound up three flights.

The thing was, the old house had leftover magic in its walls and floorboards, its pipes and wires. Blake could feel the energy pulsing just below the surface, as if the place had been built for magic. Or maybe, like dust and memories, Zora had left some behind.

Zora had raised Blake's mom, Delilah, and Remi on Oakwood Street along with their landlady, Rose, who became a surrogate auntie to the twins, and later, a surrogate grandmother to Blake. Blake loved imagining their time there, loved asking Rose and Remi about it. When Blake was little, she would even press her ears to the walls and floors, just to find out if the house would talk to her, would give up any of its secrets, anything at all, but it never did.

Blake opened the back door.

A great beech tree stood at the far end of the yard, wide and beckoning. Evergreen hedges grew in a neat manicured row along the fence, and every other inch of space on either side of the narrow brick pathways was bursting with flowers and foliage of every color: blue, purple, orange, yellow, and red.

It looked like a fairy woodland, tangled and twisted, especially at this time of year, but to Blake's uncle it was a carefully cultivated garden held together by his meticulous hands and loving heart. He even kept a small greenhouse in the far corner so he could grow vegetables and all species of flowers year-round. And underneath all that jungle Blake knew there was an impeccable garden. A world beneath a world, waiting for its chance to bask in the sun.

Blake found her aunt Remi on her knees, digging in the soil as she swayed to the Animals' bluesy rendition of "The House of the Rising Sun." *"There is a house in New Orleans,"* Remi belted out in a husky alto, *"they call the rising sun . . ."*

Blake thought her aunt was beautiful—and it wasn't just her full lips or iridescent skin. It wasn't the fact that her cheekbones were just high enough to look nothing short of royal. It was the way she moved through life—with a rhythmic grace inherited from a long-ago era. Today she wore her hair in a perfectly coiffed, flipped bob, and her dark eyes shone with a spirit that reminded Blake of her mom—which wasn't surprising since the sisters had been twins.

Sometimes Blake thought that Remi had never really recovered from her sister's death. There always seemed to be an emptiness in her, like she was nothing but an old abandoned boat drifting aimlessly out to sea.

There was a rhythm to the house on Oakwood Street. Predictable like the steady beat of a poem or song. And this was why Blake had to take a moment to process the impossibility of what she was seeing. Remi never came into Cole's floral domain. It just wasn't part of their dance.

"What are you doing?" Blake asked, going over to where her aunt was kneeling.

Remi's head snapped up. She turned down the transistor radio she had been listening to. "Oh, don't give me that look. The soil is nice and wet from the rain, and I wanted to surprise Cole and plant some tulip bulbs, so when they bloom, he'll know I was thinking of him." With a huff, she handed Blake the trowel and got to her feet. "And that I support his obsession with something other than me."

That was the thing about Remi. She was both predictable and unpredictable. Soft and hard. Chaos and order.

Studying Blake, Remi said, "I sent you a message to call me. I was worried about the rain, but you're bone-dry. You must not have walked."

"I got a ride."

"A ride."

There was a question waiting there for Blake to answer. "From Richie."

"And what does this Richie drive? Is he a safe driver? Do I know him?"

Blake laughed. "Which question do you want me to answer first?"

"All of the above." Remi's gaze hardened, a mask of controlled worry, but underneath that was the truth: She loved Blake and was terrified of losing her to a "senseless act." Which meant anything outside of Remi's control, even a simple one-mile drive home.

"A Beetle, yes, and no."

Blake was sure Remi was going to launch into her *Be careful* speech. The same one that included an entire two minutes on how bad things happen to good people. But instead she tsked and said, "Do we like this Richie?"

"We?"

Remi narrowed her dark eyes.

By way of a noncommittal answer, Blake sighed and said, "He asked me to the prom. And I said yes."

"So we do like him." Remi's right brow quirked as she set a hand on her hip. "When do I get to meet him? I need to make sure he's worthy of escorting you."

"Aunt Remi! Please don't make this a big deal. Or make him come by early or anything awkward like that. It's just the prom."

"Just the prom. Mm-hmm. Well, you know Cole and I have to approve." A small, knowing grin played on her lips. "Maybe you could invite him to your birthday dinner."

Blake suddenly felt a flip in her stomach—another reminder of the big day and all that came with it. Her birthday had always stood in the shadow of her parents' deaths. They had died this week ten years ago, killed in a car accident on a rainy night while she was curled up in bed asleep.

Ten years, she thought, and she could still remember the smell of her mother's shiny black hair (lemon rinds and chamomile) and the soft tones of her voice that was made to sing lullabies.

She remembered her dad's callused brown hands, the freckle on his right earlobe, and the way he called her Esperanza, her given name, which she had abandoned in favor of her middle name. After her parents died, she didn't want to be called Hope ever again.

To Blake, her birthday had always been a reminder of loss and grief and what might have been. But this year felt different, and she wondered if maybe grief and joy could live in the same space. She'd certainly be busy enough. Besides her interview, she had more plans than she'd had in a long time.

Blake's aunt and uncle had insisted on a special dinner despite her reservations, and Olivia had already organized a beach bash. Blake had begged her friend to just go to the movies, or to hang out and do nothing, but Olivia had just as firmly argued, "It's only a couple of people. Besides, you can't keep hiding from the world."

But Blake didn't feel like she was hiding from the world, more like she was studying its parts and her place in it. She loved Olivia, but what did her friend know about living in Blake's skin? About being wedged between three cultures, two of which carried little weight in the world. Her dad was Mexican. Her mom, half-Black, half-white. Remi always said that Blake got the best of her parents: her mom's chestnut eyes and her dad's wavy locks. It was the spirit of the blended cultures that made Blake "unique."

"I take your silence as—"

"No way," Blake argued, stopping short of *I barely know him* because all that would do was sound alarm bells. "But I promise you can meet him before the prom." Quickly. To avoid an interrogation.

"*Well* before the prom," Remi said. Then: "Oh!" She yanked off her garden gloves. From her pants pocket she produced a gold ring inlaid with tiny rubies. "Picked it up at an estate sale. I should have waited for you, but it was just too irresistible." She handed it to Blake. "Feel anything?"

This was the rhythm of excavation that they had settled into.

When Blake first came to live with her aunt and uncle, she was wandering through an antiques store and stopped in front of a still-life painting of red apples. The moment she touched its framed edge, she said, "Oranges."

"Sweetie," Remi said, "those are apples."

"I know, Aunt Remi, but I taste oranges."

And that's how Blake's role in the family began, through touching and sensing. At her aunt's urging, she had spent the rest of that day using her bits-and-pieces magic while Remi cataloged Blake's responses. Some pieces registered nothing but dusty fingertips. Others were benign or even amusing, like the silver letter opener that made Blake smell tomatoes and vomit. But then they came to a sapphire necklace. "Shadows," Blake said. "I taste shadows. Bad luck." She would never forget the taste, like brushing her teeth with ashes.

After that, Remi rarely bought any "estate" items, unless Blake didn't feel any bad mojo emanating from them. "We don't need anyone else's bad luck," her aunt had said.

The ring was warm from Remi's touch. Blake rubbed her fingers over its edges until she heard the faint traces of piano keys, echoes of a long-ago memory. She handed the piece back to her aunt. "A couple of notes, like a lullaby."

"So what kind of cake do you want?" Remi asked.

"I really don't need one."

"German chocolate it is," Remi said. "I even found a good recipe in the new Betty Crocker."

"You're going to bake?" Blake didn't want to be disrespectful, but Remi was pretty much a disaster in the kitchen.

Remi rolled her eyes, pocketing the ring. "It's a damn shame I didn't inherit the culinary gifts of my ancestors." And the way she said it made Blake think Remi was talking about more than cooking.

Remi searched Blake's eyes intently before they headed inside, where Remi washed the soil from her hands and poured herself a cup of coffee. "I heard you up last night. And the night before. Everything okay?"

"Just some bad dreams."

"Bad dreams?" Cole said, sweeping into the kitchen, where he planted a kiss on Remi's cheek. He was starched from tan cuff to white collar. His hair was tousled, a cumulous puff of sandy blond. Her uncle had a medium build with long legs that might give the illusion that he could be tripped easily. But he was as solid and anchored as an oak tree, without the rough edges.

Blake was glad for the interruption. "Hey, Uncle Cole."

He took a sip of Remi's coffee. "When I saw the rain, I tried to make it home before you got out of school."

"She got a ride," Remi practically purred. "From Richie." She enunciated his name like it was a foreign word.

Cole's eyebrows shot up. "Do we know this Richie?"

"Did you guys go to the same parenting class or something?" Blake teased.

"They're going to *the* prom," Remi said.

Cole nodded slowly, his eyes searching Remi's as if they were speaking a secret language that only they could understand. It probably went something like this: *Our baby is going to the prom, and with a boy. A boy! How did she grow up so fast? We have to meet him, his family, get their entire history.*

Blake was sure Cole would pepper her with questions, but it was Remi who changed the subject. "And what do you mean bad dreams?" She took her coffee cup back from Cole. "Of the nightmare variety or just pesky buggers?"

"Pesky." Blake leaned against the counter and mindlessly reached for her Saint Christopher medal, which hung around her neck on a gold chain. It was a gift from her parents, and she had worn it as long as she could remember.

"Uh-oh. I know that look." Remi was already wagging her finger.

"You always twist Christopher when you're thinking deep thoughts," Cole said.

"Or when you're nervous," Remi put in. "I'm surprised you haven't worn him down to his bones."

"I'm not nervous." *Not about the prom. Not about the internship. Not about my birthday.* But Remi was right. Blake always twisted her necklace when she was nervous. And when doing that didn't make her feel better, she would talk to Rose. Blake paused mid–necklace twirl. If there was anyone she could tell about the interview, it was Rose. She would keep it a secret; she wouldn't judge or fuss or belabor the issue.

She'd also probably forget two minutes after I told her, Blake thought before pivoting.

"Is Rose going to be able to come to the dinner?"

Remi shook her head sadly. "She's just not well enough, sweetie."

"But she did call last night," Cole said. "She said she has something for you."

Blake nodded, feeling more resolute than ever to pay her surrogate grandmother a visit.

She had something for Rose, too.

That night Blake fell into bed, exhausted, replaying the same three words over and over in her mind: *Look. See. Remember.*

The family cat was curled into a tight ginger ball next to her. His purring had a calming effect that slowly pulled Blake into a deep sleep. Where she dreamed . . .

The willow tree is wide, full. In motion.

Tossing its tresses from side to side as if it is trying to shake a memory loose.

Blake wants to know the secrets of the tree. Closer, *she tells herself.* Get closer.

Her steps are slow, burdened. She tries to speak, to talk to the willow, but her lips throb with a dull and old pain. She raises fingers to her mouth. Stitches. Thick, jagged stitches. And her first terrifying thought isn't Why? *Or even* How? *Her first thought is . . .* Who?

Who would sew my mouth shut?!

She falls to her knees before the tree. Pleading silently. Her ribs and spine ache with the weight of a thousand screams.

A deafening crack.

The trunk splits open to reveal . . .

Glossy moonlit water. The reflection of a forest dominated by thick trees with low-hanging branches where pale blue hearts, with the familiar eye, twist in the breeze.

Snow falls from the gloomy sky.

A girl, her face hidden by shadows. She wears a long blue-and-white dress and is beating her fists against some kind of invisible barrier. Light snowflakes whisper through the trees, scattering across the ground.

The girl stops.

As if she knows Blake is here. As if . . .

Blake startled awake. Her hands flew to her mouth. She needed to be sure it was just a bad dream. A bad recurring dream with different details each time she dreamed it. Except for what Blake now called the seeing heart and the tree. Those were always the same.

Massaging her temples, she sat up, clicked on the table lamp, and snatched her journal and pencil from the nightstand. She hated taking notes, but she didn't want to forget what she had seen, heard, felt. And the dreams had already inspired her art in new ways.

Her notes from the Deveraux dream stared back at her as she wrote down the details of tonight's dream: *girl, forest, stitched mouth, the seeing heart.*

Look. See. Remember.

Bleary-eyed, Blake twisted her fingers tighter around the pencil, concentrating. The girl, her face shrouded. Like always.

But she had almost looked at me.

And before Blake knew it, her hand had begun to sketch the heart—simple, round, clean strokes. The eye was just as basic—an almond shape with wispy lashes. "On top of spires," she whispered, "now dangling from branches." *And Deveraux—that was my grandfather's name.* She paused. *But why would I be dreaming of that?*

Blake fell back against her quilted pillow. It was three a.m., la hora de las brujas. Her father used to tell her that the witching hour was the time when the door between this world and the next thins to a fine mist.

"And then what?" she had asked him.

"What do you mean?"

"Who goes through the mist?"

She recalled his wide smile as the Spanish fell from his lips. "Solo las almas más valientes."

But what if I'm not a brave soul? Blake wondered as she swung her legs over the side of the disheveled bed restlessly. Even that wasn't enough to wake the sleeping cat. "Some help you are," she groaned.

Blake's sigh was lost in the sound of a creaking stair outside her bedroom. She went to the door and opened it, expecting to see Remi or Cole, but she saw neither. Instead, she saw a slender blond figure in a long pink robe; the figure held a finger to her lips.

"Liv?" Blake whisper-shouted. "What are you doing here?"

"I got scared."

It wasn't the first time Olivia had used the hidden key on the porch to let herself in. She'd been doing it for years. Blake admired her friend's independence. She lived with her mom after her parents got a divorce a few years ago, an event that had sent her mom back to her job as a nurse and Olivia into endless nights of unsupervised freedom.

"I can't believe you walked the entire block at this hour . . . in your robe," Blake chided.

At once, Olivia waved Blake's logic away like an annoying fly. "People who are running from the bogeyman don't take time to change their clothes, Blake." She sang the words with so much dignity and poise that Blake nearly believed that she had indeed been chased all the way to her doorstep.

"But they have time to put on shoes?"

"I couldn't exactly outrun him barefoot."

Olivia plopped onto the bed and kicked off her sneakers. The cat peeled open a single eye and glared at Olivia for invading its space before letting out a half yawn, half meow and taking his leave.

Blake said, "I called you earlier. . . ."

"Had to run some boring errands with my mom." Olivia's eyes danced around the space as if she were taking inventory: There were layers of half-painted canvases leaning against the walls, half a dozen coffee cans filled with brushes and old rags, and an easel in the corner near the window that was missing two screws. "You ever think about cleaning this place up?" she asked.

"Never," Blake argued. "This is orderly chaos."

Olivia tucked her feet beneath her with a resigned sigh. "So, why'd you call?"

"Well," Blake began, trying to act more coy than usual, "after school, it was raining."

"That isn't exactly news."

Twisting her torso to see Olivia, she smiled. "Is Richie giving me a ride home news?"

Olivia jumped onto her knees, practically shouting, "He asked you!"

"Shh..."

Liv was bouncing on the mattress. "I told you! Give me all the details. Every single one. And do not leave anything out."

After Blake told Olivia everything, including that Richie's car smelled like leather and fresh mint, Liv said, "I have two requests. First, you guys should wear blue, because you'll look amazing, and second, you have to promise me that you won't fall in love with him."

Blake pulled a face. "Liv, I don't even know him, and my only love right now is art."

Liv threw a pillow at her. "And me."

"And you."

With a pout, Olivia groaned. "I can't believe you went to bed without telling me."

"I tried calling twice, and I was tired."

"Blake," Olivia said, "that is not an excuse when something is this fab." Her eyes darted to the journal sitting open on the nightstand. Blake froze. Liv would interrogate her about her subconscious to no end if she saw those notes. Thinking quickly, she diverted Liv's attention. "I think Richie and I should definitely wear yellow to the prom."

Snapping her focus back to Blake, Olivia said, "Remember camp when we were thirteen? I sneaked out with Brad? He was a year older and I didn't tell you. I didn't tell you about my first kiss and you looked at me with so much venom that I swore—*we* swore—on our spit and locks of hair that we would never ever keep anything from each other again."

"I remember," Blake said, confused. "But I did tell you about Richie, so—"

"That's not what I mean," Olivia interrupted. "I mean you've been acting different for the last couple of weeks, and I know this is a really hard time of year for you, but I can't help but wonder if there's something you aren't telling me."

Like the weird dreams? Like the interview that could change my life? Olivia would kill her if she ever found out that Blake had kept it from her. But Blake wasn't sure that there was anything to *say* about the dreams, and she was worried that talking about the interview might jinx it.

And then that voice deep inside whispered, *We did promise on spit and hair.*

"Okay," Blake confessed, "you're right, but you have to promise me you won't be mad at me and that you won't get too excited and that—"

"I Girl Scout swear!"

"So Mr. Brown asked me to enter this art contest," she began, before spilling the rest.

"Blake! That's far-out!" Olivia socked her in the arm. "How could you even think about not telling me? But I'm not even surprised. Of course you got the interview."

Blake fell back onto the bed with a *whoosh* and stared at the ceiling. "That internship could guarantee me entrance to any art school in the country, Liv. But there are a hundred other artists, probably mostly boys, and it's such a long shot but—"

"Look." Liv held up her hand. "You can sketch and paint like no one's business, and anyone who can't see that is blind or crazy or dumb."

Blake loved Olivia's confidence, but facts were facts. Yale had the best art program in the country, but no women were ever admitted. So Blake had directed her dreams to Vassar, but to get in and earn a scholarship required an incredible portfolio and résumé, and a whole lot of luck, which always seemed to be in short supply. She needed to get this internship.

"What are you so afraid of?" Olivia asked more quietly this

time. "I know the world was built by men for men, but talent is talent."

Not in the art world, Blake thought. She could count the women in the field on one hand, and even those weren't regarded as highly as their male contemporaries. A terrible *what-if* rose inside Blake, more demanding than ever: *What if I don't get into any school? What if I fail?*

Then, in a barely-there whisper, she sat up and said, "What if I never get to be an artist?"

Silence stretched between them in the dim room. Olivia blinked as if perplexed by Blake's question. "But . . . you already are an artist."

Blake let the words sink in. Their simplicity and absolute truth. But Blake wanted more—she wanted the career, the experience, the life.

Olivia nudged Blake. "No more secrets. It's the one thing . . ." She cleared her throat. "It's the one thing I can count on. Promise me."

Blake felt the fragments of the strange dreams bubbling up inside her. She wanted to tell Olivia everything, but had no idea what *everything* was. And in the end her mouth betrayed her.

"I promise," she lied. "No more secrets."

4

Wind and gray and ghosts seemed to follow Blake's every step as she made her way down Buchanan Street, weaving between busy pedestrians who looked like they were on a mission.

Blake loved this city—with its sweeping views of the sea, the soaring skyscrapers flanked by Victorian buildings, and the forever hills that always led to something surprising. But more than anything she loved the vibrancy, the colors, and the sounds—the diversity and energy of the place that her mom had loved, too.

As she walked, her mind wandered, landing on a memory.

She was five, maybe six, and her mom had been a flurry of motion, running through the house with her hair dangling in curlers. She finally came to a stop and sat at her vanity, painting her lips and coating her lashes while she hummed a tune Blake couldn't remember. She loved the way her mom rubbed her lips together (three times) before making a pout. Her dark eyes met Blake's in the mirror, and she smiled. And the pink curlers began to unwrap gently from her mother's hair as if invisible hands were tugging them free.

Mama, Blake had said, pointing. *There's a ghost in your hair.*

Her mother turned to her and lifted her onto her lap. *Not ghosts, my love. Magic.*

Do I have magic?

Her mother tugged her into a fierce hug and whispered, *More than you know.*

The absence of her mother had left a vacant space inside Blake—a void she guarded with sharp eyes: *If you don't guard the empty spaces inside you,* her dad had warned, *you must beware what fills them.*

The senior center smelled like bleach and stale things. To most, it was where people went to die. A place of discarded dreams and broken hearts. But to Blake, it was a place of leftover joy. There were lifetimes of memories stored here, but most people didn't sit still long enough to listen.

Walking briskly down the hall, Blake passed the nurses' station, waving to the busy crew that didn't seem to notice her.

Except for Betty. The round, middle-aged nurse fell into step with Blake. "It hasn't been one of Rose's better days."

Blake stopped. Looked at Betty. The woman had thin lips and always overfilled them with bright pink lipstick, which bled into the wrinkles around her mouth.

"What do you mean?"

"She just seems to drift further and further from this world," Betty said, adjusting her white cap. "She's lucky to have you."

I'm the lucky one, Blake thought as she made her way down the corridor to Rose's room.

The eighty-nine-year-old sat with her back to the door, her face tilted toward the ghostly light pressing itself through the window.

"Is that you, Blake?"

Blake smiled. "How do you always know?"

"Because you walk with purpose. Most people don't."

With a light laugh, Blake stepped into the small room that was

Rose's world: There was a twin bed, a vine-patterned sofa, and a rosewood vanity with a cracked mirror. Rose liked having her own belongings near her, said it kept the memories close. The pale walls were lined with a couple of Blake's early sketches: birds with lopsided heads and unrealistic wings that would never carry them into the sky.

They aren't worth framing, Blake had told Rose when Rose still had her sight.

I'll be the judge of that. And when she moved from Oakwood Street to the geriatric center, she told Blake she didn't need to see them to know they were there, keeping her company.

On the nightstand, there was a photo of a young George, the man Rose had been married to for ten years before he was killed in a skiing accident. Blake felt like she knew him because he was at the center of Rose's conversations and stories. There was the time they went on an African safari. The time they rode camels and saw the Egyptian pyramids. The time she fell into the Seine River and he jumped in to save her.

Rose had once remembered all of this with amazing clarity, but now she couldn't remember what day it was, or which president occupied the White House. And lately, her memory had played cruel tricks on her, making her believe that George was still alive, that he was coming for her.

"Did George get my letter?" Rose asked, turning her face and sightless eyes to Blake.

Pulling up a chair, Blake sat next to Rose. "He did."

"Is he going to come for me now?"

Blake's heart sank, but she told herself the lie was a small kindness. "Soon," she said.

"And did he write back?"

"Of course."

Smoothing her short white curls, Rose smiled. "Read his letter to me."

Blake wrapped Rose's shawl tighter around her, then tugged the crumpled envelope out of her pocket—the one she'd been toting around until she could come see the older woman. Blake's eyes flicked to the cracked mirror, where she thought she saw a flash of light, but there was only the reflection of her and Rose. And the lie she held in her hand.

She hesitated, keeping her gaze on the mirror.... *So strange.* Maybe it was just her exhaustion playing tricks on her.

"Blake?"

"Oh, sorry," Blake said, turning back. She pulled off her knitted cap, ran her fingers through her wind-tangled hair, and began reading. "'Dear Rose, I received your letter and am filled with a longing to see you again, too. I will be home soon and, yes, we can venture to see the northern lights. Be patient. We will be together again, my love. Yours truly, George.'"

Patting her sunken cheeks, Rose said, "I should get ready. He likes me in red." She smiled a small smile. "Promise me you'll help me get ready when the time comes?"

Blake placed the letter she had written in Rose's hand and squeezed. "I promise."

"Who's making promises?" Remi announced, flying into the room with a gust of energy.

"Is that you, Remi dear?" Rose asked with a smile.

"None other," Remi said, planting a kiss on Rose's cheek.

Blake felt a twinge of disappointment that her aunt had arrived. She hadn't even gotten to tell Rose about the interview. "I didn't know you were coming," she said.

"I was in the area and knew you'd be here, too."

"I love having my girls here." Rose was beaming. Then her expression clouded over for a split second and Blake knew she was missing her other two "girls," Zora and Delilah.

Remi's gaze caught Blake's and she offered a small grin just as Rose said, "Blake, I have something for you. For your birthday. Go to the top drawer of the nightstand."

"You didn't have to—"

"Shush."

Blake went over and opened the drawer. She found a small framed photo of her mother. Delilah was standing in front of the Golden Gate Bridge with windswept hair. She wore a mischievous grin, her eyes looking beyond the lens.

"I didn't wrap it," Rose said.

"It's beautiful." Blake pressed her fingers to the glass. "I've . . . never seen it before."

"I've been saving it for you. Remi helped me frame it just so." Rose turned her face toward Blake. "I took that photo myself on her eighteenth birthday."

Blake couldn't tear her eyes from her mother's face. From the fraction of an instant caught on camera so long ago. But it was Delilah's gaze that Blake found herself searching. In that moment she wished for a sound, a taste, an image, but there was nothing. "I love it," she said as she returned to sit next to Rose. "Thank you."

Rose patted Blake's leg. "I knew you would."

They sat like that, absorbing the quiet like a summer sun, for several minutes before Rose said, "Did I ever tell you about the day Zora showed up on my doorstep?"

Blake had heard the story a million times and she never grew tired of it and loved it more each time. "It was raining," Blake said.

"Cats and dogs," Remi added as she sat in a chair across from them.

"I had an apartment for rent on the third floor of the house," Rose said. "I called it Pink Paradise because the walls were salmon colored." She closed her eyes as if she could imagine the apartment's every detail. She probably could since she had taken the apartment once Remi and Cole moved into the house. "All my rooms were named," Rose said quietly. "Did you know it was raining cats and dogs that day? I almost didn't answer the knock. And there she was, beautiful, poised, mysterious Zora. All bundled in a yellow coat."

"And she was pregnant," Blake said, trying to imagine how scared Zora must have been, expecting twins and alone in a new city.

"And you made her chamomile tea," Remi put in.

"With three heaps of sugar."

Blake wondered how Rose could remember these fine details of the past but so often lose sight of her present reality. Maybe she was better off, she thought. Living in the bright place of her best memories.

"And she was magic," Blake said, her voice a notch away from a tremble.

"Oh, and her voice. That angel could sing, and there wasn't an instrument she couldn't charm." Rose took several breaths, then: "We had good times, didn't we, Remi?"

Remi nodded. Tears pricked her eyes. "I remember the house being filled with music and dancing." She wiped her cheek and inhaled sharply. "Remember when my mom would work late at the club and you would give me and Delilah cookies for dinner? And Delilah would use her magic to lift the chocolate chips out because she felt sorry for them and didn't want to eat them?"

Blake smiled at the image of chocolate chips floating over her mom's head.

Rose was laughing. "And then Zora would come home all wrapped up in her music from the show, and give us an encore?"

Blake basked in the anecdotes. These family stories were so magical, it was as if the words themselves could sweep them all back to a single moment in time. She found herself hungry for more, leaning into the two women who possessed memories she would never have.

"And she would make up little musicals for us," Remi added with glee, "and give all of us parts, but we were a disaster compared to her brilliance."

"Her magic," Rose uttered.

Eager to take advantage of Rose's rare memory, Blake pressed for more. "Tell me about my mom's magic." *Tell me something Remi hasn't already.*

Remi stiffened. She shot Blake a look, one steeped in a subtext that Blake could only read as her protective mama-bear stance.

Rose's milky eyes circled Blake's face. "Zora threw it all out with the cows." She turned. "Do you know what you need, Blake?" she asked brightly. "A big pair of pants."

And just like that Rose's mind spiraled back into the shadows of make-believe.

Blake stood with a disheartened sigh. "Yeah, well, the world only hands those out to men."

"Eh . . . who needs pants when you have purpose?"

"I wish you would move back home with us," Blake said.

Remi patted Rose's leg. "The house misses you. We miss you."

A pause. Then: "I told George that we shouldn't buy a place with so many stairs." She shook her head. "And I don't want to be fussed over. Besides, I have Zora to look after me. You just missed her."

Blake only nodded. This wasn't the first time that Zora had "visited" Rose. But whenever Blake asked what Zora had to say, Rose always told her the same thing: *She says nothing. Nothing at all.* Blake had wanted to ask, *Then how do you know she's here?* But she didn't want to be disrespectful.

With a yawn, Rose said, "I think I'll have a nap."

A moment later she was asleep in bed, and as Blake watched

her chest rise and fall, she wished she could extract all the bright images locked away in Rose's memory.

Blake sighed and stood, heading over to the vanity drawer where she placed "George's" letter on top of the dozens of real ones that were tied up with a pink ribbon. A terrible guilt gripped her. *It's not wrong,* she told herself, *not if Rose is happy. Right?*

"Are you ready to go?" Remi asked softly.

"I'm going to stay for just a little longer."

Remi gave her a quick squeeze before she headed out.

With a heavy heart, Blake stared down at her mother's photo. *She was my age,* Blake thought. *Filled with a magic I want.*

She traced her fingertips over her mom's image.

And in the next blink the world faded. Then came a tug like being swept underwater. Cold flooded every cell in Blake's body. An image began to take shape. Hazy, shrouded in mist, like a plume of smoke dissipating.

A lake, dappled with pale sunlight.

Across the water, dozens of seeing hearts float.

The silence comes next. Snow drifts from the pale sky. Just like before.

Darkness pulses at the edges of the fading images.

Breathless and shivering, Blake found herself back in Rose's world.

Trying to feed air into her lungs. Trying to make sense of what she had seen. Trying to not split down the middle. As she rushed out of the senior center and into the cold, gloomy light, her mother's voice echoed across her memory: *More magic than you know*.

It was one thing to dream strange images and another thing to see them in what could only be described as a vision.

For the next couple of days Blake alternated between downplaying it—*Maybe I'm just tired and stressed*—to examining the enormity of it—*Is the seeing heart trying to tell me something?* She remembered that her grandfather Phillip had been able to see visions in reflective surfaces. Was that what this was? Some wishful thinking that a piece of his magic was making itself known in her? Blake pushed the thoughts away. She had too much on her plate right now, including her big interview on Saturday.

The days vibrated with a nervousness that put Blake on edge. Even when Richie was walking her to her classes (*Was he always this boring?*), even when Olivia was planning Blake's birthday beach party (*Can we not call it my birthday party?*), even when Mr. Brown was mock-interviewing her for the big day (*My heart is going to burst*).

On her birthday, Blake woke at dawn.

Somewhere deep in the house, wood creaked.

She rolled out of bed and threw on some jeans and a black turtleneck sweater, careful not to wake anyone. With her satchel in hand, she stepped into the chilled morning air.

The westerly wind nipped at her ears as she hurried through the neighborhood in desperate need of calming the butterflies that had taken up residence in her stomach. Her interview would happen in mere hours and she was way too excited to sleep.

When she arrived at Dolores Park a few blocks away, she took in the view of the San Francisco skyline. The early-morning fog wrapped itself around the belly of the city, revealing only the tops of the buildings and the silvery sky in the distance. Ever since Blake was little, she'd sketched best in the first light that pushed out the dark. There was something mystical, serene, primal, and also hungry about this time of day. Like it was always stretching toward something that wasn't there. And then the sun would appear, and the peaceful gray quiet would be swallowed whole.

Tugging the thermos of coffee from her bag, Blake took a long, warm drink, then hoisted herself into the tree, an old oak she had named Fernando when she first began sketching from its thick, steady branches. It was only six years ago, when she had been scaling the beech tree in their yard for fun, that she realized her entire perspective changed when her feet were off the ground. After that, she started looking for other welcoming trees in the city, and soon began to sketch regularly in the safety of Fernando's arms.

Settled in a wide foothold, Blake set the pencil to the page, took a deep breath, and began, allowing her heart to lead her mind and her hands. Some of her best work happened when she slipped into this sort of meditative state.

Slowly, an image began to materialize.

The willow tree—first its long, lithe branches and then its smooth, wide trunk. Wisps of soft and dark and light and angry gray strokes. And then the heart. Dangling from a fine thread like a Christmas ornament.

Blake pressed her lips together, inhaling sharply. She had two choices. She could fight the phantom tree, demanding a presence in this world, or she could see where it took her.

"Fine," she whispered, "let's see what you want to become."

For the next hour, she was lost in a world where she felt most like herself, where she felt connected to a greater whole, to the past and the present and the future all at once. To her, art was an invitation into a world of her own making.

Her hand swept over the thick paper in uninhibited, effortless strokes. Jagged branches, spinning ribbon, dangling hearts. Another iteration of the same willow tree, but this was a sketch with hungry clawlike roots erupting from a pool of water at the base of the trunk. A small, soft-edged girl knelt before it, staring at her reflection. Her face was that of a tan wolf. Blake stared into the wolf's dark eyes before averting her gaze to the seeing hearts. "What are you trying to tell me?" she asked the image as she settled against the branch and closed her burning, tired eyes. For only a moment and then . . .

A gray sky looms overhead.

Mist rises across an ocher meadow.

The willow stands at the center, its branches waving in the wind, beckoning Blake closer. The seeing heart dangles from a fine silver thread.

She takes one step. Two.

She feels the familiar push-pull deep inside her chest.

Look. See. Remember.

The dark trunk splits down the middle. Suddenly the ground drops away and Blake is falling. . . .

Falling . . .

She woke up just as she was heading into free fall. She hit the ground with a painful thud, her sketchbook landing next to her. Gripping her left arm, she thanked the saints it wasn't her painting arm, then curled into a ball and let out a small groan. She glanced up at Fernando, at the place she had tumbled from about seven feet above, and she was grateful she hadn't been any higher.

Carefully, she tried to stretch out her injured arm, but a sharp pain forced her to curl it into her body. After a quick inspection of poking and twisting, she was sure it wasn't broken.

Blake stood, brushed herself off, and leaned against the rough trunk. "You could have caught me," she said.

As she gathered her things and set them in her bag, a sudden ache pulsed deep in her eardrums. She opened and closed her jaw, then shook a finger inside her ear, but the pressure only grew.

Insistent footfalls sounded. Blake turned to find herself alone. Remi had warned her dozens of times not to go to the park at this ungodly hour, but Remi wasn't an artist.

She's going to kill me, Blake thought, hugging her left arm to her body.

A shadow danced at the corner of Blake's vision. She glanced up and saw a moving silhouette, long and lean, behind a palm tree about thirty yards away. The shadow stilled.

And waited.

Heat pulsed in her neck.

Her ears pounded like a beast wanting to break out of its cage. The air vibrated high and hurried as her hand went to St. Christopher.

Her internal voice scared her more than the idea of a stranger hiding behind the tree: *Run.*

Quickly, she took off in the opposite direction. Rhythmic footfalls reverberated behind her. Her heart thrashed wildly as she picked up her pace, gripping a sharp pencil between her fingers just in case.

And when she finally rounded the corner of Oakwood Street she risked a glance over her shoulder. There was no one there.

The pain in her ears subsided as she swept her eyes down the street, searching. For the tenth time this week she questioned herself, what she saw, what she felt, what she heard. Her senses were the one thing that she could always rely on, the one part of her bits-and-pieces magic that grounded her. And now? She wasn't so sure.

"I've told you a million and one times to stop climbing those blasted trees," Remi said as she secured the sling around Blake's arm. "You're lucky it's just a sprain. What were you thinking? You could have hit your head! Been really hurt."

"Do I really have to wear this thing?" Blake groaned. *I'm going to look ridiculous for my interview.* "My birthday party is tonight, and who wants to show up to the beach wearing a dumb sling?"

Remi deadpanned: "Yes, Blake. You do. And if it's not better in a few days, we need to go to the doc's. And please, Blake. For the love of God, promise me you'll keep your feet on the ground."

Blake blew a hair out of her face. "On one condition."

Remi smirked. "You know I don't do conditions."

"But Liv went to so much trouble, and . . ."

"Mm-hmm . . . What is it?"

"Can I get a later curfew tonight?" Eleven p.m. was ungodly for a senior, plus Richie was going to be at the beach party and she wanted to spend some real time with him outside the halls of Mission High. If only to cast out the nagging (unwanted) feeling that he was dull as a doorknob and so much better admired from afar.

Remi stood, sighing. "I'll think about it."

That afternoon, with nerves buzzing, Blake had tried on five different outfits, chosen and discarded more than twenty pieces of art, and battled at least a dozen thoughts of self-doubt. The clock was ticking, so she settled on a simple black pencil skirt and tossed a few of her sketches of the strange tree into her portfolio, because she knew that to make it big, to slay the demons of doubt, she had to be bolder, she had to take risks. At the last moment she included the piece she had begun in the tree earlier. It was unfinished, but there was something about it that called to her, and after all, wasn't art about emotion?

Thirty minutes later she hurried off the bus as the fog rolled in, turning all it touched hazy and gray. Cold Pacific winds crept over the city's steep hills like they were trying to push March on its way.

On the street, buses and cars rolled by. Pedestrians went about their wanderings like windup toys, walking past cafés and storefronts without so much as a nod in Blake's direction.

San Francisco was a thriving city. Always in motion, changing its face, smell, and touch like it was auditioning for a different role every day.

That's how Blake felt, like she was auditioning for her future. And she had approximately six minutes to get there. She readjusted the sling on her sprained arm, and with her portfolio case under her good arm, she raced up the last of the two hills, wishing she had spent more time trying in gym class.

A light drizzle began to fall as Blake climbed the last hill that led to Grayson's mansion in Pacific Heights. Her lungs ached with the cold. Her nose began to run. And her pulse hammered as she climbed the last rise, repeating *I can do this* to the rhythm of her gait.

The gray-shingled redbrick mansion sat atop a peak that on clear days captured a stunning view of the Golden Gate Bridge. But today the thieving fog had other plans.

Blake stumbled onto the columned front porch and knocked on the grand door embellished with carved grapevines and scowling cherubs. A stout, expressionless woman greeted her with "You're late" before trying to close the door in Blake's face.

"Wait!" Blake mindlessly used her sprained arm to block the door, wincing at the sharp pain.

"The letter was clear," the woman said flatly.

Winded, Blake looked at her watch. "I'm . . . only . . . a few minutes late. Please. The bus and . . . traffic." She gestured to her arm, hoping for sympathy. "And it's my birthday."

Blake cringed. Had she really just tried to use her birthday as a reason for the woman to take pity on her?

The sour woman looked unaffected. What did she care about Blake's dreams? She didn't look like she even cared about her own, at least not anymore. Blake stood straighter, wishing she had a free hand to smooth her unkempt hair. She was about to throw her pride at the woman's feet and plead again when the woman grunted, "Follow me."

Blake happily obliged and found herself trailing the woman

through the dim foyer, past a grand staircase that rose from the herringbone-patterned wood floors. Some big-band music played from down the hall as rain began to lash the roof, and for a moment Blake felt like she was in the belly of a great wooden ship heading into a storm.

That is, until she stepped through a set of double doors into an austere and empty windowless room larger than a banquet hall, complete with shiny marble floors, just like she had seen when Mr. Brown had given her the letter.

A gallery, Blake realized as the woman said, "Don't touch anything," before leaving abruptly.

Blake looked around. Brass piano lights illuminated each artwork, doing little to light the rest of the dim space. At the far end a vast gilded mirror that ran from floor to ceiling reflected the room's grandness as well as Blake's crumpled, abject form. She swept a hand over her black pencil skirt and threw her shoulders back as she began to move through the gallery.

In a barely audible whisper, she let the words flutter into the space, trying them out. "Nice to meet you, Mr. Grayson. Thank you for this opportunity. The tree is symbolic of..." Her voice trailed off. She couldn't tell him what the tree was symbolic of because she didn't know. She had been dreaming of the broad, wilting branches and gnarled roots for nearly three weeks, and every time she came to the canvas, this was the image that poured out of her. But she couldn't exactly tell him *that*.

Blake searched for the right thing she could say to Mr. Grayson, the right words to make her stand out.

God, she hated words. They were temporary, invisible things released into the air usually with little thought. But art. That was lasting. That was forever.

Blake crossed the gleaming floors to get a better look at the works displayed uniformly across the walls. Maybe she could impress Mr. Grayson with her knowledge of art. Impressionism? Pointillism? Cubism? There wasn't an ism she didn't know.

From this distance, the most recognizable piece was the silk-screen print of Elizabeth Taylor, a repeated image of the starlet by Andy Warhol, Mr. Pop Art himself.

But the most captivating, by far, was a piece of conceptual art, a rusted shovel hanging on the wall with a card that read: *Shovel: 1. To bury the dead. 2. To unbury the dead.*

So not only is he bad at marriage, he's macabre, Blake thought. *And brilliant,* she reminded herself. *With the key to my future.*

Her hand was reaching toward the splintered handle before she could acknowledge that a rule was about to be broken. Hesitating, Blake peeked over her shoulder. When she saw the coast was clear, she let her fingers graze the rough wood.

A splinter caught the skin of her finger. And then . . . salt. She tasted salt.

"Blake Estancia?"

Jerking her hand back, she spun to find Mr. Grayson, the man who had butchered her name by using a hard *C*. He was long-limbed, looked like he subsisted on crackers and lentil soup, and wore a green wool cardigan with a missing button and baggy brown slacks. Not the kind of man five beautiful women would say yes to.

"Estancia," Blake said. With a soft lilting *C*.

He grumbled and began to fidget with his sweater. "You don't look like a Blake. I thought . . ."

That I was a boy? "My mom was a fan of William Blake. The poet."

"I know who he is." Clearing his throat, Mr. Grayson added, "What's wrong with your arm?"

"Climbing a tree."

He stared blankly.

"For the art," she managed. "I think better when my feet are off the ground, and I like to change perspective."

"Well, let's hope you're a better painter than you are a climber." There was no mirth in his voice as he led her to a narrow table near the back of the room. "Show me what you have."

Blake's fingers squeezed the portfolio case's handle once before she heaved it onto the table. *I climb a lot of trees? Seriously?*

"First, can I just say thank you for this opportunity?" she said. Easy words. Safe words.

Mr. Grayson blinked behind his smudged spectacles. "Is there going to be a second?"

"A second?"

"You said 'first,' which implies there is going to be a 'second,' and I am a busy man. You aren't the only candidate."

Right. Blake rewound her brain, or at least tried to, back to Mr. Brown and their mock interview sessions, but everything was a muddied mess of a memory and now she wished she had paid closer attention to the *real* world and not the dream one.

Awkwardly, Blake unzipped the leather case her aunt Remi had bought for her last year, but it snagged at the halfway mark. All the while Mr. Grayson's pale eyes hovered on her until finally she wiggled it open.

She had painstakingly arranged her pieces from what she considered her best to perhaps her less-inspired works. The first was a bare willow tree with long black branches, stretching upward and outward to an absent sun. The tree's skeletal boughs twisted and bent like aching limbs that couldn't carry the weight of the ghosts that Blake had imagined clinging there. The trunk itself was smooth, free of any details, with the exception of a pair of golden eyes.

Trying to control the trembling that had begun in the soles of her feet and was slowly working its way up her legs, Blake said, "I call this one—"

"This is a tree."

"Well, it's symbolic—"

Mr. Grayson silenced her with a large, pallid hand. "This is nothing like the piece Mr. Brown submitted that got you this interview. That abstract was lively, meaningful." He gazed at the painting the way someone might stare at a white wall. With utter disinterest.

"Yes, but I... I think all good artists take risks and—"

With a huff, Mr. Grayson said, "Allow me." And before Blake could stop him, he began to riffle through her work, all thumbs and smears, as if her paintings and sketches were receipts to file.

Blake's confidence waned. And then Grayson tugged a piece free: the one Blake had sketched that morning of the girl/wolf.

Mr. Grayson leaned in. He smelled of mothballs and old things. The closer he leaned toward the piece, the longer Blake held her breath. Maybe he would appreciate the sketch's irony.

"What do you call this one?"

"I still need to fill in some of it, maybe some shadowing and..."

He leveled her with those pale eyes.

"I call it *The Wolf*," she said. "It's expressionism."

The moment the words left her mouth, Blake wanted to shove them back in.

Mr. Grayson straightened. "I am very familiar with expressionism. But I am not interested in your inner troubles. And even more, I am not interested in personal meaning over technical skill." He tugged off his glasses and began to polish them with the hem of his sweater. "That will be all."

Blake went stiff. "Excuse me?"

"This is a competitive internship, and your work is not suitable for my tastes."

Not. Suitable. Never. Suitable.

"But you haven't seen the others," Blake said, her voice dripping with desperation that made her want to gouge out her own eyes. "I can do other things—"

"Miss Estancia, you seem like a nice girl. Perhaps you should put your efforts into other endeavors."

Other endeavors? "But I want . . ." She lifted her chin. "I am going to be an artist."

His stony face split into a forced smile. "Do yourself a favor. Focus your energies on something more substantial, more realistic for a young woman."

Blake's eyes stung. Her insides burned with anger. His subtext was clear. *Find yourself a nice husband and settle down.* She wanted so badly to give him a piece of her mind, to tell him, *I want to be more than someone's wife*, but what good would it do? She had met people like him before, so closed-minded they didn't recognize the truth anymore. And yet he held the shiny golden key that could unlock her future. She started to argue and then stopped herself, choosing pride over desire.

She began to stuff the pieces back in the case, not caring that they were getting creased with each shove. The words rose up her throat. She shoved them down, one rotten morsel at a time: *You're not exactly an expert on marriage, Mr. Five Strikes.*

Blake jerked the zipper a few notches until it snagged. She hated how her hands quivered so obviously. Mr. Grayson could probably even see the lump forming in her throat. As she swung back around to leave, she dropped the case, sending it spinning across the shiny floors and into the gilded mirror.

"Dear Lord," Mr. Grayson muttered under his breath.

Blake rushed over to seize the portfolio. And as she stood, she caught sight of something in her periphery.

A silvery glimmer reflected in the glass, like a white moth bouncing in and out of streams of sunlight.

A sudden coldness gripped Blake, bone-deep, pinning her in place. Like at Rose's.

"Let's not start with the histrionics." She could hear Grayson's voice, but it was tight like a violin string and so far away.

A hum, rising. Vibrating through her. She shouldn't look.

But the pull was too strong.

Leaning against the wall to catch her breath, she threw her gaze straight into the mirror. Beyond her own reflection a pool of mist swirled across its surface, and then an image took shape.

The broken lines of a dark, misty forest. The tree at the center, its trunk vibrating with a golden light in the shape of a door. A voice whispers from the other side.

"Look. See. Remember."

"Miss Estancia! Do not touch the walls."

The whisper becomes a woman's voice, clear, loud, insistent. "Death approaches."

"Who's going to die?" Blake cried.

Mr. Grayson grunted. "Excuse me?!"

The glass began to ripple like water.

Blake stumbled back.

"Shall I call you a cab, Miss Estancia?" Mr. Grayson asked exasperatedly.

She had no words, couldn't push them up and into the air. A power swirled inside her, both familiar and unfamiliar.

Blake turned to the man now, her bones pulsing with fear and fading memories that were not her own.

There was a cold pause, a moment where everything stopped and whatever had been inside her receded back to wherever it had come from.

Mr. Grayson dropped his glasses to the floor with a soft click. "Please leave, Miss Estancia."

Blake spun and fled out of the gallery, through the foyer, and into the cold, where the sky had already begun to darken.

7

lake careened through the dark, tripping over a raised edge of wet concrete.

She slammed against a wide, beckoning tree with bark so rough it bit into her palm before she dumped the portfolio case onto the ground. She let it sit there so she could breathe. One breath. Two breaths. She could still feel the frantic ball of energy in her chest.

Vast and stretching and slowly waking.

What just happened? What just happened? She turned her mind back to the moment she saw the reflections in the mirror. The voice, a woman's, had risen inside her, sharp and demanding.

Look. See. Remember.

Remember WHAT?

And then there were the words that turned her cold. *Death approaches.*

Blake's fingers went to St. Christopher, tracing the scalloped edges of the medal as she tried to understand the meaning of the vision. Of the heart that kept appearing over and over and over.

Her mind was a flurry of implausibilities, all of which pointed to magic, a magic that felt dark and old. And so impossible before now.

Blake had thought that maybe the image she had seen at Rose's had been a fluke. A moment of stress and high emotion. Now she realized these weren't just images or dreams—they were visions. But were they like her grandpa Phillip's? Or was this something different?

And if I did inherit Phillip's abilities, why are they showing up now?

Remi had always told her: *Magic only appears in the first few years of childhood.*

But what if Remi had been wrong and her mom had been right? What if Blake *did* have more magic in her? What if her magic had just been lying dormant, waiting for the right moment? Waiting to fill the void?

Cars hummed in the distance. Soft moonlight scattered shadows across the road. And Blake had the sudden awareness that she was being watched.

I'm being paranoid, she thought. And yet her pulse thudded high in her throat. She could hear the beat, even taste it. It was inside her and outside her, everywhere and nowhere. This was more than instinct. This was a powerful knowing, like the lines of a sketch she could feel before she pressed the pencil to paper.

Somewhere in the shadows someone was watching. She was sure of it. Blake squeezed her arm around her ribs, eyes scanning.

A honk startled her.

Headlights stole her vision for an overwhelming moment before the long vehicle pulled alongside the curb. She immediately recognized the baby-blue Chrysler.

The driver's door swung open. Uncle Cole got out, waving at Blake. He leaned his right elbow on the roof. Easy, casual.

"What . . . what are you doing here?" Blake asked.

"I found the invitation from Mr. Grayson on your desk." Cole hesitated, then: "I've been circling the block. I thought you might want a ride."

Oh. Blake's head spun. She nodded, trying to clear it, trying to think of what to tell him first.

In the ambient light of a distant street lamp, Cole rubbed his chin, clearly giving her a moment. He wore a gray Rolling Stones T-shirt. Stretched, not starched. Rock-band tees were his uniform for regular life. But in his professional life, where he was a botanist at the university, a respectable member of society, and a servant to capitalism, he wore over-ironed button-ups and slacks, a uniform that was so inappropriate to his personality, Blake sometimes had to do a double take to make sure it was him.

Blake picked up her portfolio and walked over to the car, suddenly grateful she didn't have to keep this secret or even the humiliation to herself. Cole rounded the back bumper and took the case from her.

"I need to talk to you and Remi." Her voice shook with the aftereffects of the ominous vision.

"About the internship?"

"Not exactly."

Blake could read his slack jaw, the softened eyes, the tug of his mouth. "Are you okay?" he asked.

Okay was definitely a relative term in the moment. Okay she didn't get the internship? She would be okay. Okay she had just experienced something terrifying? No. She was not okay.

"Can we just go home?"

Once they were inside the car, Cole said, "Before we leave..." He let his words hover, inviting a response from Blake.

"Yeah?"

"Want me to go in there and teach the guy a lesson?"

"It's not his fault he didn't like my stuff."

"That's not an answer."

Cole was playing around, trying to lighten the mood. The guy wouldn't swat an angry wasp if it landed on his bare arm, stinger poised.

"He's an old man," Blake argued, but she could already feel the satisfaction of Cole's fierce loyalty spreading through her.

"Which means I could absolutely take him."

A small laugh escaped Blake. "His housekeeper might be able to take you."

Cole sighed as he brought the engine to life with a roar. "I thought you would want to know that Remi has already burned two of your birthday cakes and now there's more smoke in the house than a Vegas casino."

"That's a lot of smoke."

"It's a lot of burned cake. You sure you want to go right home?"

Blake nodded. "Does Remi know, too?"

"That you were chosen from more than a hundred students

because you're a talented artist?" He shook his head. "She would want to know, though. You know how much she hates secrets."

"I'd rather not tell her," Blake admitted. Then, with a resigned sigh, she added, "But I need to. I need to tell her about other things . . . and you, too." *That maybe I have more magic than we thought. That it wasn't what I expected.* Not the fear, or the sense of drowning, or the foreboding that came with it.

Death approaches.

Blake tried to wish the words away, but they kept replaying in her mind.

Cole gave her a knowing expression, but he didn't pry. He never did. And Blake loved him for it.

"Huh. I bet his glasses were dirty."

"How'd you know?"

"They'd have to be for him not to choose your work."

Taking two steps at a time, Blake ascended the wooden stairs with Cole right behind her. She threw open the door and rushed through the entry and into the dimly lit living room.

She hadn't thought past this point, what she would say or how she would say it. She just knew she needed to see Remi.

She stood there, catching her breath, and it was as if the world had shrunk down to this moment, a tunnel view of her aunt, alone, sitting at the desk, head bent over a jigsaw puzzle. Cole was nothing more than a faded figure in her periphery, a distant voice repeating her name.

And before Blake could get the words out, her aunt looked up. Their eyes met. Remi's face went slack, and she began to nod as if Blake had asked a question. "Blake?"

"It's happening," Blake said, feeling the rush and weight of the words in her chest. "The magic. I've got *more*."

Blake could tell Remi was processing. Her mouth opened and closed on words she wanted to say, questions she wanted to ask but didn't. She took a breath. Two. "Sit down."

Cole inched into the frame. A newly lit cigarette hung from his fingers as he pulled a side chair up and eased into the thing like it was made of glass. To Blake, he and Remi were like two bookends, holding a treasure trove of knowledge between them.

Blake sat on the blue velvet sofa as Remi's dark brown eyes studied her through a thin haze of smoke. A knowing expression passed over her aunt's face as she settled next to her. "Tell me."

Blake told her aunt and uncle everything—the dreams, the visions, the symbols that had accompanied them . . . that terrifying voice in the last one. "What does it all mean?" she asked. "Who's going to die?" Tears burned her eyes as her stomach clenched.

Cole ran a hand over his sandy hair and exhaled loudly. Remi's brows came together.

Remi's gaze cut to Cole's long enough to convey a message that caused him to nod almost imperceptibly.

Blake stiffened. "What is it?"

Cole drew in a lungful of smoke and blew it into the air in a long stream.

"Remi?" Blake said, tightness pulling at her chest.

"It's time you learned the truth."

Words can be loaded or empty.

They can be flat or sharp, beautiful or painful. They're only words, sounds strung together on the tongue. But it's their meaning that determines whether your world is crashing in around you—*your parents are gone*—or whether your heart will sing—*your art has been chosen for display at the city art show.*

And tonight Aunt Remi's words both terrified Blake and filled in blanks from her life she'd always known were missing.

Remi grabbed Cole's cigarette and took a long drag. The last time Blake had seen her aunt smoke was two years ago, after President Kennedy's assassination.

Remi reached across the space between them and gripped Blake's hand. Her touch was warm and soothing. "Your grandma Zora turned her back on our family's magic. She thought... she believed that it was the source of all of our family's suffering. She had this idea that our family is cursed, something about broken promises. And she thought that the magic was some kind of link to this darkness. She even forbade your mom to use her abilities."

Remi's words landed with force and danger and possibility. *Curse? A link to darkness?* Then, recalling the moments of magic that illuminated her memory, Blake said, "My mom didn't listen, did she?"

A small smile formed on Remi's lips. "She didn't."

Cole said, "Zora thought that if she could vanish the magic, tragedy couldn't find us."

Blake thought about the way tragedy had touched her family, followed it like a shadow. First her grandparents, then her parents. And even Remi and Cole had had their share of sorrow. They had wanted their own children, but it wasn't in the cards. Remi had always told Blake that it was because the good Lord wanted all of her love to be reserved for her, but Blake knew her aunt and uncle would have loved a larger family.

"Do *you* believe we're cursed?" Blake asked, thinking the question seemed ridiculous but necessary.

Remi chewed her bottom lip. "According to my mother, our family has lived under this strange sort of spell of threes."

"What do you mean threes?"

"Two good things always followed by a bad one."

Like getting the interview and Richie asking me to the prom followed by spraining my arm.

"Listen," Remi went on, "our world . . . it has a strange way of making people like us feel cursed, making us feel like we don't belong."

"People like us," Blake said. "Black people. Mexican people." All she had to do was turn on the news to see the way people of color were treated—deplorably, cruelly. There weren't enough negative adjectives to describe the pain and suffering and injustices in this world.

"And you know where that kind of treatment comes from," Remi asked, keeping her voice even. "Fear. Deep dark fear."

Cole's jaw was clenched. "And ignorance," he said.

And darkness, Blake thought.

"But this curse," Blake pressed, "it sounds like it's about more than our society."

Remi threw her gaze to Cole—there was a hidden message there. One that said, *Should we tell her?*

"Aunt Remi," Blake said, speaking quickly. "I need to know everything. I need to understand what's happening. Why I'm getting these visions."

"Let's start at the beginning," Cole suggested. He reached for his cigarette and inhaled sharply as he turned to Blake. Ashes fell onto the table. "Tell us what you were doing right before you had the vision today, and the one at Rose's."

Blake gave her aunt and uncle every detail she could remember. The way Mr. Grayson made her feel small and unworthy. "I was embarrassed, emotional," she said, remembering. "And at Rose's it was more sadness."

"Are there any details of the dreams or visions you haven't mentioned?" Cole asked.

"The gates with Deveraux—"

"That was my father's house in New Orleans," Remi interjected.

"Why would I see his . . . Wait," Blake said. "Does it snow in New Orleans?"

"Rarely." Remi began twisting her fingers. A mask of pain covered her beauty, and Blake could tell she was processing not only the newly arrived magic, but the mystery of the seeing heart. But if anyone could put the pieces together, it was Remi. Her mind was built for puzzles. The question was: *Would she want to?* Blake watched her aunt. She waited. And when Remi said nothing, Blake blurted, "Well?"

"I'm thinking!" Remi snapped. "I'm sorry . . . it's just that magic doesn't come in a neatly wrapped package. Sometimes there is no rhyme or reason for it. No keys. No answers. It just is."

Blake could feel the frustration rising in her chest. She had come to her aunt for a solution. Not meaningless speculation. *It just is?* She took a breath and tried a different direction. "Both visions—at Rose's, then at Grayson's—I got cold and dizzy. Why?"

Remi cast a tender look at Blake. "Magic requires energy, a give-and-take. Your mom used to get tremendous headaches. She often said the magic took more than it gave . . . though as her power grew, the headaches went away."

But there was something other than the cold and the dizziness Blake experienced with each vision. Something she couldn't quite name—a push and pull like there was another power struggling inside her. Something inching toward the void that she wished she could grab hold of.

Remi went on: "My dad could see things in reflective surfaces, but he couldn't control them."

Blake nodded, remembering how she'd also immediately thought about her grandfather Phillip and what she'd always been told about his magic. "Do you think I have his powers?" she asked. "I mean with seeing things in mirrors?"

Remi paced, rubbing her forehead. "Oh, Blake, I wish I knew."

She could see her aunt's hesitation. "Please, Aunt Remi."

Remi's eyes flicked to Cole's before she added, "My dad had a mirror—a special one. It had been in his family for generations, dating back to our ancestors in Germany. . . ."

"Were they cursed, too?" Blake asked.

"I don't know. But the mirror showed the past, present, and future . . . if you asked the right questions, that is."

There was no way to mask the frustration that bubbled up inside Blake. "A curse and a magic mirror? I . . . I don't . . . How come you never told me any of this?" The moment the words left her mouth she knew they sounded like an accusation.

"Your dad," Cole said, his voice turning soft and quiet. "He had asked us . . . that if anything ever happened to him and Delilah, we would protect you from the curse and its tragedies."

Blake struggled to keep her thoughts coherent, logical. "You think the *curse* killed them." She felt like hitting something. *No,* she thought. *People kill. Curses . . .* She let the thought evaporate. She knew nothing of curses or what they did or how they did it.

"No . . . I mean . . . we were trying to forget." Remi's voice took on a pleading tone. "To go on with our lives, and as each day passed without more misfortunes, we felt lucky. Like we had escaped something."

"To dredge it all up . . . to talk about the curse," Cole added, "would have been for nothing, a burden you didn't need to carry."

Blake paused. "So where is the mirror now?" she asked, thinking maybe seeing into the past would give her answers about her parents. Maybe let her relive memories of them.

"No one knows," Cole said.

"My mother was the last person who had it," Remi said. "We think she hid it."

"Why would she hide something that powerful?" Blake's voice rose.

"When your grandfather died, it broke her," Remi said. "Something snapped in her and . . ." Her mouth trembled. "And she grew bitter over the years, and the more bitter she grew, the more she buried the magic. She stopped talking about it."

"Because of the curse?" Blake could hardly bring herself to say the words.

"And because of Phillip," Cole said. Blake had never met her grandfather. He had died in prison before she was born, serving time for a murder he didn't commit. It had always felt like a stain on the family, a dark spot that could never be washed clean.

Cole reached for Remi's hand, squeezing it tight. "We don't have to talk about this right now."

Clearing her throat, Remi said, "We absolutely do. This is important, and as much as my mother wanted the magic to vanish, to spare us more pain, it's here and we have to face it." She shifted her gaze to Blake. "I saw the mirror when I was a child. It was gold with an ornate frame. My mom kept it in the back of her closet in a hatbox and only showed it to us once. I think she wanted to see if your mom or I could use its magic. And when we saw nothing but our own reflections, she never showed it to us again."

Blake asked, "How do you know it was enchanted?"

"One night when I was little," Remi said, "I had a bad dream and slipped down the hall to my mother's room. When I saw her light was on, I started to push the door open, but then I heard her talking like someone was in the room with her, so I peeked through the door's crack. She was sitting at her desk with the mirror held up to her face. I only had a side view, but, Blake..." She paused and pressed her lips together. "There were sparks and flashes of light coming from the mirror. The thing glowed like it was conducting electricity. And she was asking it to show her things."

Blake took a moment to process what Remi was telling her before she launched the next question: "But that still doesn't explain why she would hide it."

Remi cut her a glance. "I don't know. Maybe she hadn't meant to hide it forever. Or maybe it has something to do with creating distance from the magic or . . ."

The curse, Blake thought.

Death approaches.

Blake shuddered.

Cole stood and began to pace. "There were others who knew about the mirror. We don't know how they found out about it, but they sent a letter to Zora before she came to San Francisco demanding that she give it up. Maybe that's who she was hiding it from."

Others. Power. Want.

"But why would anyone want it if it doesn't work for everyone?"

"I have no idea," Remi said with a sigh. "Maybe they knew something we don't—about its origins or powers or . . ." She let her voice trail off.

"What happened to whoever sent the letter?"

Remi gave a small shrug. "As far as I know, my mom never heard from them again."

Blake's mind was spinning. "So you're telling me that our family is probably cursed, Zora hated magic because of this curse, and she hid some enchanted mirror that some bad guys were after. . . ." She took a breath. "And my visions might have something to do with all this?"

"That's about right, honey," Remi said.

Blake averted her gaze to the dying embers of the cigarette in the ashtray while Remi began to pull apart the pieces of her jigsaw puzzle like she didn't have the heart to work on it anymore. "My mother saw something else in the mirror," she said. "She told me and Delilah that she saw a woman who was trapped and . . . her face was shrouded."

"Shrouded?" Blake felt all the muscles in her body tense. She tucked her sprained arm closer to her body. "Like my dream," she muttered. "The lady's face is covered under a hood and no matter how hard I try I can't see her. Do you think"—she hesitated—"it's the same woman?"

Remi shrugged. "Does she talk to you in the dreams?"

"No, but it's like she knows I'm there."

Remi and Cole shared a glance before Remi said, "I found some letters from my parents a long time ago. It seems at one point my mother was fixated on releasing the woman in the mirror. She thought that if she could free her, our family would be whole again, that the curse would be broken."

"Then why didn't Zora release her?"

"Perhaps she tried," Cole put in. He lit another cigarette and resumed a professorial stance. "These images and dreams, as odd and random as they seem, are likely pieces of a greater whole."

"Like the magic is trying to tell me something. Maybe to do what Zora couldn't do? Free the girl, break the curse?"

A layer of silence pressed down on the room.

Blake was the first to speak. "But the visions are more like weird surreal paintings." She thought about her art training. "Like they symbolize something. So the heart with the eye must mean something. Like someone is watching?"

Was that why she'd felt so weird at the park and then outside Grayson's?

"Or your heart needs to be awake?" Remi put in.

There were way too many possibilities. "And . . . my mouth was stitched together. Maybe that means there's a secret or . . ." Frustration mounted and Blake felt like she was just grasping at straws.

Cole uttered something under his breath that Blake didn't catch as Remi stood and began to pace across the worn rug. "The woman that my mother saw was wearing red shoes. Have you ever seen those in your dreams?"

"No, why?"

Remi glanced at Cole.

"Maybe we should show you."

Cole hurried down the hallway, returning a couple of seconds later with a glossy white shoe box cradled under his arm.

He opened the box, showing Blake a pair of flat red shoes lined with fur. They rested on a bed of matching satin and had ribbons sewn onto each side of the heel, so the wearer could tie them around her ankles like a ballerina. "They belonged to Zora," he said.

"They're enchanted," Remi added. "Like the mirror."

"Enchanted?"

Remi said, "They make the wearer silent as a mouse and they leave no footprints." She inhaled sharply. "After your grandmother died, your mom and I found them hidden under the floorboards in her room, along with some letters between my parents." Then, as if anticipating the thought already forming in Blake's mind, she added, "The mirror wasn't there—"

"Or anywhere in this house," Cole put in.

"But why would she keep the shoes here and not the mirror?" Blake asked.

Remi reached for a cigarette, then seemed to change her mind. "The shoes helped keep her off the grid, and it makes sense that she kept them close in case she needed them in a pinch."

Blake turned her attention back to the shoes. She was transfixed by their simple beauty, and even though she had never seen them in her dreams, they looked familiar. It was like staring at a long-lost object you thought you would never see again.

Every thought in Blake's mind retreated to make room for the surging doubt. It was one thing to hear about great magic, to have strange dreams and fragmented visions. It was another thing entirely to hold the magic in your hands.

"Have you worn them?" Blake asked.

"They never fit me."

Blake's skin prickled. Suddenly she felt a hand heavier than

Fate's pressing down on her. She stood and paced in front of the shoe box. "What if my magic is the answer to finding the mirror?"

"Magic does attract magic," Remi conceded. "It's what attracted my parents to each other." Her words floated across the room like a forgotten whisper, and Blake felt something brush the back of her neck, causing her to shudder.

Cole gave Blake a long and steady gaze. "Maybe your power is a magnet, drawing the symbols—and whatever they mean—closer."

"Repeated symbols like the heart always have a message," Remi said.

"It did have a message." Blake groaned. "*Look. See. Remember.* What is that even supposed to mean? And don't you think *look* and *see* are the same thing?"

"Not always," Cole said. "For example, when I am studying a flower species, I am *seeing* it, understanding it. But to *look* at it is to merely acknowledge it exists."

"Kind of like a painting in a museum," Blake said. "Anyone can look at it as they pass by, but only some people will really *see* its meaning?"

"Exactly."

Blake sighed. "Couldn't the magic have given me a clearer message, something I knew what to do with?"

"Magic is often fractured in the hands of those who haven't had proper training," Remi said.

"Well, where am I supposed to get training?" And as soon as the words were out, Blake could see the pain they caused her aunt. Remi's face fell. Blake blurted, "I'm sorry . . . I didn't mean . . ."

"It's all right," Remi said gently. "I wish I were able to teach you."

"So . . . what do we do next?" Cole mused.

Blake didn't want to imagine a life of worry, a life of constantly looking over her shoulder, waiting for the other shoe to drop. And a large part of her was curious—about the mirror and its powers. Maybe it could show her or teach her more about her own magic. What if her magic was a direct link to the mirror? What if it was the answer to her *why*? "We have to find the mirror and help the woman inside," she said. "We have to break this curse."

"Whoa!" Remi held up a hand. "Let's take a beat."

"Can I see those letters from Zora and Phillip?" Blake's mind was already racing ahead.

"I'll have to dig them out of the closet," Remi said. "But, Blake, we need to think this through, come up with a plan. One that is as safe and responsible as possible."

Cole reached out his hand, a bridge between them. "We're going to figure this out—together."

Blake nodded, feeling a surge of confidence that Cole was right. After all, she had *actual magic* trying to tell her something, maybe even trying to help her. Plus, she had the shoes, and Remi would get the letters. Surely, the combination of all three would point her in the right direction. She'd find a way to tap into her new powers and break the family curse. No one was going to die on her watch.

"Okay, we will work together to figure out what your visions mean, to see how it's all connected," Remi started. Blake stood up. *"But,"* Remi continued, "we have to be honest with each other. And, Blake, that also means no unnecessary risks. We'll be with you every step of the way, all right? You'll tell us if you have more visions or if anything seems dangerous or overwhelming or untenable. Promise me you won't do anything foolish."

Blake paused. She thought about the feeling of being watched at the park and her vision at Grayson's, wondering if she should say anything. But she had no hard proof anyone else had actually been there. And if Blake told Remi about it now, it would only worry her, and she might want to call the whole thing off.

Cole's and Remi's expectant eyes fell on Blake.

She looked down at the shoes. "Nothing foolish," she said. "I promise."

"The cake!" Remi shouted as the smell of burning reached the living room.

She ran into the kitchen with Cole right behind her.

After taking a deep breath, Blake drew closer to the shoe box. She kicked off her shoes and began to ease a bare foot into one of the slippers. The fur was soft and warm. But the shoe was too narrow. She couldn't get her foot more than halfway. She plopped onto the sofa and, with her one good arm, tried to shove her foot inside, but the shoe wouldn't budge.

As Blake started to slide her foot out, she felt suddenly disoriented, as though she had stepped outside the present moment. Then she felt a jolt of warmth between her toes that ran up her arch and into her leg. A tremor traveled through her. Blake felt all the blood drain from her face.

And her foot slipped into the shoe.

The satin shoes, smooth as a placid lake, hugged her feet like they were made for her. And then, in half a blink, the slippers transformed. Gone were the fur-lined ballet flats. In their place, a pair of Mary Janes with a rounded toe, a single strap, and a flat, square heel.

"How in the . . . ?"

Blake looked up to find Remi and Cole walking back into the room, staring at her in awe. As if Remi could read her mind, she said, "Their magic adjusts to the wearer." Cole draped his arm around Remi's shoulders and gave her a tight squeeze before kissing her temple and whispering something Blake didn't catch. Then, to Blake, he said with a smile, "Very modern."

Blake's heart pounded in her chest, and for a moment she found it hard to breathe.

The doorbell rang. But no one moved to answer it.

"Blake?" A deep crease formed between Cole's brows. "Are you all right?"

She nodded, feeling a bit off-kilter. Heat and cold rushed through her simultaneously, vying for dominance. And then she was somewhere else. Voices echoed. Light glinted off a body of water. Images spun like a roulette wheel.

There was the taste of warm raspberries. Summer sun. Freezing wind. And tenderness. Turned to fear. Turned to dread. And love. So much love.

Like dainty butterfly feet, all of this touched each of Blake's senses in a simultaneous rapture that stole her breath. And then the sensations were gone, leaving her feeling empty and cold. Blake stared down at the shoes, wondering how many feet they had protected. How many steps had they taken? How many paths had they walked?

An insistent energy buzzed about the room, as if each word, each hope, each longing were bound up together in a swell of *what-ifs*.

A slow stirring worked its way up Blake's legs, through her stomach, and into her chest. And for the first time since she lost her mother, she felt connected to her, by a single shared thread that neither death nor time could break.

She felt invigorated. Yes, the curse was a terrifying realization, and the visions she'd experienced were far from pleasant. But the idea that she had greater magic than she'd ever imagined coursing through her veins, that she could use it to do something *big* and *purposeful*—it was what she had hoped for her entire life.

The doorbell rang a second time, followed by an insistent knock.

Blake's footsteps were silent across the wood floors as she rushed to answer it.

She threw open the door to find Olivia on the porch, looking her up and down. Her friend was decked out in tight black pedal pushers, an adjustable hemp belt detailed with tiny plastic Life Savers candies, and a pale yellow sweater. "What happened to your arm?"

"I fell out of a tree."

"You really need to stop climbing them."

Blake smiled reflexively. "That's not going to happen."

Then Olivia seemed to take in the rest of Blake's appearance. "You're wearing *that*?"

"The party—" Blake whispered.

"You forgot."

"No . . . I . . ."

Remi appeared and placed an arm around Blake's shoulders. "Olivia, is it time already?"

Blake heard their small talk. Their words flying back and forth felt muted, and all of a sudden nothing else mattered. Not the party. Not the time. Not her birthday. Not any of it but the magic.

"Earth to Blake," Olivia scolded. "You in there?"

Snapping out of her trance, Blake nodded, ran upstairs, and changed out of the pencil skirt into a pair of pedal pushers and a flouncy blouse. She was about to kick off the red shoes when she hesitated, realizing she liked the feel of their magic around her feet. Leaving them on, she headed back downstairs, where everyone was standing in the darkened entry, which was lit only by the eighteen flickering candles atop her very lopsided unfrosted birthday cake. Remi balanced its plate carefully.

"You have to make a wish before you leave," Cole said.

With flutters in her stomach, Blake stepped off the last stair, leaned over the cake, closed her eyes, and silently said, *I wish to find the mirror and set the girl free.*

"You didn't call me about Grayflea guy!" Olivia growled the second they were alone in the car. "What happened?"

Blake blinked. The internship dreams dashed, the awful interview—it felt like a lifetime ago now. "I didn't get it."

Olivia was already shaking her head. "He's a buffoon. He doesn't deserve you."

Blake nodded, squeezing her toes inside the shoes. She wanted so badly to tell Olivia *everything* that had happened with Grayson, including the strange vision. But she couldn't think of a good enough place to start. *You know that little thing I can do with objects? Yeah, well, there's more. A lot more.*

Besides, Remi had pulled her aside before she left the house, whispering, "Make sure you keep all of this between us." Then, as if Blake needed clarification, she added, *"In the family."*

Blake wondered how she would ever keep something this big from her best friend. Weird dreams and interview nerves were one thing. But this—

"Blake?" Liv's voice brought her back to the moment. "Aren't you going to agree that he's a buffoon?"

"Right. Yes. And he practically told me to go find a good husband. Can you believe that?"

Olivia barked out a laugh. "Maybe you should send him a copy of *The Feminine Mystique*."

"Humph. He wouldn't understand a word of it."

Olivia sighed. "I'm really sorry, but I promise you that someday he's going to regret it. You're going to be a big deal. Mark my words."

"Thanks for the vote of confidence."

"And when you *do* make it big, can I get invited to all the fancy parties?"

"Liv . . . you and I both know I will *not* be going to fancy parties."

"I said me, Blake. Can I use your invites?"

Blake laughed. "Deal."

Olivia drove like a madwoman, weaving in and out of traffic down Sloat Boulevard while she prattled on about how late they were, and why were there so many traffic lights and bad drivers in the world?

Blake's mind drifted to her grandmother.

A part of her could understand how Zora would blame magic for the tragedies in her life. She had watched her husband go to prison and die there; she had raised her children alone. Awful, yes, but what about the good? Her gift for music. Her daughters. Her friendship with Rose. So many people needed to place blame when something terrible happened. It was their way of trying to understand, of naming the faceless monster under the bed. Sure, there were curses, but didn't that also mean that there was *good* magic that could fight them?

Olivia parked the car along the highway, squeezing between a station wagon and a Beetle. With her hand on the door handle, Blake turned to Olivia, who was putting the finishing touches on her perfectly applied red lipstick. "Only a few people, right?" she asked.

Olivia smiled and hopped out of the car.

Outside, the air was wet and chilled, carrying the faint scent of sweet blossoms from somewhere down the shore. The sky was a dark canvas illuminated by the full moon.

Blake tugged her coat tighter, feeling suddenly itchy and uncomfortable in her own skin. God, she hated being the center of attention. And yet she was walking across the sand, toward a looming crowd near a bonfire, toward the Rolling Stones singing "You Can Make It If You Try."

A few people noticed her and Olivia and shouted, "Happy birthday!"

Heat bloomed across Blake's neck and chest. And as much as she hated parties and wished she could go home and process what she'd learned about her newfound magic, she knew Olivia had done all of it out of love. And she couldn't exactly skip her own birthday party. So she put on her best smile as she cast her gaze across the thirty or so familiar faces, and instantly transported from magic mirrors and curses to real life.

"Isn't it outta sight?" Olivia said, sweeping out a long arm. And before Blake could utter the words that would support the lie, Olivia said, "Look, I know you hate surprises, and crowds, and, well, if you're going to be a famous artist, you need to mingle more. Learn how to walk among the commoners." She began to stroll like an exaggerated ballerina, which only made Blake laugh.

"Or I could just paint."

"To be great, people need to see your art. They need to buy it, and guess what? Your art is an extension of YOU, so you better learn to sell yourself and be charming."

Blake scoffed affectionately. "I *am* charming." She knew Olivia was right, of course, but she hated the idea of selling any part of who she was. It occurred to her that maybe if she had been more charming, Grayson would have given her the internship. On second thought, she knew no amount of charm would have won her the position he had always intended for a boy.

Olivia chirped, "Come on." She squeezed through the smoky, shadowy horde, leading Blake by the hand. A group of guys kept their eyes glued to her as she walked past. And it wasn't because she was the most beautiful girl there. It was some unnamable quality that shifted the energy of any room or place that Olivia occupied. It made Blake think of her mom.

"How do you do that?" Blake asked. "They love you."

"They love the *idea* of me," Olivia said. "And someday, if I'm going to be the world's best lawyer, juries have to love me." She sighed, then added, "People matter, Blake. You have to find your way into their hearts."

An image of the seeing heart immediately came to mind. "Seems kind of manipulative," Blake said.

"Strategic," Olivia countered.

The full moon threw down a sliver of buttery light, illuminating the black sea, as waves formed, crested, and crashed with thundering force. Blake had always loved the ocean. Its endless darkness and mysterious moods. The way it was forever changing yet eternally the same.

A few paces beyond the bonfire, Olivia halted, turning Blake a hundred and eighty degrees. "Don't look now, but Richie is to the left of us, two o'clock. He's with that Santana guy."

"Carlos Santana from bio?"

"That's not even the point," Olivia said exasperatedly. "You should for sure play hard to get. Make Richie come to you."

"You just said to be charming."

"Exactly."

Tugging her coat closer, Blake said, "Can I tell you a secret?" There was at least one confession she could share with her best friend tonight.

"Is that a real question?"

"I wonder if . . . Richie is kind of all show and no go." The thought had been eating away at her, and maybe a small part of her wanted Olivia to sing his praises, to tell her she was crazy, that she wasn't dumb for saying yes to the prom so quickly.

Olivia nodded, pressing her red painted lips together. "I could definitely see that."

Oh.

Blake grimaced. "He's just so boring, Liv. And I touched a key in his car and guess what I sensed?"

"You saw a dagger?"

"No, Liv. Mud. Boring old mud. And now I have to go to the prom with him, and I wish I had thought about more than—"

"Him being a hunk?"

Blake nodded. "And I'm really hoping he's not a drag tonight or maybe shows another side of himself?"

"Like not mud?" When Blake didn't return the laugh, Liv shrugged and added, "Well, like I said, at least you'll have awesome prom pictures."

Blake let out a light laugh and glanced around. "I don't know half these people."

"What does it matter?" Olivia said, tossing a blond strand over her shoulder. "It's great music, a few drinks, laughs."

"So, we can pretend it isn't my birthday party?" Blake asked, wondering if Richie had seen her yet.

"If you lose that coat."

"Not happening. I'm freezing!"

"Beauty and style are painful, dear." Her eyes dropped to Blake's feet. "Dig the shoes, though. New?"

Blake glanced down at her Mary Janes covered in sand and a thrill went through her at the thought of the magic tied to her feet. "A gift."

Olivia smiled, that effervescent warm smile that had made Blake like her instantly in second grade. "Okay, tree climber, did you get a curfew extension?"

"Eleven forty-five."

"Perfect." Olivia gave her a catlike grin. "I admit," she said, scanning the party, "this thing got a little out of control."

"A little?" Blake offered a small laugh. "Well, if the whole lawyer thing doesn't pan out, you can always be a party planner."

Olivia scoffed. "That might be the meanest thing you have ever said to me."

Just then there was a loud commotion up the shore toward the pier. Blake started to walk over, when Olivia tugged her back. "What are you doing?"

"Checking it out." And before Olivia could say another word, Blake rushed down the beach, where she found two guys, one white, one Black, on the ground, all fists and grunts and hate. She recognized both from school but couldn't remember their names.

There was a small group gathered around the fighters, watching, waiting to see who would emerge the victor. It made Blake sick.

"Hey!" Olivia yelled, coming up behind Blake. "Someone stop them!"

But they kept swinging. Blake felt helpless. And then she saw Richie, front and center, watching with captivated eyes and egging the guys on as they pummeled each other. He jumped back when the fighters rolled too close, his expression filled with a sick glee, and in that moment Blake was sure that she was *not* going to the prom with this guy.

Without thinking, she hurried over and began to thrash the guys with her coat and one good arm. "Stop!" she shouted.

The next thing she knew, Dean and another guy Blake had never seen raced over, grabbed hold of the guys' shoulders, and yanked them off each other. An arm jerked out, striking the stranger square on the chin and nearly knocking him down, but he stood his ground. And just when Blake thought he might retaliate, he opened and closed his mouth, rubbing his jaw gingerly.

The fighters' chests heaved up and down like the world had run out of air. Dean had the white guy in a headlock.

"Let them fight!" Richie shouted.

Dean scowled, scanning the crowd. "How about you fight *me*?"

There was silence after that. At least until Olivia shouted, "Get them out of here!" Her words were directed at Dean, who didn't argue, but it was the tall stranger who made the first move. He lowered his head and said a few words under his breath to the Black guy before leading him up the shore. As he passed Blake, she heard him say, "Just go cool off. It's not worth it," in a British accent.

Meanwhile, Dean was shoving the other fighter in the opposite direction and Olivia was trailing them, chewing the white guy out.

Richie came over, more amped up than Blake had ever seen him. "Did you see that?"

"I saw how much you enjoyed it," Blake said, still seething.

"The guy deserved it." Blake didn't need to ask to know Richie meant the Black guy. "He let his eyes wander to the wrong thing," Richie added.

"Thing?"

"Some chick."

Blake was shaking with anger. She knew she should have waited for a better, less emotional moment, but the words came before she could stop them. "I don't think we should go to the prom together."

Richie smirked, half grunted. "You already said yes."

"And now I'm saying no."

"Blake . . ." He took a few steps too close, forcing her to jump back out of his reach. "You already said yes," he repeated.

Blake felt sick to her stomach.

Then the distinctly British voice said, "Everything okay here?"

Startled, Blake snapped her eyes to the stranger who had helped Dean break up the fight. He was holding her coat, which must have been lost in the shuffle.

"Mind your own business," Richie said.

Without thinking, Blake blurted, "This *is* his business."

Richie's blue eyes narrowed hatefully. "You know this guy?"

The stranger looked a couple of years older than Blake. He was lanky, with broad shoulders, and looked like a runner or at the very least an athlete who scored points by being fast. His wavy brown hair was in need of a trim, and his nose was a bit off-center. He was wearing a black sweatshirt with the white words *Royston Town Football Club*. Arms folded over her coat, he switched his weight to a single leg, smirking at Blake like he wanted to hear her answer, too.

Blake hesitated, then realized the Brit could be her out, so she went all in with "He's taking me to the prom instead of you."

The stranger's eyes went wide, and Blake thought he might ruin the ruse, but then his expression relaxed into a knowing smile.

"Looking forward to it."

11

Richie's face went slack. And before he could recover, he took off, muttering, "You're such a bitch."

Blake, seething with anger and adrenaline, turned to the stranger. "Sorry about all that."

"The bloke's an ass," he said. Then, with a smile: "The prom, eh?"

"I didn't really mean . . ."

"I'm Ian, by the way."

"I'm Blake."

"Like the English poet?"

Blake let the surprise wash over her. No one had ever guessed the origin of her name. "How did you know?"

"Oh," Ian said, looking as stunned as she felt, "I was just kidding. You mean you're really named after the poet?"

"Yeah."

"Blake," he repeated. Then, with a snap of his fingers: "You're the birthday girl. Which means I should say happy birthday."

For the first time, Blake noticed his swelling jaw. "Um . . . your jaw looks like a grapefruit. Are you all right?"

"Well, I didn't get beaten by your coat."

Olivia appeared from the shadows just then with a soda can and handed it to Ian. "It's cold. For your face."

Ian took the can and pressed it to his jaw with a wince. "Thanks."

"So, you know Dean?" Olivia asked.

Ian nodded.

"He's British," Blake said to Olivia and instantly regretted the words. Or at least how stupid they sounded. Definitely *not* charming.

"Does the Brit have a name?" Olivia was frowning now. Blake knew that expression. Olivia was getting ready to cross-examine Ian. "Because Dean's had a few brews and doesn't seem to remember it."

"I'm Ian West," he said, extending a hand that Olivia left hanging in midair.

"But why are you here?" she asked.

"Uh . . . I just moved to San Francisco a couple of months ago. . . . Live over in Haight-Ashbury."

"I meant why are you here at this party?"

"Oh, right. I met Dean at the pool, and he told me to check things out."

Blake didn't know if it was his smooth accent or composed stance that softened Olivia, but she went from Doberman to poodle in two point three seconds. "Well, thanks for . . . breaking things up," she said before turning to Blake. "We're going to play volleyball if . . ." She hesitated as her eyes drifted to Blake's arm. "Damn. Okay. We can roast s'mores or something."

"Go have fun," Blake said. "I'm good here."

Surprise registered in Olivia's eyes and she nearly smiled. "Just don't let James Bond here bleed out all over the beach." And then she was gone.

Ian smirked. "She's . . ."

"Not very trusting," Blake said.

"She should be a private investigator."

Blake laughed. "She's going to be a lawyer."

"Even better." With his free hand, Ian tugged a white handkerchief out of his pants pocket and patted his jaw.

Blake considered the fact that she was standing on the shore with a British guy who not only broke up a fight that he didn't have to break up, but who knew William Blake, had gone toe-to-toe with Olivia . . . and he carried a handkerchief? He probably drank tea and quoted Shakespeare, too.

"Do you always carry one of those?" Blake asked.

Ian turned to her. In the dim shadows, his eyes took on a hint of gray, but she was sure they would be hazel in the light of day. "It was my mum's."

Was?

Maybe it was in the way his voice dropped to a near whisper or the way his shoulders softened, but Blake was sure that the handkerchief was simply a memory. Lots of people carried memories in their pockets or wore them around their necks. She traced her fingers over her St. Christopher medal as they stood there in silence watching the sea toss and turn.

Ian added, "She died when I was a kid."

Even though Blake had anticipated the truth, the sincerity of his delivery threw her off-balance. "Oh, I'm sorry." *I know how you feel.*

Blake always thought it was a ridiculous thing to tell people you were sorry when someone died. There had to be better, more meaningful words, but she couldn't think of any.

Ian pocketed the handkerchief, picked up a twisted chunk of driftwood, and threw it into the sea. "This isn't how I thought today was going to go."

"I don't think anyone ever thinks they're going to get clocked in the jaw," Blake said, hoping for lighter conversation.

"Right, because then everyone would stay in bed all day and that's sadly pessimistic," he said. "Am I really bleeding?"

After a quick inspection, Blake said, "It's just a nick."

"And a grapefruit." Ian attempted a smile but grimaced instead.

"So, you've only been here a couple of months?"

"And I've already seen the Golden Gate, the wharf, Chinatown, most of the museums, and Coy Tower."

"Coit."

"Right. And I've braved the cable cars."

He held the can to his face and glanced around like he was expecting someone to emerge from the shadows. "Truth?"

Oh God, was he one of those guys who always needed to get something off his chest? "It depends on whether I'm going to hate it or not."

He looked like he might laugh, a show of appreciation for Blake's humor, but then he pulled it back and said, "Dean likes Olivia, and he asked me to come to this party as backup. He thought the whole

British thing might make him seem worldly and score him some points." Ian's eyes lifted to the full moon, then dropped back to Blake. "I was pretty terrified when she started in on me. Sure I was going to say something I shouldn't. I'm really appalling at secrets."

His confession wasn't exactly a surprise to Blake. Dean had had a crush on Olivia since the ninth grade. "So you don't usually crash parties?"

"Not ever," Ian said resolutely. "But don't tell your friend. Dean would kill me."

"Olivia's my best friend," she said, walking closer to the waves. She remembered what Remi had said about the shoes leaving no footprints, and as the sea retreated, Blake furtively pressed the shoes into the shallow sand. There wasn't a single mark. If it weren't for the adrenaline still coursing through her body, she might have felt like a ghost.

"So you're going to tell her and have my death on your hands?" Ian said, tugging her back to their conversation.

"I already agreed not to let you bleed out," she said with a playful shrug, "so I guess for now your secret is safe with me."

Ian let out a small laugh. "Good. You seem like someone I can trust."

"You just met me."

"You learn a lot about a person in the first few minutes."

"The first time you saw me I was whacking those guys with my coat," Blake reminded him.

"You didn't want to see anyone get hurt," he said, so matter-of-factly that Blake was already nodding her agreement. "So, what happened?" He gestured to her sprained arm.

Blake looked down at the sling, then back to Ian. "I fell out of a tree."

"A tree." There was no question, but Blake sensed a challenge, as if he didn't believe her story. She felt a flicker of annoyance.

She said, "A very tall one."

"Do you climb a lot of trees?"

Blake could barely stop her eyes from rolling. She didn't owe him an explanation, so why, then, was her mouth already moving to give him one? "I'm a painter. I was changing perspectives."

At this, Ian popped the can open but didn't take a drink. "Let me guess," he said, eyeing her intently. "A realist. No, wait. That doesn't seem right. Surrealist."

Blake was momentarily impressed, but he was wrong on both counts. There in the moonlight she decided that if Ian were a painting, he would be muted tones, watercolor, not oil. "Expressionist," she said lightly.

He stared at her expectantly, and rather than make him ask,

she gave him the most basic version she could give: "I don't paint things to look like themselves. More like the way I see them, if that makes sense."

"Right," he said with a knowing look, as if the answer he had been searching for had finally made its way into his mind.

There was a strange, luminous expression on Ian's face. One of triumph? Pride? If Blake had known him better, she was sure she could have decoded the message.

"So you're like Munch," Ian said cheerfully.

A pleasant warmth radiated through Blake. "You know him?"

"Doesn't everyone know that creepy iconic image of the man screaming like his soul is being torn from his body?"

"No," Blake said assuredly, "not everyone knows it."

They headed back toward the party, where the volleyball game was in full swing at the edge of the fire, making Blake wonder if she might have a fun time at the party after all. A glow-in-the-dark ball flew from one side of the net to the other. A few kids were hanging down near the waves while two others were shouting dares to dive in. Empty blankets and towels were strewn about. At the base of a small dune, Ian stopped, reached down toward a striped blanket, and picked up a guitar. And by the way he traced idle fingers over its curved body, as if he were asking its permission to strum the strings, Blake knew it belonged to him.

A shiver thrilled up her back as he began to play a slow melody, one she was sure she had heard before.

"What's that song?" she asked as they wandered closer to an outcrop of rocks that jutted from the sea.

"'Stardust,'" Ian said in a low, almost reverent voice. "First recorded by Hoagy Carmichael and since been remade by greats like Louis Armstrong, John Coltrane, and Nat King Cole."

"You like the oldies." Blake found herself drawing closer.

"I like great music." Ian strummed the sad notes like he was one with the guitar, standing in a grand music hall playing for no one but himself.

Soon Blake was lost in the melody. She became aware of the music's effect on her, how it tugged on a memory in which she danced on her dad's shifting feet while her mom sang the lyrics.

Sometimes I wonder why I spend

The lonely night dreaming of a song

She squeezed her toes inside the red shoes. Then, as thoughts of the day's wonder and magic and enchantments began to drift through her mind, Blake found herself gazing at the moonlit sea. Beyond the waves toward the dark, glassy surface. A thread of light. An image began to materialize, an image she couldn't see from the shore. A familiar cold swept through her like an arctic wind, gripping her. Forcing her to look.

"Blake?"

Ignoring Ian, she ran up the shore to the pier, hoping, praying that whatever was in the sea would wait for her. Once she reached it, she charged to the dock's edge and peered out.

The world fell away, the sound of the waves vanished, and even the wood beneath her feet felt like nothing more than a dream. In that moment, as she searched for the apparition, it felt like an entire lifetime was passing between each heartbeat.

There, across the glossy moonlit water, Blake saw the reflection of what she couldn't see from below: a forest dominated by thick trees with low-hanging branches where seeing hearts, translucent as glass, twisted in the breeze. As if dozens of eyes were watching.

A girl, her face hidden by shadows. She wears a long blue-and-white dress and is beating her fists against some kind of invisible boundary. Light snowflakes whisper through the trees, scattering across the ground.

Across the red shoes on the girl's feet.

Shock waves roll through Blake as she inches to the edge. She wants to reach for the girl, to console her. A sharp gust of wind sweeps across her face, urging her closer. She takes slow steps toward the water. One step. Two.

Three.

"Blake!" Ian threw an arm around Blake's waist, rooting her firmly to the spot. All at once the world returned to her with violent force. Tears pricked her eyes, and she was overcome with what she had been about to do. She had nearly thrown herself off the pier.

"Are you all right?" Ian said, still holding her in his grasp.

Blake was quivering down to her bones, trying to stand upright as confusion and fear vibrated through her body. "I just got a little dizzy." She tugged out of his grip, blinking away the tears.

Ian, shifting his weight uneasily, remained an arm's length away, as if he thought she might attempt to thrust herself into the frantic sea again. "What happened to you?" he asked in a low voice. "You were saying something."

Blake froze. "What do you mean?"

"Words... over and over like a chant. Like..." Blake thought his voice was about to trail off to a faraway place when he added, "Like someone who didn't want to forget something."

"What did I say?"

"'Look, see, remember.' Over and over. You sure you're okay?"

"I'm fine," she said before her gaze returned to the ocean. The girl and the forest and the blue hearts were gone, and all Blake could see was the dark, glossy sea churning...

churning...

churning...

Daring Blake to look beneath the surface.

It was well after midnight, and still Blake couldn't sleep.

She paced her room, taking herself through every moment of the party.

Trying to find a connection, a clue that maybe she had missed among the other visions.

Deveraux. Death approaches. Look. See. Remember. A stitched mouth. The seeing hearts, always watching. And the girl. She had to be the one trapped in the mirror.

There was no doubting that the visions were getting more intense. Tonight's had felt different, more vivid than the others. It had called to her as if it had wanted to be seen, studied, analyzed from every angle.

What are you trying to tell me?

It was Blake's nature to figure things out on her own. When she struggled with a sketch, she relied not on reason but on instinct and intuition to lead her to an answer. Where red could be blue, and rain could be gold, and love could be forever.

With a frustrated sigh, Blake flipped through the crinkled pages of her journal, looking for answers.

The first fifteen pages were filled with notes made with the same pen, all in a frenzied half-asleep cursive that made the letters look like they were hiding from something. Finding a blank page, she now wrote down all the details she knew about the curse, the mirror, and the shoes, trying to find a connection, to make sense of what it all meant. She pressed her pencil to the page to sketch the seeing hearts that twisted from long silk ribbons in the trees, but the moment the lead touched the paper, her hand trembled, unable to create the shapes she could see so clearly in her mind.

From her right shoulder to the tips of her fingers, she felt a strange tingling.

Blake waited a moment, shook out her arm, and tried again.

This time she was able to create a rudimentary version of the heart, but the curves were all wrong.

It was one of the first shapes she'd ever drawn—before a square or a circle. Before she even knew what a heart was. Or what it could do.

But no matter how hard she tried, she couldn't bring what was in her memory to the page.

Maybe I'm in a dream right now, she thought sardonically.

An artist who couldn't create.

Her gaze lifted to the shoes near the foot of her bed. In their original form, they looked to be the exact same as the ones that had been tied to the girl's feet in her visions. The snow-covered ground had only deepened their shade to a bold, deep crimson like fresh blood.

The girl.

Even though Blake knew nothing about her, she felt a strange connection to her. She knew what it was to beat her fists against an invisible boundary. Was the girl an ancestor of hers? Remi had never confirmed who the shoes belonged to before Zora. Which side of the family had they come from? Blake knew so little about any of her heritages. Not Zora's mixed Black and Anglo-European ancestry or Phillip's German roots. Could this girl have made the shoes? Was she their first wearer?

And if the girl had worn these shoes, then maybe . . . The idea burned to life so quickly Blake was afraid it would extinguish itself if she so much as breathed wrong.

She snatched up the shoes, slipped them on, and stretched her toes inside the magic. She fell back against her pillow and took deep, cleansing breaths to relax. *The mystery of it all is just like a blank canvas,* she told herself. *A blank canvas I have to fill. One stroke at a time.*

It wasn't long before she fell asleep. And this time she dreamed.

And she dreamed.

Dark green vines grow across an endless night sky. There is no light, no sparkling stars or majestic moon. Only Blake's ability to see through the shadows to the magnificently strange sculptures that tower at least ten feet above her. She's in a garden of stone gods, angels, and warriors. Each one is naked, so she can see the brute strength in their muscles. They look like sculptures from a museum. David. The Thinker. Aphrodite. Satan.

And as Blake moves, their eyes follow.

A deeper darkness folds in.

"You're here," comes the first whisper.

"Who are you?" Blake's voice is small and quiet.

"Who are you*?" the voice repeats, neither a man's nor a woman's voice. This time from the opposite end of the garden.*

"What do you want?"

Silence.

Blake takes a few trepidatious steps and realizes she is barefoot. Her bare soles tread across frosty grass. Everything feels heightened. Intense. Unpredictable.

A low and steady hum follows closely as she steps through the stone garden, surveying, studying, searching. For what? Clues? Answers? Ghosts?

Finally she comes to a statue so familiar it stops her in her tracks. A young woman, wavy hair, deep-set eyes, her stone arms cut off at the elbows. She peers closer. The statue looks like her. Its chest is split open, and in the center? An orb, spinning slowly on an invisible axis, glowing with a bone-colored light. And on top of it is the pale blue heart. The eye at its center blinks.

Breathless, she reaches for it.

The moment her fingers touch it, a whisper floats overhead: "Find. Find. Find."

Then comes the growl.

Her gaze shoots up into the blanket of darkness.

There is a pair of golden eyes, floating like two flames. Then a face emerges. A wolf.

Bits of snow shiver in the air.

Another growl, and then: "I've been waiting a long time for you."

Blake woke up gasping for air. She understood. She had to *find* the seeing heart somewhere in the real world.

Between second and third periods, Olivia found Blake at her locker, cornering her immediately. "You look like hell."

"I didn't sleep much."

Olivia narrowed her finely lined eyes. There were so many questions there, questions Blake couldn't, wouldn't begin to answer. "Right. So, about Ian."

"What about him?" Blake retrieved her English textbook and closed the locker door.

"He asked for your number. I, of course, didn't give it to him."

"He did?" Blake considered Olivia's words. Her thoughts pulsed with the memory of the way he played the guitar like a centuries-old ghost. She also remembered his intense stare after he saved her from walking off the pier. The cold she'd felt when he let go of her waist. She had wanted to explain to him that she had stepped out of herself, that she hadn't been acting rationally, that the magic had taken hold and wouldn't let go. But she didn't owe him an explanation. Even if he had saved her from herself.

Olivia smirked. "Should I have given your number to him?"

"I mean, he's nice," Blake said, choosing her words carefully because one mention of *cute* would send Olivia into matchmaking mode and Blake had zero time for that.

"Nice?" Olivia smirked. "Did you see those eyes and hear that accent?"

"There's more to life than eyes and accents."

Olivia looked like she was about to argue but changed her mind. "By the way," she offered, "I got you that really pretty blue sweater you wanted at the Emporium for your birthday, and forgot to bring it to the party. I ran out of tape, so I didn't wrap it. I'll bring it by later."

At the same moment, Dean came over, wearing a deep scowl. "Hey, Blake." The guy looked like he wanted to crawl out of his own skin.

"Hi," Blake said.

"Um . . . Ian . . . He wants to ask you a question."

Olivia snorted. "You mean the guy you invited to my party without asking?"

Dean cut his sharp eyes at Olivia. "The guy who helped break up a fight at your party."

"Then he should ask the question himself," Olivia put in. But Dean had hit a nerve. No ordinary person would notice, but Blake did. The quick flash of heat in Olivia's cheeks. The rush of words from her mouth. The way she tilted her head an inch too far to the left.

"You wouldn't give him her number," Dean argued.

Olivia started to frown, but then her expression relaxed. "Touché."

Dean scanned the crowded hall like he couldn't believe he'd been chosen for this errand. "So, do you want to see him or not?"

Blake gave him a quizzical look. "Is that his question?"

Olivia was already nodding. "We'll meet you guys at Whiz Burgers Friday."

"We will?" Blake gawked at Olivia.

"Meet us at seven p.m.," Olivia said to Dean, ignoring Blake.

"Meet *us*?" Dean grunted.

"Blake's not going alone," Olivia argued, resting her hand on her hip. "And I never really thanked you for breaking up the fight at my party, so I should buy you a milk shake or something."

Big, brawny Dean—correction, big, brawny, terrified-looking Dean—said, "I'm allergic to milk."

Olivia waved her hand nonchalantly. "You're missing the point, Sixty-Five."

Dean glanced at Blake, clueless. She wasn't sure if he was confused about the nickname or Olivia's point. "It's your football number," she explained, wanting to strangle Olivia as she sauntered away, swinging her straw bag by its shiny handle.

On her way to English, Blake was stopped in the corridor by Mr. Brown. He glanced down at her arm. "What happened?"

"Long story."

Mr. Brown looked like he might ask another question but then seemed to think better of it. "Listen, I got a call from Mr. Grayson this morning," he began. "I'm sorry, Blake."

Blake hardened her armor and forced a smile. "Rejection's part of the gig, right?"

"Right. But it doesn't matter, because I have a wonderful new opportunity for you," he said as he escorted her down the crowded corridor. Blake cringed. She had heard those exact words before when he told her about the Grayson contest.

They weaved between throngs of students, him raising his voice to be heard over the near-end-of-day chatter.

"Her name is Ms. Ivanov," he said. "She just opened a new gallery. Mostly Russian art, but she wants three students for an up-and-coming art section for the gallery. It's a one-time showing for some fundraiser. She's extremely well connected in the art world. This could be wonderful exposure."

Three? Blake's heart leaped from side to side, despite herself. She liked those numbers. "What do I have to do?" she asked, stopping just outside her English class.

Mr. Brown grinned as he reached into the chest pocket of his blazer, retrieved a white business card, and handed it to her. It was made of fine linen stock, which told Blake that Ms. Ivanov didn't cut corners. On the front, she found the address, and on the back, a handwritten date and time. It wasn't lost on her that Ms. Ivanov's name wasn't on the card. Only *Ivanov Gallery*.

"That's your appointment, ten a.m.," Mr. Brown said, pointing at the card. Then, with a chuckle, he added, "I knew you'd say yes."

Blake studied the card, the weight of it as light as air, but the magnitude of it as big as the moon. Tracing her fingers over the edges, she took a deep breath, focusing. Notes of warm jasmine and subtle cedarwood drifted through the air, there and gone. The perfume was pleasant without demanding attention. "This is the Saturday after next," she said to Mr. Brown.

"I know it's spring break, but you'll be in town, right?"

Blake nodded. She felt feverish. To show her art in a *real* gallery? A gallery owned by a woman? The thought of it sent a rush of bubbling warmth through her. Then she smiled, a wide, welcoming, *I can do this* smile. "Thank you. Thank you. Yes, I'll be there."

Mr. Brown nodded politely, but she could tell he was excited, too. He had always believed in her art, in her vision, in her ability to "create magic."

If he only knew.

"Make sure to bring your entire portfolio," he said. "Unlike Mr. Grayson, Ms. Ivanov is open-minded, keen on inventiveness, and above all, she likes a risk-taker. But," he said with added emphasis, "she's also a stickler for punctuality."

"Got it." And before Mr. Brown walked away, Blake said, "Hey, um . . . do you know of any famous paintings with a heart that has an eye in the center?" It was a long shot, but she was determined to figure out what the symbol meant, and what it was trying to point her to.

Mr. Brown paused. He narrowed his eyes like he always did when he was in deep thought. "Not off the top of my head. Why?"

"Just wondering," Blake said defeatedly before she swept into the classroom.

Blake stayed after school in the library, flipping through books on art, history, symbolism, and ancient relics. Feeling trapped by the sling, she took it off, relieved she could move and stretch her arm with no pain. She searched indexes for *seeing heart*, or *eye in the heart*. But she found nothing. *I'm looking,* she thought. *Help me see.* And then her mind snagged on *remember* and the usual *remember what* that always followed.

When she got home the house was empty. She set her book bag down in the kitchen just as the phone rang. "Hello?"

"Hey," Liv said, sounding like she was far away from the receiver. "I think we need to plan out spring break. I was thinking some shopping, maybe a beauty day—my nails are kind of awful. And it sounds like Kyle Flannigan is having a bash."

Blake leaned against the kitchen wall, her eyes alighting on a note on the fridge from Remi: *Check your room.*

"Sure," she told Liv. "Okay."

"So, if I make all our plans you're cool with it? Even parties?"

What did Remi leave in my room?

"Uh-huh."

"Do you think Martians should be invited to the party, too?"

Then she remembered: Zora and Phillip's letters!

"Blake! You're not even listening! What's gotten into you?"

Snapping out of it, Blake said, "Sorry, Liv. I'm just . . . I was looking at a note Remi left. I have to go, but I'll call you later."

Upstairs Blake found a stack of envelopes on her bed. She hurried over, planting herself atop the brown-and-yellow quilt. A strange quiet wrapped itself around her, and then she remembered the red shoes, thinking that they might connect her to Zora. She slipped her feet into them, repositioned herself on the bed, and untied the gold ribbon that held the letters together.

Blake decided to start at the top, regardless of the postmark date. With a deep breath, she removed the first letter from the creased envelope. A deep shudder ran through her, and she tasted something sharp and pungent, like chewing aspirin.

Zora's handwriting was tight and controlled.

Her words blurred on the page. The sunlight streaming in from the window faded to a distant glint. Thunderous heartbeats pounded within Blake, and the overpowering taste in her mouth increased.

She felt herself falling. Heat swept through her with such intensity that she squeezed her eyes shut and took a deep breath until the sensation subsided.

Opening her eyes, Blake saw that the world had changed. With each blink the room cracked, splitting like a mirror. Shattering until a new scene emerged.

A darkened room lit only by a single candle comes into view. The walls are lined in paper decorated with pink roses and ivy.

In the corner a woman with curly brown hair sits at a desk with her head tipped down. From this vantage, Blake can only see her profile. But even so she knows that this is her grandmother.

Zora lifts a handheld mirror from the desk and peers into it. The looking glass is etched with delicate scrolls that look like tangled vines. She is whispering something, talking to the mirror that is pressed closely to her face, but what she is muttering, Blake can't hear.

The candles flicker. Shadows dance at the edges of the vision. The scents of wood smoke and sage float into the space.

Then, suddenly, Zora's head jerks up. Blake studies the fine curve of her jaw. The way her warm skin glistens in the candlelight. Zora turns her gaze toward Blake. Time stands still. The flame. The heart. And then . . . she whispers, "Follow."

Footsteps sound outside. A knock on the door and then the sound of a familiar voice: "Mama, are you awake?"

Blake's breath hitches in her throat.

Mama?

Focus. Stay focused.

She feels the vision fading. Its edges blurring. No! Not yet. *With single-minded determination, she refocuses her energies, willing herself to remain a second longer. A sharp pain bursts behind her left eye.*

Just then Zora turns and shifts the mirror, and by way of reflection Blake sees her face. Zora's dark, penetrating eyes zero in on her. A hardened stare, both daring and stunned. In that moment, when their eyes lock, Blake feels a stirring deep within telling her that she is connected to Zora by more than blood or magic. She is connected by secrets.

Another knock on the door.

Zora shoves the mirror into an armoire just as a long-fingered hand curves around the door's edge, pushing it open. And there, floating at the edge of the door, is a blue seeing heart, so faint it looks like mist.

Whispers swirl all around Zora's voice. Blake's mother's voice.

"Wake up. Wake up. Wake up."

The vision quivered in tremulous silence, fading into nothing.

14

Blake was thrust back into awareness of this world with deafening force.

She was on her knees on the floor. The letters scattered like yesterday's news.

Sweat dripped down her neck. Bitterness rose in her throat. She stumbled to the trash can and vomited. Her mind couldn't begin to process what she had seen and heard. The past, another symbol, her mom, a moment in time strewn with memories that didn't belong to Blake. Until today.

"Blake!"

In what felt like a single motion, Remi swept into the room, helped Blake up, and guided her to the bed to sit down.

"I'm . . . okay." Blake's voice came out slow and shaky.

Wordlessly, Remi pulled her into a gentle hug, allowing Blake a moment to breathe. To wash herself of the shock that came in violent waves. She broke free and bent down, sweeping the letter into her grasp, half expecting the vision to reappear.

Remi's eyes stayed glued to Blake. "Tell me what happened."

"Zora," she began, and spilled the details, every scent, sound, touch, until she finished with "Remi, I . . . I saw the past with nothing more than touching this paper. There was no water or mirror or . . . reflection. It was . . . it was like the air was a mirror cracking right in front of me. And Zora . . . she was . . ."

"What?"

"She seemed to look at me in the reflection."

Remi was quiet. Her expression a blend of emotions Blake couldn't read. Fear? Confusion? Anger?

After a moment, Remi nodded, acknowledging Blake's words, and got to her feet. She went to the window, where threads of almost-spring sunlight began to slip behind a dark cloud. Her shoulders rose and fell with her deep breaths. She turned back to Blake. Her fixed expression frightened Blake. It was the kind of expression that could break anyone's resolve. "Maybe this was a mistake."

Blake could feel the wall of resistance rising inside her aunt, and still she asked the question she knew she wasn't going to like the answer to. "What do you mean?"

"Look at you, Blake. You're drenched in sweat. You . . ." Remi stared into the wastebasket. "You vomited. You were on the floor, for God's sake!" She inhaled sharply. "We don't know anything about your magic and how it affects you. You said it yourself. Your magic . . . You didn't even need a reflection this time."

Which means my magic is getting stronger.

"I think I just overdid it. I'm fine," Blake countered, but it came out more like a plea than a statement of fact. Glancing down at the red shoes, she suddenly felt like the fractured statue she had seen in her dreams. With the seeing heart at the center of her chest.

Remi's gaze followed Blake's to the shoes. She breathed through her mouth a few times until . . . "That's it."

"What?"

"The shoes . . . What if they're increasing your power?"

There was a visceral truth to Remi's words. Blake could feel it down to her bones. Not the kind of knowledge that comes from books or even experiences, but from ancestral memory, passed down through blood. "I think you're right; the visions are getting more desperate," Blake said before spilling what happened at the beach, leaving out her near plunge into the sea.

"Are you sure the girl in your vision was wearing these shoes?" Remi said.

Blake nodded numbly. "I think she might be a part of our family from way back. Do you know where the shoes came from?"

"My mom only said she got them from *her* mother." Remi began to pace. Her jaw was tight; her nostrils flared. "I had no idea the magic would have this kind of effect on you, and I can't . . . I can't ask you to use your powers to go in search of something that risks your well-being and safety."

"The curse risks all of our well-being and safety." Blake's words were coming at a frenzied pace now. Waves of nausea spilled over her, and she fought to keep them at bay, away from Remi's careful gaze. She stared at the envelopes still strewn across her floor. "I can't just forget my dreams or what these visions are trying to tell me," she uttered, lost in a trance of desperate longing to know the truth, to know what it all meant.

"Listen to me. There's something you don't know. This magic—it's dangerous."

"I know. But Zora and . . . my mom . . . they told me—"

"Blake."

"'Wake up. Wake up.' Maybe it means—"

"Your grandmother's magic killed people, Blake!"

In that single instant, all the air was sucked out of the room. Blake stood silent, staring at Remi.

Remi came over, gesturing for her to sit on the edge of the bed with her.

"The night it happened," Remi began, "they..." She swallowed. "My parents were trying to catch a boat to Paris. They were betrayed by a friend of theirs and there was a fight. She didn't mean to do it. It was an act of self-defense, and my dad... he couldn't bear to see her go to jail, so he took the fall for her."

Blake needed a moment to process what her aunt was telling her about her family history, a history hidden behind a mask of lies. In her mind, her grandfather had been framed for a murder he didn't commit, and the real killer was still out there. She had no idea that the killer was her grandmother.

"How did she do it?" Blake's voice was timorous and small. Her nausea waned.

Remi took her niece's hand in her own. "Your grandmother used telekinetic magic. Do you hear what I am telling you? She lost control of her power and people died. And..."

"What?"

Remi wore a pained expression. "And her best friend died, too."

Blake couldn't begin to fathom that kind of horror. The idea of ever being responsible for something happening to Liv was too much to think about.

"I know I should have told you," Remi said, "but I didn't want to ruin her memory and I thought her brand of magic would never touch you, that if we only used your power to find the mirror, it would be okay."

"I'm not Zora," Blake said angrily, jerking her hand free. "My magic is different. You said so yourself."

"I know that, but—" Remi massaged her temples in slow circles and took a long breath. "If something happened to you, I would never forgive myself."

"Nothing is going to happen to me. I can learn how to do this, Remi. And I have you."

Remi's expression was unchanged. It would take more than pleading to move her.

"So, what?" Blake argued, getting to her feet abruptly. "You think I can open the door to this magic and now just close it? Lock it away? Pretend it never happened? It's trying to tell me something!"

"I don't know what to think, Blake. I just . . ." Remi's expression grew somber. "There was a time I didn't really believe in curses, bad luck, that sort of thing. Or maybe I just didn't want to believe and then—" She hesitated as if she were measuring her words carefully. "Now I'm not so sure. And we cannot ignore the rule—"

"Of threes," Blake finished. It was so easy now to track the good followed by the bad. But Blake didn't want to wait for some horrible thing to happen. And besides, she wanted to see the mirror, to touch its power. She wanted to see her parents again, even if only in the past.

Blake studied her aunt, sensing her fear. A fear that she knew was speaking for her, twisting her words into impossibility. She placed her hand on Remi's shoulder, forcing her to look her in the eye. "There's no putting the magic back now. I can't ignore what's happening to me."

Remi picked at one of the quilt's loose threads. "I don't want to open a door to darkness."

Staring down at Zora's shoes, Blake knew that Remi was right: The shoes had increased her powers; they had made the vision sharper, had made the taste of fear more bitter. Had made Blake feel like she was in the room with Zora. The power, while painful, had also been intoxicating. A feeling she wanted to return to again and again. "You said magic acts as a magnet, and that means that even if I want to, I can't stop seeing the visions. I can't stop dreaming. And I get it now. I'm supposed to find the seeing heart in the real world," Blake said.

Remi began to gather the letters from the floor as if her hands needed a distraction. She set them on the desk and turned to face Blake, sighing. "Find it how? An image? A sculpture, a shape?"

"I don't know, but I think . . . I hope that my magic will guide me," Blake responded quickly, encouraged by the fact that her aunt was even entertaining the idea.

"'I left my heart in San Francisco.'"

"Remi! Maybe that's a clue."

"You think Tony Bennett is a clue? It just came to mind with all this talk of hearts."

They went through the rest of the lyrics about the blue and windy sea, about coming home to the city by the bay. But nothing stood out for Blake. Besides, the heart Bennett sang about didn't have eyes.

"And you're telling me everything?" Remi asked.

"Of course," Blake lied. Her mind was a storm of possibilities and terrors. She wasn't about to tell her aunt that she could still feel the leftover effects of the magic, the way it had struggled inside her, made her sick. It was as if her body was rejecting the magic. But how could that be?

Remi pressed the heels of her palms against her eyes and let out an exasperated breath. "I wish my mother had armed me with more knowledge. So I could help you and keep you safe."

"What about Rose?" Blake asked. "She was Zora's best friend, and they lived in the same house all those years."

"Even if she told Rose anything, Rose's memory isn't reliable."

That was true, Blake thought. But if Zora's spirit had really gone to see Rose, then maybe she could find answers there.

Beyond the bus window, the city looked colorless, draped in a thick fog that crawled up the streets like an uninvited guest. Blake had always loved the mist. The breath of ghosts, she used to call it. It always felt so moody, so otherworldly. So mysterious. Now she thought it was just a thief of sight.

By the time Blake arrived at the senior center, it had started to rain. A soft pitter-patter like hundreds of tiny bird feet dancing across a rooftop.

Rose's room was shadowed in darkness. Empty.

With the magic wrapped around her feet, Blake hurried to the dining hall. But Rose wasn't there. She wasn't in the library or the game room either.

The rain was falling faster now. Lights flickered overhead. Phones rang. Voices mingled, becoming indecipherable reverberations.

Silent as a whisper, Blake rushed up the corridor stairs to the fifth floor. The atrium was empty except for Rose. Relief flooded

Blake as she stood at the entrance a moment, catching her breath and reining in her runaway fear.

At the center of the circular room Rose sat in a chrome wheelchair, a sobering contrast to the lush green plants that surrounded her like the dwelling of a fairy queen. On her lap was a mountain of brown yarn and in her hands two metal knitting needles. The rain fell in a steady rhythm that seemed to match the beat of Rose's knitting.

Rose turned. "Is that you, George?"

Blake stood dumbfounded for a moment, puzzling over how Rose could have sensed her presence when she was wearing the shoes and her approach had been silent as the rising moon.

"It's Blake," she finally said as she headed over, pulled up a thin wooden chair, and sat next to Rose.

Setting her needles to rest, Rose said, "Did you come to get me ready?"

"Actually," Blake said, "I came . . . I wanted to ask you about Zora."

"Who?"

"Your best friend."

Rose's face split into a smile. "I'm making a hat," she said. "For George. His ears are always cold."

Blake felt the weight of defeat as thunder bellowed in the distance. A low, rolling sound.

Tilting her face to the ceiling, Rose cried, "Oh my! The clothing. It's on the line out back. You must bring it in. But be careful. Don't slip on the steps."

"Don't worry, Rose," Blake said dejectedly. "I brought it in already."

Rain pelted the windows like small stones and Blake cursed herself for not bringing an umbrella.

Leaning closer, Rose whispered, "Are the girls asleep?"

Blake froze. *Girls?*

"How could anyone sleep with all this ruckus, Zora?"

Rose's mind was a dense forest Blake would never find her way through. She had had moments of astonishing clarity, and moments of utter confusion. But never, not once, had she mistaken Blake for anyone else. A part of Blake wanted to set her straight. Another part wanted to follow this through to see if maybe . . .

Blake guided the conversation cautiously, slowly, afraid that one wrong word would disrupt Rose's memory. "Yes, it's quite a storm," she said. It took a moment for her to find her voice. Zora's voice. The lie twisted her stomach. "I need to talk to you about the mirror."

"The looking glass?"

"I . . . I can't find it."

Rose quirked a single brow. "I don't know about a mirror."

Blake hesitated, inhaled. "What about a heart?" she said, her pulse racing. "It's pale blue and has an eye in the center. Have you ever seen that?"

Rose's vacant eyes stared across the room. "A heart with an eye . . ."

Blake held her breath. *Don't lose the moment. Don't lose the moment.*

They sat in silence until Rose whispered, "Zora?"

Blake followed the woman's gaze to the corner near the sweeping palm. There was no one there. "I can't hear you very well," Rose said, directing her attention to the tree. "So much static. Come closer."

Blake wanted to speak, but she was too afraid to shatter the moment. Her heart pounded wildly, its reverberations thudding across her entire body.

"She wants to tell you something . . ." Rose began. She opened her mouth, confounded, but no words came out.

The mirror. Tell me where the mirror is. Or the seeing heart—at least tell me where to find that.

Rose pressed her lips into a thin line and shook her head vigorously as she reached for Blake's hand. "Zora says, 'It will cost you. Will you pay the price?'"

Just then a nurse waltzed in, pointing at her watch. "Time for her bath."

A knitting needle fell to the floor with a clank. Rose startled.

"Just one second," Blake told the nurse as she took hold of Rose's hand and waited expectantly for her to say more. "What price?"

Rose tilted her face to the ceiling. "I don't care for storms."

Blake knew the moment was lost. "Zora?"

Rose started to hum and Blake slumped back, discouraged. Why wouldn't Zora talk to *her*? Was it because of Rose's condition? Could she reach those places between life and death more readily? Or perhaps because the two of them had known each other in life?

"If Zora comes back," Blake said, turning to Rose, "ask her about the looking glass. Ask her—" She broke off, catching her breath. "Ask her where she hid it."

Rose inhaled slowly, her expression faded.

"Rose! Tell me you'll ask her."

"I want to go home," Rose said, burying her face in her hands. "I want to see George."

The nurse cast an annoyed glance Blake's way. "Please, miss. She needs to take her bath. It will calm her."

Warily, Blake stood and kissed the top of Rose's head, regretting her outburst. "I'm sorry. It's going to be okay, Rose. I love you. It's going to be okay."

The nurse retrieved the fallen needle and wheeled Rose from the atrium. As soon as they got to the entrance, Rose's arm shot out, stopping herself on the doorframe. She turned her face so Blake could only see the sharp points of her profile.

"Be careful, Blake. Some doors should stay closed."

The landscape of Blake's mind had become a forest dense with shadows, mist, and unanswered questions.

By Friday, she had gone through Cole's encyclopedias, had combed through magazines, even flipped through the Yellow Pages ads. She walked the neighborhood looking at menus, billboards, storefront posters, but she found nothing. She even put up "Have You Seen Me" flyers around the neighborhood with a sketch of the seeing heart and her phone number.

So far, she had had three phone calls. One woman told her she had seen a similar heart once in France at a small church, but she couldn't be sure. Another person told her they had seen it on a T-shirt but *that* heart had two eyes. And the most recent call came from a woman who said she had seen the image on a tarot card when she was twelve.

That happened to be Blake's best lead, so she went back to the Yellow Pages and found a new-agey kind of store called the Sword that sold tarot cards. It was a dusty, dim place no bigger than a small classroom. The owner was an older woman with white hair that hung to her waist. When Blake showed her the sketch, the woman shook her head. "Nothing like that here."

"Can I just take a look around?"

"Suit yourself."

Thirty minutes into her search, Blake had found nothing, and when she flipped through the last deck of tarot cards, the woman grunted and said, "I told you there is nothing like that heart here. It must be one of a kind. What do you even want it for?"

"It's just... I've been dreaming about it."

"Well, just ask the question you want answered before you fall asleep," the woman said as if it was the most obvious solution. "Dreams will talk to you if you let them."

But will visions? Blake wondered as she made her way home, feeling more defeated than ever.

Maybe her attempts were too small. Too few. She needed to be bolder, riskier. She had to connect with her magic if she was ever to find the seeing heart. But how could she grow her bits-and-pieces magic into something concrete, something big and powerful? Something that didn't make her sick. Something she could control.

Back home she plopped onto her bed and cast her gaze toward her mother's photo on the nightstand.

"I wish you were here," she whispered. "To tell me what to do. To teach me how to use this magic. To help me find the mirror."

While the newly awakened magic came from her mom's side of the family, Blake's father came from a long line of curanderas, including his grandmother, whom Remi recalled as a gifted intuitive healer. She wasn't surprised Delilah would have attracted a man with magic in his ancestry, too.

Magic attracts magic.

There was a strange comfort knowing that her parents shared a lineage of magic regardless of their different backgrounds.

Maybe I missed something in my sketches, Blake thought.

She tugged her book bag free, looking for her sketchbook, but it wasn't there. Then she remembered she had left it at school. *Shoot.* Any other day, this wouldn't have been the end of the world, but the school would be closed for spring break and Blake needed to review some pieces in there for her meeting with Ms. Ivanov.

Blake glanced at the clock on her nightstand: 6:30. And she was supposed to meet Olivia, Ian, and Dean at Whiz Burgers at seven.

Praying the school custodians were still working, she flew out of her room in search of Remi or Cole, hoping one of them could save her time by driving her.

Thankfully, she found Cole carrying a ladder across the backyard.

"Hey, are you busy? Can you give me a quick ride to school?" Blake asked.

Cole set the ladder against the porch. "Now?"

"If that's okay. I'm kind of in a hurry."

With a smile, he shook his head. "Kids are always in a hurry, and then when you're all grown up, all you want to do is slow down." He gave a mock frown of concern. "Or do you think that's just me?"

A few minutes later, they were in the car. Too bad Cole drove like a slug.

"So," he began, "Remi tells me you have a prom date."

"Had."

An expression of surprise swept across Cole's face. "I can only guess that *you* pulled the plug?"

"He wasn't who I thought he was."

Cole threw a sidelong glance at Blake. "And are you okay with that?"

Blake let out a light laugh. "With him being a world-class skuzz or with me being dateless?"

"Nah, I don't care about the *skuzz,* as you put it, only you. And you know what? I'm proud of you for knowing what you want and what you don't want." He pulled up to the school. The engine idled. "Do you want me to wait?"

Blake didn't want to explain that she was going to Whiz Burgers to meet a boy—and not even her ex–prom date but a different boy, at that. "No thanks," she said as she hopped out of the car. "Oh, and tell Remi I'm hanging out with Olivia and will be home later."

Before she shut the door, Cole said, "Hey, Blake?"

"Yeah?"

"I love you, kiddo."

"I love you, too."

Blake raced up the steps to the main doors only to find them locked. Quickly, she went around to the north side of the building, relieved to find the door held ajar by a trash can. She slipped inside and saw one of the custodians sweeping the hall.

"I forgot something in my locker," she said as she swept past.

Her footsteps were silent as she hurried down the empty corridor. A deep throbbing began to pound in her ears the moment she opened her locker and grabbed her sketchbook.

Disembodied whispers swirled all around her. She could feel the eyes on her before she even looked up. It was the same feeling she had experienced at the park, and now...

She snapped her head up just in time to catch the edge of something, a figure in a tattered green dress darting into an adjacent hall.

"Hello?" she called.

Her voice was sucked into the vacant space. Blake's scalp prickled.

Quickly, she headed back the way she had come. And then she paused midstep, remembering the word from her vision... *follow*.

She spun and ran in the direction of the figure. Her pulse pounded. The throbbing intensified.

There.

At the end of a smaller hall, a side door flew open. The woman in the green dress moved through the space like a puppet connected to invisible threads. Her hair was a tangle of darkness with cold ashy-gray streaks. And the skin of her arms looked burned. Bits of flesh hung loosely.

She stopped in the doorway. Turned.

She raised a finger to her lips. "Shhhh."

The door closed with a hush.

Ears pounding, whispers rising, Blake hurried after the stranger. When she stepped outside, the woman was gone. And so were the creepy sensations.

Blake felt like she was standing outside herself, peering down at the gray scenery that seemed to vibrate with undeniable magic. A flutter of wind swept across the landscape, lifting a piece of paper from the ground and delivering it to Blake's feet.

She stooped and picked it up: a half-torn flyer for the St. Patrick's festival at Dolores Park tonight.

And there . . . at the torn edge . . .

Blake blinked, peering closer.

There was no mistaking the shape. It was half of the seeing heart.

Blake shivered at the unexpected warmth radiating from the paper. Closing her eyes, she connected to her magic, pulling it closer.

Suddenly the air began to split like glass, a crack in the world's veneer. Blake's field of vision melted away, revealing a scene.

A crowd of people walk leisurely through the festival at Dolores Park. There is no sound, no color, only the movement of the wanderers.

And it is as if Blake is there and not here. Aimlessly drifting alongside the people, with no control of where her legs are taking her.

She arrives at a sign that says "Readings for Lost Souls," and on the sign there is a seeing heart.

Snow flutters from the sky, twisting, tumbling flakes gentle and silent. Floating to the ground like tiny ghosts. And then she sees. This isn't snow. The sky is raining flowers: small white blooms shaped like tiny stars. Her eyes scan the sky as she reaches out a hand to catch one, but the vision is swept away like smoke in the wind.

Blake felt as if she was being reabsorbed into the present moment. Her breathing was erratic, her heart was pounding, but at least she wasn't vomiting.

Look. See. Remember.

Suddenly that part of the message made sense. Cole had been right. *See* as in realize, as in understand. As in *see* the truth.

As she stared down at the paper still in her hand, her skin began to tingle all over.

Not snow, she thought. *Flowers*. In all the visions, the sky had been raining flowers!

Looking at her watch, she sucked in a sharp breath and whispered, "Shit." She was due at Whiz Burgers twenty minutes ago. Olivia was going to kill her.

But the heart had spoken. This was Blake's first true lead, and she had to follow it. Adrenaline pumping, she raced to the festival at Dolores Park, to the answer she knew was waiting there.

16

Blake headed down the windswept street.

What was usually a quiet road had turned into a cyclone of activity, colors, and music. At least the side that was Dolores Park, which was packed with people for the St. Patrick's Day festival.

She passed the Mission Dolores Basilica, all its turrets and spires and grandeur dwarfing the mission next to it. And beside that? A little graveyard of forgotten souls and rotting bones, some of which had been moved to sites outside of the city, an act that Blake thought had to be sacrilegious at best. A ticket to hell at worst.

The festival air carried the scent of smoke and spices. Bells rang, music played, people laughed, and screams bounded down the midway. Unlike her vision, the place was an explosion of color and life.

Blake walked through the carnival at a brisk pace, searching for the sign: "Readings for Lost Souls."

Was that what she was? A lost soul? Maybe she had always felt a bit adrift, a small boat in an endless ocean of unseen boundaries and unanswered questions. She wondered if she was being too impetuous. Maybe the half heart was just a coincidence. *No*, a little voice told her. *There are no coincidences where magic is concerned.*

Her mind jumped to the image of the strange woman in green, and now that she had time to process it, she found the figure frightening.

Was she the same person who had been watching her at Grayson's and the park? And then there was the unnerving pounding in her ears and distant whispers that accompanied each visit. Like a warning bell before the first bomb hits.

Refocusing on the task at hand, Blake pressed on, searching, picking up her pace. Hope, hope, *hoping* that the tent from her vision would result in a significant lead.

With each step she felt her heart beat a little faster, as if to say *Hurry.*

I've been waiting a long time for you.

Row by row, tent by tent, Blake searched for the wooden sign from her vision. Her head swam with possibilities. The world felt as if it were on fire. She turned down another row and slammed directly into—

Ian.

Seeing him under the bright lights of the carnival confirmed that his eyes were hazel, not brown or gray. And his jaw showed only the fading remnants of a greenish bruise from last weekend.

"Blake," he said with a note of surprise. "This isn't Whiz Burgers."

"Ian?" It was all she could think to say, including the lilt at the end of his name indicating the question: *What are you doing here?*

Around them the crowd moved with the rhythm of the swelling ocean. But Ian stood firm.

He looked amused, like he hadn't just been stood up by the girl whose life he had saved. His wandering gaze swung back to meet Blake's. "I guess we were meant to meet tonight after all."

Blake swallowed. "Right. I'm sorry. I got . . . I was busy . . ."

Ian didn't seem annoyed or even put off. If anything, he acted like he was enjoying this. Or maybe he was pleased he had found the runaway girl. "Carnivals are a good place to be busy."

A giant beach ball bounced over their heads as some kids laughed and ran after it. Suddenly and desperately, Blake wanted to be anywhere but here. She was about to respond with a retort of her own, except she had none. The idea of it, though, brought Olivia into her mind, and that's when Blake realized her friend was MIA. She glanced over Ian's shoulder. "Where's Olivia?"

"She headed back to her house. With Dean. I guess her mom made a dinner better than burgers."

If the idea of Olivia and Dean together was supposed to shock Blake, it worked. Olivia had liked plenty of guys over the years, but she had never taken one home to her mom, and Blake never would have guessed the first one would be Dean. Did she really like him that much? Had Blake missed the signs along the way? Had something happened that she didn't know about? All of a sudden she felt like nothing more than an observer of her life and the people in it. A mannequin in a store window.

"Oh" was all Blake could think to say. And then she found herself talking. "The other night..." she began. "I'm not usually like that." Lie. Lie. Lie. *I am always like that. Or at least lately.*

"You nearly fell," Ian said, instantly serious. "I was there. End of story."

Blake appreciated that he was giving her an out, helping her save face.

"So," he began, "want to check out the Ferris wheel? I mean, since we're here?"

"I can't. I have to go."

He looked surprised by her quick rejection, which made her cringe inside. The last thing she wanted to do was be rude or make things awkward.

"No problem," he said. "Another time."

"It's just that—"

"Really, Blake . . ." He flashed a warm smile. "You don't have to explain anything to me."

Blake felt instantly guilty that she had stood Ian up. And guilt always made room for second thoughts.

"It would be fun to ride the Ferris wheel," she said. "It's just that I came here to look for something."

"Does this have to do with the other night when you said, 'Look, see, remember'?"

Blake froze. She held Ian's gaze, searching his eyes—for what, she didn't know. And then she remembered that she had chanted those words on the cliff, out loud, openly. In front of a stranger.

Blake found herself taking a small step toward Ian before she stopped. "I wasn't myself," she echoed with a finality she hoped he understood as *I don't want to talk about that.*

She began to walk and Ian fell into step beside her. And then her eyes were drawn to the thing she had come here for.

The sign sat in front of a curtained booth. The wood was painted a peacock blue, in long, careful strokes, like whoever painted it wanted the words to do more than be read. They wanted the words to hypnotize.

Blake felt a thrill scuttle up her spine at the discovery while Ian's gaze followed hers to the sign. His eyes glittered with an unexpected interest.

"I have a nan who reads tea leaves," Ian said. "She foretold my journey to America."

"Seriously?" Blake didn't know him well enough to tell if he was kidding or if he was in the habit of using words like *foretold* in everyday conversation.

With a dash of humor in his voice, Ian said, "So you stood me up for a psychic?"

Blake twisted her mouth to one side, considering Ian. "It's not like that."

"I guess if you're looking for your future, she's the better choice."

What was that supposed to mean? Blake didn't have time for this, or Ian's word games. Or his damn smile.

"I can wait for you here," he suggested.

"You don't have to."

"Look, I'm a chivalrous guy. I should make sure you're okay." Then, with a raised eyebrow, he leaned closer and added, "Besides, I want to know what she tells you. Maybe she'll say you're going to meet a charming chap from across the pond."

Despite the inky sky and the faint mist, despite the vision and the scary woman and the starflowers, Blake returned the smile. And then she headed over to the booth.

The moment she stepped up to the ribbon that cordoned off the entrance, a woman appeared from behind a shimmery drape. She wore a pale peach scarf that covered her head and was tied off in a knot at the nape of her neck; her eyes were so sunken it was as if the weight of her eyeballs was too much for her small frame to handle.

"I am Martina." The woman cradled her hands like she was waiting for something to drop into them. "You come for a limpia? To find love? To know your future?"

Blake had no idea how this worked or if there was something she was supposed to say or do. "I... I was hoping you could tell me why I'm here." She thought her words sounded brazen, even ridiculous, the moment they left her mouth, but the woman didn't seem fazed. Instead she unhooked the ribbon and waved Blake to step behind the drape.

Blake stole a glance at Ian over her shoulder. He stood with his hands deep in his pockets, grinning at her as if he had expected her to give him one last look.

The private area was dim, lit only by candles. An old woman, wearing a sky-blue dress that reached the dirt floor, sat in the corner eating a burrito and stroking a tiny gray mouse perched in her lap. The mouse snapped at the bits of tortilla the woman cupped in her palm.

"One dollar for a fifteen-minute reading," Martina said.

Blake nodded slowly.

"Come. Sit," Martina said. "And tell me your name."

"Blake," she said as she sank into a rickety chair. The straw seat sagged beneath her, poking into the back of her thighs. Her mouth went suddenly dry as she dug a bill out of her purse and set it on a table, its mirrored surface distorted with ashy swirls running through it like storm clouds gathering.

Martina swept the money into her lap, then took Blake's hand in her own. Closing her eyes, she took a deep breath. When she opened them a moment later, she said, "You are here for a purpose, Blake."

There was a long pause. Really? Blake had come here for this? She dropped her gaze to the smoky mirror, wondering if something might appear. But there was nothing more than the skewed reflections of the tented roof and Martina's and her clasped hands.

Two whispers of air tickled Blake's cheek before a stronger draft landed. Remi was calling her. *Come home.*

But why did Remi need Blake to come home? Blake hadn't been gone that long.

Martina spoke lightly. "You will fall in love, move away from here. Oh, and there are children. Three. No. Two."

That could be anyone's fortune, Blake thought, her expectations sinking lower and lower with every word the woman spoke.

"Ah, you're an artista," Martina breathed.

A morsel that stoked the fire of hope.

Still, Blake remained poker-faced, waiting to see if the woman might prove her worth and tell her why she had been led here. Another sweep of magic air, this time more insistent.

Martina added, "I see a very large horizon for you. A difficult journey."

Blake shifted in her seat, trying to relax. "Journey to where?"

"To the answers you and so many others before you have been looking for."

The last thing Blake wanted to do was be rude or insult Martina, but she had to hurry this along. "Uh . . . can you be more specific?"

"Ghosts . . . so many ghosts." Martina cast a cool gaze at the old woman in the corner, who stood on shaky legs and drew closer with the mouse still in her hand.

The old woman's voice was barely above a whisper. "Mira a los muertos."

Blake had once spoken Spanish—she could still recall speaking to her father, the way the words rolled off her tongue smooth and beautiful and effortless. But after he died, she had no one to speak to, and her knowledge of the language had died, too. Now all she had were scattered words.

Heat rose in Blake's cheeks. "I . . . I don't understand." But she did. She knew one word: *muertos*.

Martina translated: "My mother says to look to the dead." Martina's mother spoke freely and quickly, one word tumbling over the next as Martina translated. "It is the ghosts who have put you under what we call hechizo de proteccíon, a protection spell, but now the spell's magic is being overwhelmed by another, more powerful magic."

A dozen warning bells rang out in Blake's head. "Protection spell?" Her mind immediately went to the push-pull feeling that had only grown stronger. "What does that mean?"

The old woman's eyes bored into Blake, and as she spoke, Martina repeated the words in English as quickly as if they were her own: "It is a way to protect you, to . . ." She inhaled deeply. "To keep you hidden."

"Hidden from who?" Blake asked as she reached for the medal around her neck.

This time the old woman said nothing. It was Martina who provided the answer. "Hidden from yourself."

It took a moment for Blake to process Martina's words. After several long seconds, she blinked, found her voice. "Why would I need to be hidden from myself?"

Martina took a slow, deep breath. "You have great magic coursing through your blood."

Blake's whole being went still. How could this woman know that?

"You had a birthday recently?"

Blake nodded.

"Birthdays have a way of opening doors to magic, and *this* magic comes from more than one source," Martina continued. "Do you understand?"

Blake thought about what Martina was telling her. And as much as she wanted to dismiss her words outright, she could feel the truth as easily as she could hear her heart thrumming in her ears. She knew she had inherited magic from her mother and Zora, but now she felt something she had always known but never recognized. It was like walking past a small statue in a park for years and never noticing it, until one day the statue spoke to you. "My grandmother on my dad's side," Blake began, and the words flowed before she could even think them, "she was a curandera."

"I do not know where the magic comes from," Martina admitted. "That is for you to discover."

The old woman frowned, then said something to Martina, speaking in low tones. Martina shook her head as if she didn't want to relay her mother's message. The old woman clenched her jaw, waiting. Finally Martina closed her eyes and wiped a few beads of sweat off her brow. "Tanta emoción."

"What about emotion?"

"It flies around you, circling you. Such love . . ." Martina said. "You must connect. The thread is there. Waiting for you to find it." She stood and walked over to a low table, where she retrieved a canvas sack. Inside, she tugged out a small lavender pouch tied with a silver string.

"Create a circle around yourself with this," Martina said as she set the pouch on the mirrored table.

Blake reached for it, but Martina stopped her. "Not here. What is inside must only see the light once. Do you understand? Take this home. Create a circle and sit in the middle. What is unknown will become known."

The logical side of Blake's mind was scolding her, telling her to leave, that Martina was just an entertainer, a woman at a carnival selling tricks and stories and lies. She was probably going to charge

Blake more for the pouch. But the magic slippers on her feet begged her to listen, to try to understand.

"How much for this?" Blake wrapped her fingers around the sack. It felt . . . empty.

Martina's face softened, creating a sagging effect that made her look older than she had just moments ago. "It is my gift to you, a birthday present. From one bruja to another."

I'm not a bruja, Blake was about to say, but her time was up and there was no use arguing.

Outside, a light drizzle had begun. Blake turned her eyes to the sky, half expecting the starflowers to descend.

"Blake?" She looked over to find Olivia rushing toward her. Ian was right behind her. Olivia's face was tense. Her eyes filled with fear.

"There's been an accident."

The night Blake's parents left this world, she was startled from her sleep by whispering voices resonating from down the hall.

Curious, she tiptoed to her bedroom door and opened it, forgetting that the bottom scraped across the threshold with an annoying screech.

The voices stopped. A shadow surfaced, rising up the wall near the stairs, and then Remi appeared. For half a second Blake mistook her aunt for her mother, except that tears were rolling down Remi's face and Blake had never seen her mother cry.

"Go back to bed, baby," Remi said gently.

"Where's Mama and Papi?" Blake asked.

Blake didn't remember the moments that followed, but she remembered the words *accident* and *gone*. And she remembered the way her breath was knocked from her chest as if she had fallen from the top of the oak tree in her backyard. She couldn't inhale or exhale. It was as if she had forgotten how to breathe.

That's what this moment felt like.

But Olivia had only been half-right. Yes, there had been an accident. Cole had fallen off the ladder while trimming a tree branch in the garden. But he had fallen because he'd had a heart attack, and that felt somehow intentional, like some preplanned, well-timed moment Blake wished she had seen coming.

The image of Cole dropping her at the school flashed across her mind. His last words to her replaying over and over.

I love you, kiddo.

When they arrived at the hospital, Blake fell into Remi's arms. Remi held her so tight she thought she might shatter into a thousand pieces if her aunt ever let go.

Clinging to Remi, Blake suddenly felt Olivia's and Ian's absence.

They weren't allowed in this area of the hospital and had insisted they were staying, until Blake urged them to go home.

"Tell me what happened," Blake said through stinging tears as Remi released her.

Remi looked blank. Empty. A body without a soul as she shared the details of the fall through erratic breaths. The blow to the head, the gash over Cole's right eye, and the broken ribs, the minutes he lay there helpless and unconscious until Remi had found him. The long and torturous wait for the ambulance. The call to Olivia's, hoping Remi could reach her niece.

This is why she tried to reach me, Blake thought. *And I ignored her. I ignored her magic!*

Remi concluded with "He's in surgery now."

"He's going to be okay," Blake said, but it came out more like a question lost between hope and terror.

Remi led her to a sofa. Leftover crumbs were scattered across the scratchy seat. "He's young," Remi said, as if she were trying to convince more people than Blake. "And he's strong. We just have to pray and . . . focus hard on his healing."

The idea of losing Cole was too much to bear. He had been the one to teach Blake how to stand on her head, snap her fingers, and eat cereal without her spoon ever scraping the bowl. And he believed in their family magic without question.

There was a dragon in the hospital with them that night. Fierce and bold. Terrifying and deadly. A dragon in the form of a thought that Blake knew they couldn't hide from forever. Someone needed to say it, even if it meant opening a door to the unknown. "What if this is my fault?" Blake whispered.

Remi only stared, as if the awful thought carried too much weight for her to stomach.

Blake's mind went into hyperspeed as she thought about the rule of threes. She should have been paying attention! *What two good things have happened? The interview coming up with Ms. Ivanov? Learning about the protection spell?*

And then she remembered the words: *Death approaches.*

Blake's mouth filled with warm saliva; she thought she might throw up. Had she ignored the warning? Were those words for Cole? *If only I could put the pieces together faster.*

"No, Blake," Remi insisted. "This was no one's fault. Do you hear me? This was an accident."

Accident. Blake turned the word over in her mind angrily as she imagined the tools at Fate's disposal: accidents, misfortunes, coincidences, strokes of luck. Whatever anyone wanted to call them, everyone bowed down to the twisted whims of Fate, and Blake was sick of it. She didn't want to go through this life always feeling afraid and waiting for tragedy. She wanted to rise up and meet joy and fresh possibilities at every turn. She wanted to captain her own ship. But there was no doubt in her mind that coincidence had no part in this evening's events. She felt like the curse was taunting them: *I could have taken his life. I can take all of your lives.*

More than ever Blake knew she had to find the mirror, to release the girl and end this misery once and for all.

Blake wanted so badly to tell Remi about the scary woman at the school, about how she had been wrong about the snow, about how the seeing heart had led her to Martina's. She wanted to tell Remi about the magic that was being smothered by another, more powerful spell. She reached into her coat pocket and wrapped her hand around the pouch that still felt as if it only contained air.

How many doors will I have to open to get to the mirror?

That was the moment she decided she wouldn't clutter her aunt's head and heart space right now. Not when Cole needed her.

What if Cole's heart attack was a warning? A warning for Blake to hurry, to pay closer attention.

Will you pay the price?

No, she wanted to scream. *Not if the price is Cole.*

Intent on turning off her mind, Blake asked a nurse for a piece of paper and a pencil so she could sketch. Remi paced around the room as Blake set the pencil to the page. Her hand shook like it had before, quivering as if it were afraid to draw the image blooming in Blake's mind. Finally she wrestled a flower onto the paper. And when she had drawn the gentle flower, she hated its rough edges, its poor shadowing, its overly realistic form.

Something inside her froze as the question took hold of her, shaking her, forcing her to look at what she had so badly wanted to ignore: *Why can't I sketch the way I used to?* Was this the same thing as the tree insisting on being drawn?

It's the adrenaline, she told herself. *It'll pass. I'm an artist. I'll always be an artist. That doesn't just go away.*

It was another two hours before Cole's doctor walked into the waiting room with slumped, tired shoulders. And then he spoke, seemingly insignificant words, none of which were the ones Blake wanted to hear. She wanted to hear that Cole was going to be okay. He was going to have a long and healthy life. But all she heard was *blocked artery, bed rest, observation, no more cigarettes, lucky to be alive.*

"Can we see him?" Remi asked.

"He won't be awake for a while," the doctor said. "Go home. Get some rest. Come back tomorrow."

"I need to see my husband," Remi said so forcefully that Blake knew the doctor didn't stand a chance.

He sighed. "You have two minutes."

A nurse escorted them to the barren room. Cole looked frail, ashen. His blankets were pulled tightly around him. Remi choked back a sob, rushed over, and whispered, "I'm here, baby. I'm here. Everything is going to be okay. Do you hear me? Everything is going to be okay."

The nurse said quietly, "He needs to rest now."

As Remi stepped away from Cole, Blake tossed the pathetic flower sketch into the trash can.

The moment Blake slipped into her bedroom she was startled to find Olivia asleep on her bed. Olivia's hair was twisted in rows of pink curlers.

The needle on the record player scratched repeatedly at the album's center. An incessant plea that would never be answered. Blake lifted the needle and tugged the Beatles record *Meet the Beatles!* off the turntable. The silence was enough to wake Olivia.

"Blake?" Olivia said in a sleepy voice. "How is he?"

"He's going to be fine," she said hopefully, easing herself onto the bed. "Thanks for being here, but you didn't have to . . ."

"My mom's working all night anyway," Olivia said. "I saw her on the way to the hospital. She said she would check on him."

Blake stared at her best friend, filled not only with love but with appreciation that Olivia had always been there. Always.

"Thanks," she finally said, because she was all out of words. Or at least the heavy ones. Then, to lighten the mood, she said, "How was Dean?"

Olivia sat up and rolled her eyes. "He's an oaf."

"So you like him."

"He has no manners."

"And you like him," Blake repeated.

"Did I say that?"

"You didn't have to."

Olivia tossed a pillow at Blake and smiled. "Sixty-five. It's probably an unlucky number or something."

After Olivia fell back asleep, Blake eased herself out of the bed, careful not to wake her friend. With the pouch in hand and the shoes on her feet, she headed to Zora's old room on the third floor and flicked on the small lamp. She sat on the wood floor and set the pouch in front of her, gently untying the silver thread.

Inside, she found a handful of sand, white as a summer cloud. But how? The pouch weighed nothing and sand weighed something.

Just as Martina had instructed, Blake created a circle with the sand and sat in the center. "Now what?" she whispered.

She felt a pressing hopelessness, like she was a weak river trying to shape granite stones, as she closed her eyes and waited, focusing on Martina's words: *What is unknown will become known.*

Would this ritual show her where the mirror was? Could it be as simple as that?

Mindlessly, Blake rubbed the edges of her St. Christopher medal, and before her next thought could form, the boundaries of the room splintered and split like broken glass.

Then slowly the image materialized.

A single wedge of moonlight illuminates the dim, sparsely furnished bedroom. A yellow dollhouse is perched atop a dresser near the twin bed where a small girl sleeps.

The vision flickers. Blake knows this place, this room.

The door creaks open, and an old woman steps inside. She carries a tall candle contained in a column of glass. A golden eight-pointed crown is etched in the center of the glass. Her loose dress trails across the floor and her face is wilted from what looks like a hundred years of life. In her free hand, she carries a bundle of sage.

A man walks into the room behind her.

His dark hair looks even blacker in the candlelight. His face youthful and handsome. He sits on the edge of the bed. Young Blake stirs. "Papi?"

"I'm sorry to wake you."

"Why is Abuela here?"

"To wish you sweet dreams." He bends down and kisses the top of Blake's head before placing St. Christopher around her neck. He begins to speak

in Spanish, soft, storylike words directed at Blake. And it is as if the last ten years of loss have vanished and she can understand every single word he speaks.

"This will always protect you, Esperanza," he says. "Promise me you will never take it off."

With small fingers, she touches the medal. Her voice comes out small, but the beauty and the bigness of the Spanish falls from her lips easily. "What if it falls off?"

"It won't. It's meant to keep you safe."

"Do you have one, too?"

"Daddies don't need protection. Do you promise?"

Blake yawns and tugs on her blanket. "I'll never take it off," she promises as she drifts back to sleep.

Her father's eyes flick to his mother. "And you're sure the medal..."

"Will act as the charm, sí." Her Spanish is clipped and rapid. Her eyes bore into her son.

"What if it breaks?" he asks.

"Only she can remove it," she says barely above a whisper. "Are you certain about this?"

"I've seen what it's done to Zora," he says, releasing Blake's small hand.

"It is a dangerous thing to bind her magic."

"It's more dangerous for her to wield it," he says. "I need to protect her."

"Do you understand that she will be shielded from any powerful magic

in her path?" Abuela warns. "She will not recognize it. Instead she will fear it. And she will reject it."

"Just do as I ask."

"And if Delilah finds out?"

"She won't."

"That is a big risk."

"She's my daughter, too," her father says, his voice desperate. "And you're the one who told me that her powers are only going to get stronger. We've run out of time."

A single thread of black smoke plumes from the candle. The crown pulses with a lavender light so bright Blake can't take her eyes off it until she hears her dad say, "Do it now."

NO! *her mind screams.*

But the vision was gone. Blake sat dumbfounded in the circle of sand.

Hot, stinging tears rolled down her face.

He bound my magic.

My dad bound my magic!

She understood now. The image of her stitched mouth—it represented the binding spell. And the words *look, see, remember* were asking her to *look* for the heart, to *see* the truth, and to *remember* the night of the binding.

Unsteadily, she got to her feet and went to the window because she needed to see out, to observe the real world. Maybe it was the anger or the shock, but Blake didn't feel the usual effects of her visions. Her pulse stuttered as she stared beyond the glass at the darkened street and she thought about all the lies, the lingering, unnoticed half-truths that were out there, silent as fantasmas. Waiting.

"But now what?" she whispered.

There was a small tube of blue paint on the windowsill, left over from months ago when she had sat at this very window, painting the sky.

She opened the tube, accidentally releasing a drop of blue onto her fingers. The paint smelled of possibility. Blake rubbed it between her fingers until it dried in long smears. She thought about the crown bathed in lavender light that she had seen in the last vision, how it had drawn attention to itself, demanding to be seen. She knew then that the crown was another clue. And if the seeing heart led her to the truth, to the protection spell, she was sure the crown was leading her somewhere, too.... But where?

She reached for the medal. For St. Christopher, the protector. Her face was hot. Her hands cold. Martina's words circled the space between then and now. *Such love.*

But Blake didn't feel any love. Her shock ignited sorrow, and her sorrow ignited rage. And it was the rage that woke the sleeping beast. She could feel it. The connection was instant. One magic wanted out. The other wanted to keep it locked away.

Blake considered and weighed her options. To find the mirror and break the curse, she needed power. To stay safe, she would need the protection spell.

Her grandmother's words drifted into the space. *She will be shielded from any powerful magic in her path. She will not recognize it. Instead she will fear it. And she will reject it.*

Blake understood now.

The push and pull she had been feeling was nothing more than two opposing sources of magic. The magic that protected her. And the magic that demanded to be set free.

Only one could remain.

Blake's chest rose and fell in tiny rapid bursts. Bursts of fear and curiosity. The feeling jostled loose a memory of Mr. Jones, her tenth-grade history teacher: "Those who are afraid never make important discoveries," he had told the class. "They never reach greatness."

He was talking only to the young men in the classroom, and if memory served, he even said so. And that was the reality Blake lived in, a world that told women to be scared, that they needed a man to protect them, care for them, to provide a roof over their heads, so that their fear would keep them satisfied baking meat loaf, scrubbing floors, and laying out silk slippers for their husbands, who had navigated their way through their own days *unafraid*.

And afraid women don't become artists.

The thought wasn't big enough for a breath and yet it was there. Blake momentarily wondered if fear were sometimes the better option. Fear keeps you safe. Fear keeps the genie in the bottle. Fear eats magic whole until it's nothing more than a lion carcass picked clean.

But Blake didn't want a corpse of a life. She wanted to find her magic—all of it. To touch it and wield it. Was that what this fractured path had always been? A way to find the missing parts of herself? And now she saw what she hadn't seen before: *I can fix everything if I can just figure out what the magic is trying to tell me and why.*

She swept her hair over her shoulder and unclasped the necklace. Clutched it for a moment. The medal pulsed in her hand, its warmth coursing through her. Then she let it go.

And watched it fall to the floor.

Blake spent the entire night writing down the details of the latest vision, including the crown. "Where do I find a crown in a city this big?" she whispered to the cat that had curled up next to her by Zora's window. *If the heart found me, should I wait for the crown to find me, too?* Something about that felt wrong. Blake had a sense that she was running out of time, and the woman's voice that had swept through the Deveraux gates was always present, always reminding her *"Death approaches."*

Rubbing the cat between the ears, Blake whispered, “But who is going to die?”

She stretched out on the floor, staring out at the near-dawn sky, waiting to feel a greater magic, waiting to see if taking off the necklace would make her feel any different.

When the exhaustion overtook her, she fell into a deep sleep, but this time she didn’t dream.

The morning felt nothing like the one before.

Yesterday Cole’s heart was beating like normal. Yesterday, Blake wore a spell around her neck. But yesterday was gone and so were the moments that had led her to this point.

Remi had left for the hospital and called twice already, asking Blake to bring the things she had forgotten. And now Blake sat at the dining table, dressed for the day, gripping a cup of coffee that had gone cold as she let the memories of last night surface in the morning light.

For the first time Blake not only longed for her mother, she yearned for Zora. A grandmother she had never met. A woman with whom she shared only a recent magical memory and an entire history.

"Where is the mirror?" Blake whispered, holding tight to a childish hope that her grandmother was somehow listening. That, like Rose, Zora would visit Blake. "Where do I find the crown?" But there was no answer.

Just then, Olivia walked in wearing Blake's fluffy blue robe and a towel wrapped around her hair. "Tell me there's more coffee," she said as she shuffled into the kitchen before reappearing with a giant mug of steaming brew. She sat across the table from Blake and blew a cloud of steam away from her mug. Her eyes were pinned to Blake. "Are you okay?"

"I'm fine," Blake said. "I mean I'm worried about Cole, but—"

"That's not what I'm talking about." Olivia took a sip of coffee. "I'm worried about *you*."

"Since when do you worry?"

Olivia lowered her gaze to the mug in her hands. "You might get mad, but I have to tell you something."

In all their years of friendship, Blake couldn't remember more than a couple of disagreements between them, and even then, the two were able to sweep any differences aside almost instantly.

"Mad about what?" Blake was curious but not entirely sure she wanted to hear the answer.

"First, promise you won't hate me."

"I could never hate you. Well," Blake corrected herself, "unless you don't give me back the sweater you borrowed last month." Her attempt at humor went unvalidated.

"That's not a promise."

"Fine." Blake sat back, as if her body knew it was time to create distance between herself and whatever Olivia had to tell her. "I promise I could never hate you. Now tell me."

"I sort of . . . I mean, I didn't do it on purpose. . . ."

"Olivia."

"Last night, before you came home, I couldn't get comfortable, like there was something bulky under the pillow, so I looked and . . . I saw your journal." She lifted the mug to hide her face. "And everything in it."

Blake felt a punch to the throat. If Olivia had read through the scribbled pages, scanned the sketches, she would know about the dreams and the magic and the curse.

Shifting in her chair uneasily, she said, "It's . . . just a dream journal. I have nightmares sometimes."

"A dream journal," Olivia repeated, lowering her mug.

Blake tried to read Olivia. Her wide honey eyes. The twitch of her mouth. The curved ridge of her tightened jaw. She was definitely going to be hard to convince.

"Who is the girl in the mirror?" Olivia asked.

"I don't know. It's just a dream."

"And the curse?" Olivia said, more forceful this time. "And your grandmother Zora? And the shoes? The seeing heart? Those are all dreams?"

There was a curious glee in Liv's eyes. Blake had seen it before. A relentless pursuit of the truth that was going to make her a brilliant lawyer someday.

"Yes," she lied. She couldn't push the breath past her throat. "Where is the journal now?" She started to get up, when Olivia said, "I stuck it back under the pillow, and just for the record, I don't believe you."

Blake tried a different tactic. She laughed. A forced, ugly sound that she regretted the moment it left her mouth. "Seriously, Liv? You think all that stuff about curses is real?"

"I think you have a gift that connects you to things, to the past. I think Remi can send messages to you with a single breath. And I think these abilities come from somewhere or someone. And I think you're hiding something because you hate words and therefore would never keep a journal."

Ah, yes. The uncharacteristic evidence gets you every time.

Blake's mind turned to last night when she took off the necklace. Sitting straighter, she asked, "Do I look different to you?"

Olivia seemed surprised by the question. "Are you trying to

change the subject? Seriously? You think that's going to work on me?"

"Can you just answer the question?"

"Different how?"

Like someone who'd broken a spell? Like someone with significant magic coursing through her veins? Like someone who, through a single vision, had been able to reclaim a language she had known and forgotten? "Like..." Blake began just as the phone rang. She picked up the handset, and before she could even say hello, Remi fired off, "Why aren't you on your way to the hospital?"

"I'm leaving now. How is he?"

"Awake. He wants his crossword book and—"

"Fries," Cole said in the background, which only made Blake smile as a wave of relief swept through her along with the hope that maybe, just maybe, they had skirted the dangers of the curse on their way to finding the mirror.

"Ignore him," Remi said. "And hurry."

After setting the phone back on the receiver, Blake turned back to Olivia. "I have to go."

"Fine," Olivia said. "But we aren't done talking about this." Then, with a pleading expression: "Just tell me one thing that's true—it isn't just a dream journal, is it?"

The phone rang again. With a grunt, Blake answered, "I can't leave if you keep calling."

"Blake?"

"Ian?"

Olivia groaned. "Tell him he has terrible timing."

"Olivia gave me your number," Ian said. "I just wanted to ask . . . to find out . . . how's your uncle?"

"He's out of surgery." She felt like she needed to say more, to say thank you for going to the tarot-card reader with her, for driving her to the hospital.

"I'm glad he's okay."

A thin silence stretched between them.

"Well . . ." Blake finally said.

"Well . . ."

"I, um . . . I have to get to the hospital."

"Right. Okay. One more question."

"Yeah?"

"Did you find what you were looking for last night?"

Blake paused, gripped the phone cord, and took a deep breath. Had she found what she was looking for? No, she had only found part of it, the part she hadn't even been seeking, and yet there it was, the ugly truth of a binding spell hidden behind a mask of love. "Sort of," she said.

"Good, okay." Ian paused like he wanted to say more but knew the timing was off. "Do you need a ride to the hospital? I could pick you up."

Blake considered the offer for a moment. She could feel herself being pulled into Ian's orbit, and if she let herself go, she knew she could so easily float away. There was an effortlessness to him, but more importantly he was someone who knew very little about her and she liked the idea of being a blank canvas. "It's fine," she said. She didn't need to complicate an already complicated morning. "But thanks."

"Well, how about a burger later? Or whatever you want."

There was something so normal about his request, and right now Blake needed to feel *some* kind of normal. "Okay," she agreed. "How about I call you after I go to the hospital."

As Blake wrote down his number, Olivia was gesturing wildly, as if to say, *Tell me.*

After Blake hung up the phone, Olivia squealed. "Did Ian just ask you out?"

"It's just a burger."

"Right. Do Brits even eat burgers?" Olivia rolled her eyes and sighed. "So?"

"So what?"

"I'm right, aren't I?" Olivia asked.

It isn't just a dream journal, is it?

"About Brits and burgers?"

"Blake."

Blake hesitated. She studied Olivia, realizing that no lie would be good enough to throw her best friend off the trail of magic. Then, slowly, because she couldn't find the words, or maybe because she couldn't contain the lies, she nodded.

"I knew it!" Olivia gripped Blake's shoulders, grinning like a kid on Christmas morning. "I won't let you drown all by yourself."

"So you'll drown with me?"

"Never," Olivia said. "I'll bring the lifeboat. Now, where do we start?"

"Start? No . . . I mean I can't," Blake argued. "Not now. It's too long and too strange and I have to get to the hospital."

"You're stubborn."

"And you're demanding."

A sly smile turned up the corners of Olivia's mouth. "Then we'll make excellent detectives." She unwrapped the towel from her head and shook out her damp hair, eyeing Blake the entire time. "And don't even think of concocting some ridiculous story to cover your tracks. I'll be back Monday and you'll tell me everything. Right?"

"Back from where?"

"My mom decided to surprise me with an overnight trip down

the coast," Liv said airily. "Sorry to ditch you, but she said something about mother-daughter bonding and I couldn't exactly say no."

Monday—a couple of days from now. At least that would give Blake some time to figure things out and determine just how much she would tell her best friend. Remi wouldn't like it, and Blake didn't want to put her friend in harm's way. But then again . . . she wasn't sure her heart had room for any more secrets.

Remi's and Cole's banter could be heard all the way down the dreary corridor.

But the moment Blake stepped into the room, Remi's face brightened. "He thinks he can make all the rules," she said to Blake, shaking her head. "Thinks he knows better than the doctors. Thinks he can eat bacon lard for dinner."

"I never said that," Cole said, his voice weak but his spirits high, if you judged by the beaming expression on his face. It was almost enough to erase his pallor. Almost. "Bacon lard for breakfast is just fine," he said.

Remi rolled her eyes. "Do you see what I have to deal with?" she asked Blake.

Blake understood that Remi's confrontational attitude was her way of expressing her fear. It was her way of saying, *I almost lost you, and now I'm in charge of every beat of your heart from here on out.*

Blake stood at the foot of Cole's bed. A swell of emotions swept through her: relief, love, fear. Guilt. "Bacon lard is probably a bad idea," she said as she patted his leg, afraid a hug would snap him in two. "You look good."

"You're a bad liar."

Blake smiled. "Did they say when you can go home?"

"Another week at least," Remi huffed. "But I think it's too soon. He should stay here, where they can observe him better."

"Well," Blake said, "he won't be in danger of falling off a ladder if he stays here."

"The doctors said I'm a miracle patient. And miracles get to go home." Cole attempted a laugh but grimaced instead.

Miracle? Was there room for such things in the spaces between the curses and the magic? "Es un milagro," Blake whispered, startled she had said the words aloud. Thankfully, Remi was too worked up to have noticed.

"This is not a laughing matter," Remi cried. "You could have died."

"But I didn't," Cole said. "My ticker is too strong to go kaput so easily."

Remi launched into the details of the new lifestyle she was already planning for him. "No more lard. No more fat."

"You mean rabbit food," Cole said glumly, "and no cigarettes, no drinking, and no stress."

"You forgot exercise," Blake added.

"I don't have to exercise?" Cole smiled wide.

"Mm-hmm." Remi fluffed his pillows. "Keep on, Mr. Funny Man. Isn't it time for your medication? Where is that nurse?" she blustered, and hurried out of the room.

When Blake turned her attention back to Cole, he was holding out the sketch she had tossed in the wastebasket last night. "Did you draw this? The nurse picked it out of the trash."

Blake wrinkled her nose to show her distaste for the piece of not-quite-art. "It's awful, I know, but my hands were pretty shaky last night."

"Sorry to have put you through that."

"*You're* sorry?" Blake scoffed at the idea that Cole was to blame when they both knew better. She swung to the window, then back again, feeling incredibly lost. "The curse did this."

"No," Cole blurted. "Put that out of your mind. This had nothing to do with the curse."

"You don't know that."

Cole sat up a couple of inches. "Do you remember that time we went sailing? I think you were eleven. We ran into bad weather."

Blake nodded, clueless as to where he was going with this.

"That wasn't the curse, either," he announced. "Neither was the time you got lost in the grocery store or the time my car broke down or the time Remi twisted her ankle."

"But the rule of threes," Blake reminded him. "For every two good things, there's always a bad."

"That may be, but, Blake . . . not every bad thing is because of a curse that Zora was afraid of."

"If that's true," Blake argued, "then what's the point of finding the mirror and trying to break a curse you don't even believe in?"

"I never said I didn't believe. I've seen enough magic and tragedy to tell me otherwise." Cole exhaled. "Listen, we don't know how this works, but there's a reason your magic showed up like it did. And I'm going to make sure I get back to one hundred percent quickly so I can help you sort it all out."

Blake's father's words swept into the room at just that moment. *Her powers are only going to get stronger.* More than ever, Blake could feel the truth in those words. By habit, her hand went to her now-naked throat. *But where are the rest of my powers if I broke the spell?*

The moment she saw Cole's eyes alight on her neck, she regretted the gesture.

"Where's your medal?" he asked.

Blake's heart went still. Did Cole know about the protection spell? His words came back to her with a sickening dread: *Your dad had asked us . . . that if anything ever happened to him and Delilah, we would protect you from the curse and its tragedies.*

Blake scrutinized Cole's expression, looking for any traces of betrayal. "The clasp broke." She paused, waiting for the shock to register. Surely, if he knew about the medal, he'd have a reaction, but he only eyed her warily like he was expecting her to say more. Or maybe he was just trying to decide if he believed her. His eyes flicked to the window. And that was the moment when Blake was certain Cole knew nothing about the medal's power.

"Remi told me about the vision you had of Zora," Cole said. "Have there been others?"

"Just some dreams." With stone gardens and a lurking wolf and not-snow. Flowers. *And my next clue, an eight-pointed crown.*

"Tell me about them," Cole said gently.

Blake lowered herself onto the edge of the bed. "I don't want to worry Remi."

"Then worry me."

"I don't want to worry you, either," Blake argued. "You just had a heart attack."

"Who said it was an attack anyway?" Cole said. "It was really more of a blip."

"That landed you in surgery."

Cole looked like he was preparing a witty comeback, but then his expression relaxed and, in his eyes, Blake saw understanding and love. "When you came to live with us, I swore I would never try to replace your father. But..." He glanced at the floor, then back at Blake. "But I've raised you and loved you, and that means I get to worry."

But he was in the hospital with a half-healed ticker and some broken ribs. Not exactly the kind of guy you want to saddle with all your burdens.

"Can you trust me?" he asked.

It wasn't lost on Blake that her father's love blocked her magic and Cole's love was trying to help her find it.

She needed to give Cole a morsel. Something to chew on. "The dreams and visions are clues trying to get me somewhere."

"Like bread crumbs."

Bread crumbs. Yes, that's exactly what the clues were. Crumbs to lead her down a path. But to where? To the mirror? To the full assumption of her magic? To a sea of more unknown truths?

Cole eased himself back into his pillows cautiously like they were made of glass. "And?"

"And what?"

"How do you know this? Have any of these visions led you somewhere specific?" He quirked an inquisitive brow.

That's the problem with morsels, Blake thought. *They're too small to appease anyone as clever and curious as Cole.* "The seeing heart appeared on a flyer for the carnival and . . ." Blake hesitated, groping for the right words.

"You followed the lead." Cole's eyes glittered with an excitement that didn't match his condition or this stale, cold room. "And what did you find?"

"A psychic," Blake offered carefully, taking her time so as not to trip over her own words. "She told me that I was on a journey looking for the answers that so many others before me have tried to find, and she knew . . ." This last part required control and careful articulation. "She said I had magic flowing in my veins."

Cole wasn't blinking. He didn't even look like he was breathing. His expression was one of both fascination and apprehension. He spoke slowly, carefully. "Did she say anything about the mirror?"

Blake shook her head, realizing at once that she had set this dance in motion. She had created the stage and the rules and the tone. She had chosen the music and now here they were. She—dancing around her own lies; Cole—trying to learn the steps that would lead to the truth, and the single question hanging in the air: "Why would the symbol lead you to something we already know?" Cole asked.

It didn't.

But Blake didn't want to talk about the protection spell, or about her uncertainty that it had really been broken. What she couldn't pin down was the frequency vibrating in the deepest recesses of her heart and mind, one that told her that the magic was trying to communicate with her. She had thought that maybe once she broke the binding spell, the magic would be able to tell her exactly what it wanted to say. And now she was second-guessing all of it, wondering if her laser focus on finding the mirror was making her miss other bits of info, other clues.

In response to her uncle's question, she gave a shrug.

"Did the psychic say anything else? Anything that could be a clue?" His voice was high-pitched and alert. "Another bread crumb that maybe you overlooked?"

Cole's desperation for answers carved a hole in Blake's heart. But she told herself she was doing this to protect him, to keep him safe. Maybe the curse was done with him. Maybe the further away her family was from touching its sharp destructive edges, the safer they'd be.

Maybe.

"Nothing," Blake lied, quickly shifting the conversation to something simpler as she edged closer to the bed to fluff his pillows. "But there was something else that was weird—in my vision of the festival, I realized that the snow I told you about? It wasn't snow at all, but these small white flowers."

"Like the drawing?"

Blake nodded.

Cole was silent, ruminating. She had seen the look before. The way he studied an exotic flower with equal parts reverence and curiosity, as if the bloom would open its petals and tell him all its secrets. Underneath it all he was a scientist, and scientists are excellent at deduction. "I'll have to give that some thought, see if we can identify the flowers specifically. Maybe there's another answer there."

His eyes dropped to her hand, resting at her side. "You've been painting."

Blake lifted her hand, noticing the flecks of azure paint under her nails from last night. "Actually, I have some good news. I have an interview with a gallery owner. Mr. Brown set it up for a week from today," she said, before filling her uncle in on all the details.

Cole smiled, and for a split second he didn't look like a man who had just returned from death's door. He looked healthy and happy and whole. "That's wonderful! See?"

"See what?"

"Blessings. Not curses."

Two good. One bad. And despite what her uncle said, if Blake didn't find the crown soon, she was sure more of the bad were going to arrive.

19

Blake didn't want to go home and be alone with her buzzing thoughts and millions of questions. So she stopped at a pay phone in the hospital lobby and called Ian to see if he still wanted to hang out.

"I know the perfect place," he said. "Do you like to bowl?"

"I thought we were talking burgers." Blake hadn't been bowling since last summer when her class took a field trip. And even then, she was mediocre at best.

"Burgers and bowling." Ian laughed. "From what I hear, it's the perfect combo."

When Blake arrived at the bowling alley, Ian was standing near the shoe rental. He waved her over. "I didn't know what size you wear," he said, glancing down at her red shoes. She hated the idea of taking them off, thinking they would enhance her magic or lead her to the crown, but she was already here, and it would only be an hour or so.

The place was bustling, packed with families, other teens, and a few older folks who were playing in lanes at the far end. An expected turnout for a Saturday. The scent of buttery popcorn filled the air. And a jukebox played an old Elvis tune.

This is exactly what I needed, Blake thought. *A chance to clear my head and be* normal *for a moment.* Ian took a lane in the center and they began to change into their bowling shoes.

Ian said, "Are you hungry now?"

"Not yet. So, tell me, are you really good at this? Should I prepare myself to get whipped?"

"I'm bloody awful." Ian laughed as he laced a shoe.

"Do people in England not bowl?"

"We've got a very long history of bowling," he said, grinning.

"And I'm pretty sure we had it way before we came to America. So, really I have no good excuse. I just thought it would be a gas, and like I said..."

"The burgers."

Ian's face tightened. "Uh—I have a confession to make."

"That doesn't sound good."

"I don't really like burgers."

"So you're bad at bowling and you hate burgers," Blake teased as she double-knotted her shoes, hating how tightly they pinched her toes. "Tell me again why we're here?"

Ian stood, grabbed a ball, and inspected it. "I thought it would be a very proper American date." His gaze fell to Blake's. "Did I get that wrong?"

Blake's cheeks warmed and she felt a surge of shyness that threw her off-balance. Had he just said *date*? Was that what this was? Did she want it to be? And before she could finish the thought, a voice inside was telling her, *Yes. Yes. Yes.* She stood and grabbed her own ball. "Depends on if you lose."

Within fifteen minutes, Blake saw that Ian hadn't been exaggerating. His bowling skills were awful. Most of the time he landed his ball in the gutter, then spun back toward Blake, hands thrown to his head in hilarious defeat as he grunted, "Bugger all," and swore he'd get a strike at his next turn.

Not that Blake was much better. Although at least she could knock down a pin or two. And for the next hour, they laughed and kidded, bowled and groaned, enough to make Blake momentarily forget about the weight of magic.

Or at least until she and Ian were seated in the food court waiting for their order. Ian raised his plastic cup. "To the victor."

Blake knocked her cup against his. "It wasn't exactly hard," she teased, thinking both their scores were awful: 70 and 120.

Ian hovered his soda cup over the table, turning suddenly serious. "I have a question."

"Okay?"

He paused like a theater actor timing his lines for maximum effect. "Did you find your future?"

It took Blake a moment to realize what he meant, and then she remembered. "Oh . . . right." Martina. "I guess time will tell."

Leaning closer, elbows on the table, Ian said in a conspiratorial tone, "Or you could just follow the signs."

"Signs?"

He settled back in his chair. "Remember when I told you my nan reads tea leaves?" He didn't wait for Blake to answer. "Well, she *is* a big believer in signs, too. That's how she knew I should come here."

"What kinds of signs?"

"You'd have to ask her, but she says they're all around," Ian said. Swirling a straw through his soda, he stared into his cup as if he could conjure the future his nan had seen. "Truth?" He lifted his gaze slowly.

Blake's throat tightened. She nodded.

"My nan told me some other things," Ian continued. "She said that I would meet a girl here. Someone with secrets."

Blake felt the air shift, as if a quiet storm were brewing in the space between them. She didn't know what to say, how to react, what to do to dim the glittering light in Ian's hazel eyes. Trying to defuse the intensity of his expression, she let out a light laugh. "A mystery woman."

Ignoring her tone, Ian said, "And . . ." There was a long pause. The thunderous sound of falling pins echoed all around them.

"And what?"

"And you won't believe me."

The server brought them their burgers in baskets. The scent of the meat suddenly made Blake nauseous. "Try me." She was holding her breath.

"She said I would see . . . magic."

A coil of searing energy sprang to life inside Blake. And before she could ask another question, Ian laughed. "I know it sounds bonkers. But maybe . . . you're the mysterious girl with secrets."

Blake's cheeks felt like they were on fire. Was it possible that Ian's nan really had predicted Ian meeting her? "I'm not mysterious," she said.

Ian smiled and shrugged. "If the crown fits..."

Blake froze. "What did you just say?"

"Which part?"

Blake felt like the world was spinning on hyperspeed all around her. No. It was a coincidence, Ian—British Ian—came from a country with a monarchy, so his use of the word *crown* made sense. Blake dismissed the far-fetched idea. Then again, her vision had been clear—a crown in a shaft of lavender light.

"Blake?"

She turned her attention back to him.

"Did I scare you off with all this talk?"

Blake pushed her sweater sleeves higher, leaning in. She knew once she started talking there was no taking it back. But she had to follow her hunch. "Listen, I am going to tell you something that is going to sound really crazy, but...you said something about signs and following them. What if I told you I'm looking for a sign, a symbol really?"

"What kind of symbol?"

"A crown."

Ian blinked. "As in a real one?"

"I . . . I think so. Or maybe an image. I'm not sure yet. But where would you look?"

Folding his arms across his chest, Ian considered the question. "In a castle? A palace?"

Blake leaped to her feet as the thought simultaneously flashed across her mind. "Can we take your car?"

"Where?"

"The Palace of Fine Arts."

Ian drove through the city toward the Marina District, where the Palace of Fine Arts was nothing more than a crumbling ruin that had been a world's fair decades earlier. Still, it was the best lead Blake had at the moment and just maybe . . .

Ian parked on a residential street with a view of the lagoon and the crumbling half dome beyond. A large crane hovered over the structure; piles of rubble stretched across the construction site.

Steel-barred columns at the north end rose from the demolition, and Blake tried to imagine what it might become when the renovations were completed.

"*This* is a palace?" Ian said as they hopped out of the car.

"It was built for a world's fair a long time ago and now it's being restored."

They crossed the road and stood at the edge of the lagoon, where a single swan floated. "So what now?" Ian asked.

"We look for anything that looks like a crown."

"I'm pretty sure we aren't allowed to just walk around a construction site. There's a fence for a reason."

Blake hurried along the edge of the water. "I don't see anyone who might stop us. How about you go in that direction and I'll check things out on the north end. I'll meet you back here in twenty?"

Ian raised a disapproving eyebrow. "I should go with you."

"I'll scream if I need you." In a rush, Blake rounded the water's edge, coming to a fence with a sign reading "Keep Out." She glanced over her shoulder to make sure she was alone and then pushed on the locked gate. That's when she saw a small opening to her right, big enough to crawl through. Before she could change her mind, she let herself into the restricted area.

The steel bars and half-built structure loomed above her as

she pressed on through dust and debris in total silence. Her heart began to sink as she realized there was nothing here that looked like anything other than useless wreckage.

"A dead end," she muttered as a deep throbbing began in her ears. The world shifted, pulsed, screamed at a frequency that shook Blake to her bones.

Immediately her eyes flicked from one side of the large area to the next.

And then a man stepped out from behind one of the columns. For a split second, Blake thought maybe he worked here, but then her eyes registered what exactly she was seeing. His face was riddled with the same wounds as the woman in the green dress. He sparked the same sense of magic—a sharp-edged power. He stood there motionless with his gaze fixed on Blake. Bits of burned flesh fell from his chin. Heat rushed over her skin.

His mouth was moving now, slowly, mechanically, forming a single word: *Blake.*

All sound fell away and all Blake could hear, could feel, was a trembling deep in her bones.

She ran. Around the debris, through the fence, and smack-dab into Ian.

"Blake?"

Unexpectedly she threw her arms around his neck, gripping

him tight. His arms were around her waist in an instant. "Hey." His voice was soft, calming. "You look like you've seen a ghost."

Blake stayed like that for a moment longer than any good sense would have allowed, but for the first time she felt veiled, protected. And she didn't want to move from his arms. She took a steadying breath. Ian smelled like chicory coffee, the kind they sold down by the wharf. And he smelled of the sea. Fall, not winter.

She pulled back, her cheeks warm with embarrassment. "I'm sorry," she said, feeling like the world had turned on a slant and there was no toehold to keep her grounded. And then the dam of lies broke and the truth rushed out. "I was scared and . . . there was a man."

He knew my name.

Ian's alert eyes lifted to look over her shoulder. "A man? Did he try to hurt you?"

Blake shook her head. When she glanced back there was no one.

"What did he look like?"

That was where Blake drew the line. No way could she tell Ian that the man had looked like a leper with the stiffness of a corpse. Ian's hand was still on her shoulder in a protective sort of way that sparked something in her—a wave of gratitude that she wasn't alone, perhaps. She relaxed into his touch as he told her he hadn't found a crown, and then . . .

Silence. A lake dappled with sunlight that glitters like bits of gold sand. Grand, sweeping trees bask at the edges. There is a dock, long and lazy, that hovers over the water, and a fair-haired boy with small, bent shoulders perches on the end, his bare feet dangling over the side. He holds something in his hands.

The vision vanished. With a shudder, Blake stepped back.

"What's wrong?" Ian asked.

When Blake looked up, Ian was studying her, and for a split second, she thought he had sensed the memory that had gone through her. His memory. But how was that possible? Blake's magic worked with objects, not people. Or at least that was how it had always been before, but before had to make room for now. And there was no doubt that her magic was growing.

And there in the shadow of a half-ruined palace, the idea took root: *I really did break the binding spell.* Or at the very least, Blake knew that whatever power had bound her magic was loosening its grip.

A few minutes later they were at a small café in North Beach. It was a quiet, charming place—the kind you might find in a European village, replete with classical music, buttery scents, and miniature potted roses sitting in the windowsills. The gray afternoon had skewed darker, although there wasn't a cloud in the sky.

After they each ordered coffee, Blake swept her coat off, twisted her torso to hang it over her chair, then turned to face Ian and the dozen questions she knew he was waiting to ask. He had been thoughtful in the car, careful not to approach the subject of the scary man too closely. Instead he played the radio and was silent, as if he was waiting for Blake to make the first move. She had been lost in the allure of her own magic, of encroaching on Ian's memories as if they were nothing. But they were something. She didn't want to possess the key that opened doors marked "Private." She didn't want that kind of power. Or did she? A part of her worried that Ian could see the guilt scrawled across her face. And that he would somehow sense that she was a trespasser.

But when her eyes met his across the table, there was no hint at an interrogation. Only a sincere expression that said, *Are you sure you're okay?*

Blake wondered how many times Ian would have to ask that question before she caved and told him the truth. *No, I am not okay. I'm a broken piece of magic that might never get fixed.*

"Well," she began, and was interrupted by a soft breath brushing across her cheek, like the landing of a blown kiss. Sometimes, when Blake was outside, it was hard to discern Remi's touch from nature's. But here in this café, there was no mistaking that Remi was calling her.

And just as Ian said, "We don't have to talk about it if you don't want to," the waitress arrived with their drinks and the second breath brushed against Blake's cheek.

Blake wrapped her hands around the steaming cup, trying to ignore Remi. She wasn't ready to leave the warm cocoon of the café. If it was important, Remi would send another message, Blake reasoned.

"You must think I'm crazy," she said to Ian.

"I think you're interesting."

Blake laughed in spite of herself.

Two hurried breaths crossed her cheek. God, Remi had the worst timing.

Blake said, "I have to make a quick call."

"Now?"

"I just need to check on Cole."

Blake found a pay phone in a darkened hall at the back of the café, looked up the hospital's number in the Yellow Pages, then dialed the number and was connected to Cole's room. Remi picked up on the first ring. "Blake?"

"Is everything okay?"

"Why did you take so long? Where are you?"

"I'm . . . I'm just having a coffee. What's wrong? Is it Cole?"

Remi took a breath. There was rustling in the background. "It's

Rose. I called to check on her and she was out of sorts, going on and on about how she had to talk to you immediately. Something about the price. She said she knows the price. Does that mean something to you?"

Blake gripped the phone tighter. "No," she lied. Her heart pounded in her chest with a ferocity that made her dizzy. "I'll go see her tomorrow."

"She said it had to be tonight." A pause stretched too thin. "I'm worried about her, Blake. Can you go over now?"

Blake agreed before setting the phone down. As she headed back to Ian, Rose's words followed like a bitter squall: *It will cost you. Will you pay the price?*

When she returned to the table Ian was in a lively conversation with a burly, middle-aged man. They were talking about Martin Luther King Jr.'s upcoming visit to Grace Cathedral.

"He's done a lot for America," Ian was saying.

"An admirable effort, but not sure how much good it'll do." The man held up the newspaper with King's picture, jabbing it with his index finger. "These beliefs run deep."

Blake froze, then peered closer at the newspaper photo. The man had doodled half a dozen little crowns in a circle around King's face.

Blake rushed toward the man. "Can I . . . see that for a second?"

The man gave her a quizzical look before handing the paper over. She gripped its edges, hoping for a vision, the same way the heart had shown her Dolores Park. The café was filled with voices and activity and clanking dishes, frustrating Blake.

"Blake?" Ian's voice came to her right before she said, "I'll be right back."

Hurriedly, she returned to the pay phone, to the shadowed corner where there was some semblance of quiet. "Come on," she whispered, staring at the crowns, willing the truth to reveal itself.

A voice travels to Blake from far off. King's voice bellows down the steps of Grace Cathedral. She's there, moving up the stairs, closer and closer, until she reaches the bronze doors. Slowly they open, but before she can look inside, the world evaporates.

Clutching the paper, Blake breathed heavily. "That's it," she said, nearly smiling. "The next clue will be when King visits Grace Cathedral." *More than a week from now. Ugh.* How was she ever going to wait that long?

Returning to the table, Blake handed the man his paper, thanking him. He studied it like she had laced it with poison. "Uh, you can keep it if you like."

"Thanks, I got what I needed," she said as she sat down.

"Is Cole okay?" Ian asked.

"He's fine."

"Then why do you look so stricken? Is it the man?"

"Not exactly." She swallowed the words she so desperately wanted to say. *Your nan was right about the magic, about me and my secrets.* "I found the crown. It's Dr. King," she said, holding up the paper.

Ian's expression was one of confusion. "You really are a mystery."

"I need to go. Do you think you can give me a ride?"

"To the hospital?"

"No, I have to go see a friend. It's not too far."

A few minutes later they were back in the car driving through a thick curtain of fog that made their pace agonizingly slow.

"I hope I didn't freak you out about the magic." Ian tapped his thumbs on the steering wheel. "I don't usually tell people that sort of thing. Just forget I said anything. My nan is a little bonkers."

"It's not bonkers."

Ian threw her a sideways glance. "Yeah? Do you know anyone who makes wild predictions that come true?"

No, just one who messages me with magic. "I have a friend who hears ghosts," Blake said, before considering the weight of her words. She hadn't meant to grant their freedom, but a part of her wanted to find common ground with Ian. To show him he wasn't crazy for believing in something most people thought never existed. She added, "That's where I'm going now."

Ian didn't balk or blink. As if he were used to hearing about ghosts. He merely nodded and kept his eyes on the dreary afternoon beyond the windshield.

"Turn in to the parking lot here," Blake said, pointing.

Ian pulled along the curb at the senior center's entrance.

"Thanks for the ride."

Ian took hold of her hand, slowing the moment. Outside, the mist was shifting, stippling the building with shadows and hazy silhouettes. "What exactly did you see at the palace?"

Those eyes again. Lulling her, drawing her into his false idea of sparkling magic: Safe magic. Good magic. Exciting magic. The kind that spins dreams and grants wishes. "I have to go."

As if Ian sensed Blake's intention to cut him loose, he said, "Hang on." He put the car in park, jumped out, and ran around to Blake's side, where he held the door open.

A voice reverberated down the walkway. "You can't park here, son. Emergency vehicles only."

"I'm moving right now," Ian called out. Then, turning to Blake: "Can I see you again?"

The voice belonged to a cop who emerged from the fog and was walking faster now, swinging his arms like he was on a mission bigger than ticketing someone for illegal parking. "Hey, son!"

Without taking his eyes off of Blake, Ian said, "Tell me I can see you, so I don't have to spend the night in jail."

"Hold on there!" the cop, now fifteen feet away, shouted.

Ian raised a single eyebrow. "Well?"

Blake felt like she was teetering on the thin line between the shallow and deep ends of a pool, torn between logic and emotion. It would be selfish to invite him into her world. *But what if his nan really is a gifted seer? What if Ian can help me?*

"At least let me tell you the rest," Ian said.

"The rest of what?"

Ian smiled. "The magic. There's so much more to my story. I think you're why I'm here, and I think I'm supposed to help you, and if you say no, then my destiny might be ruined. But no pressure if you absolutely never want to see me again."

Blake returned the smile. She wanted to see him again. And again. In a single unguarded breath, she said yes to Ian and to the rest of the magic, before she vanished into the center.

The light inside the center was heavier, gloomier than usual. As if the curse inhabited the very air Blake breathed and was pressing in through every window, every door.

Rose was sitting up in bed with a pillow clutched to her chest, worrying its edges, when Blake walked into the room.

"Blake?"

"It's me." The moment Blake reached the edge of Rose's bed and sat down, she could see the brightness in the woman's eyes, electric with memory. An instant wave of relief spread through her. "Remi said you have something to tell me."

"Zora came again." Rose's voice was eerily composed. "She told me to tell you . . ." A pause. A tilt of her head. "Are we alone?"

On edge, Blake nodded before adding impatiently, "Rose, tell me what Zora said."

Rose's gaze returned to Blake's face, holding her there with the promise of what she was about to say. "She was so far away. I tried to hear."

The sound of a squeaky wheel ricocheted down the corridor, unnerving Blake. Everything felt suddenly amplified, the buzz of the cold, bare lights, the scent of decaying flowers and sweat, the stiff prickling of the sheets.

"Blake?" Rose's voice brought her back to the moment.

Blake took the woman's hand in her own. "Yes . . . I'm here. What did Zora say?"

The pleas rose up inside Blake as if she were actively negotiating with someone, or something. *Please. Please. Please. Give me something real. Something that matters.*

Rose whispered, "The wolf is here, and so are the birds."

Blake's insides twisted. Her breathing grew shallow. Had she hurried here for this? For birds and wolves and . . . ? Then, recalling the golden eyes of her dreams, she asked, "Who is the wolf?"

Snapping her fingers, Rose shook her head determinedly. "Not birds. Crows. Yes, the crows with the serpent."

The air in the room thinned to near nothingness, and Blake felt a terrible pressure in her chest beyond what her frame could contain.

"Did Zora tell you anything else?" Her voice was high and tight. "About the mirror or where it is?"

Rose shook her head, squeezing Blake's hand. "I'm scared for you, Blake. Zora said you're in danger."

Blake thought about the strange man she had seen earlier. He knew her name, but how? Was he the crow or the wolf or . . . ? And what about the terrifying woman from school? "Rose," she said gently. "Did Zora say anything about a curse or the mirror?"

"The looking glass," Rose whispered. Her eyes glazed over. "The curse. They are the same. Don't you see?"

Too afraid to speak and break the spell, Blake waited, breath held.

Rose put the pillow down, clenching Blake's hand. "The curse will keep coming for you. Touching the lives around you. Until it hurts. Until there is nothing left."

Blake knew this was true, but hearing the words fall from

Rose's lips was like being plunged into icy waters. Still, she had to stay focused, she had to stay on track before Rose's memory retreated into the dark. "Which is why I have to find the mirror so I can break the curse!"

Rose stared, nodding. "They are the same. Inside the glass," she said, "that's where it all began."

"Did she say what these crows . . . look like?" Blake cried. "Do they have wounds like burns or . . ."

"Zora said there are three. She said—"

Just then a fire alarm blared. Blake startled, only half catching what Rose had said before the old woman shouted, "Is it a bomb?"

Blake ran to the door, opened it, and poked her head into the hall. A nurse rushed down the corridor hollering orders for everyone to evacuate in an orderly fashion.

And by the time the closet blaze was put out, the light had left Rose's eyes and she'd retreated back into her unremembering world, leaving Blake alone in her nightmare with only these words: "You'll know them by their claws."

That night when Remi asked about Rose, Blake made a show of her disappointment to brand the lie as believable. "It was nothing," she lamented. "By the time I got there, she didn't remember even talking to you." Then she added the bit about the closet fire to cement the story.

Remi stood there silent, appraising. "What aren't you telling me?"

"I—"

Remi held up a hand. "Please do not lie to me, Blake. I know there is more going on."

It was no use. Blake had to give her aunt something.

"Did you know that my dad bound my magic?"

There it was. Out in the open. A painful, ugly truth.

Remi's hand flew to her mouth. "He what?"

After Blake relayed what had happened with Martina and the vision she had, Remi blinked once, twice, three times. There seemed to be no end to her blinking, or her shock. "Dear Lord, why didn't you tell me?"

"Everything happened with Cole, and I didn't want to worry you."

Blake could see the anger in her aunt's stance, in her pulsing jaw, in her grim expression, and she was pretty sure it was not only because of Blake keeping the truth from her but because of her dad's even bigger lie. "I had no idea," Remi said bitterly, "And now we know why your magic has been repressed for so long. And we know that the heart led you to the truth." Her eyes flicked to Blake's naked throat. "You tried to break the spell."

Blake nodded.

"And did you?"

"I don't know. I still feel the same tug-of-war, like the two magics are fighting for territory or something."

Unexpectedly, Remi pulled Blake into a fierce hug. "I'm so, so sorry."

"It isn't your fault."

Remi pulled back, wiping a lone tear. "That doesn't mean I can't be sorry."

The first words out of Olivia's mouth when she got back into town a couple of days later were "Tell me all about the journal."

Blake was glad Remi had already left for the hospital. She and Olivia sat on the screened-in porch that overlooked Cole's garden. The great beech tree's branches swayed in the wind.

"What do you want to know first?"

Olivia threw her legs over the arm of a rattan chair. "Do you want some wine? It might make this easier."

"I hate wine."

"I meant easier for me." Olivia inhaled sharply. "You're right. Wine will only muddle my mind. Okay, lay it on me and don't leave out a single detail. The devil is always in the details."

Blake paced while trying to collect the right words. She had never been good at stories. Not their beginnings or middles or ends. And where was she supposed to begin anyway? With her family magic? With the curse? With Zora or the girl in the mirror? There were so many entry points and not enough exits.

Slowly, she said, "Are you absolutely sure you want to know?" Blake wanted to give Olivia a way out, even though she knew she would never take it.

Olivia gave her a shocked expression. "I just told you . . ."

"You could get hurt."

"I could get hurt stepping off the curb. No one gets a guarantee. Listen." She sat up, her sharp gaze speaking volumes about her intentions before the words ever left her mouth. "I know this is freaky stuff, but you shouldn't do it alone, and I love whodunits, and from what I read in your journal, you've got a lot of questions that need answers."

"Liv, this isn't *Perry Mason*."

Olivia smirked. "I was talking about *The Twilight Zone*. Remember when I figured out the 'Invaders' episode before the ending? I knew the bad guys weren't really the bad guys," she went on. "It was a total shift in perception. Here we thought the poor old lady living in her cabin was trying to protect herself and get rid of tiny aliens when she was the alien all along!"

So Blake told her best friend everything.

When Blake was done, Olivia sat still. Unblinking and focused.

Ten seconds ticked by. Fifteen.

"Well?" Blake finally said. There was a small knot in the pit of her stomach.

Olivia got to her feet. "So, where do we start?"

"Liv," Blake began, only to be shut down by Olivia.

"Don't say another word. I told you I'd bring the lifeboat, and I won't take no for an answer. Now," Olivia said, "we need to focus on the most important elements of the case."

"Are we back to *The Twilight Zone*?"

Olivia's eyes went wide. "Of course not. I meant *Perry Mason*. He always gets his man." She folded her arms and began to pace. "So, we know several key things. First, your family has a history of magic. They also possess magical artifacts that someone else wants. Second, the only way to break the curse is to find the mirror, but no one knows where it is. And third, you're seeing symbols in visions and dreams and the heart led you to the psychic lady and the crown is leading you to King's visit, which . . . I'm going with you. And also there are creepy people following you." She took a breath. "And what did Rose say? The wolf and the crows are here?"

"Yeah. Sounds worse when you say it like that."

"Okay," Liv said, already in spy mode. "So, next step—we find out what the crown wants this Sunday and make sure not to get killed in the process."

"Liv, you can back out of this."

"Not a chance."

For the rest of the week, Blake fell asleep with the phone cradled to her ear, stretching the hall phone cord to its limit. She and Ian talked deep into the nights, him telling her what it was like to grow up in England, her telling him about her dreams of being a great painter.

"I have an idea," he said that Friday night, his words followed by a disturbing thump.

"Ian?"

Through a half groan, half breath he said, "Argh—I ran into the sofa, stubbed my big toe."

"Are you okay?"

"It's dark, and I'd rather not look in case there's blood."

Blake laughed quietly, careful not to wake Remi in the other room. "So what's your idea?" she said, hugging the receiver tighter to her ear.

"Well, I've always wanted one of those proper portraits. It's a very English thing to do. You could paint me in a smoking jacket and maybe with a pipe. It would be amazing."

Blake rolled her eyes, biting back the laugh. "I can't picture you in a smoking jacket."

"I most definitely have one." After the spilled laughter, there was a moment of silence and then: "Blake?"

"Mm-hmm?"

"I think even if my nan hadn't told me to come here... I think that we would have found each other."

Blake's heart expanded in her chest. "I think so, too."

Moments later she fell into the dark world of her dreams. Fractured images, one superimposed over the next, like a painting over a painting.

There is only the armless statue of Blake. The stone shatters into white flowers. The blooms are inhaled by a wolf, which bares its fangs as a murder of crows explodes into the air.

Blake woke with a start.

Sunlight flooded her room as she snatched her sketchbook from the nightstand, and began to draw the crows. Her fingers quivered. She shook out her hand, thinking she had slept on her arm wrong. After a few more maddening tries, she brought the crows out of the dream and into her reality.

Swimming at the edge of her vision was the silver clock on her nightstand, its relentless ticking growing incessantly louder. Blake glanced up. Froze. The shock of the moment didn't register in real time, more like a slow-motion wave rising, rising, rising before it came crashing down.

Saturday. The second-chance interview she had not prepared for.

Ms. Ivanov!

23

Blake leaped out of bed, washed up, then dressed in a pair of red slacks and a black sweater before tying her hair in a haphazard ponytail. She fumbled with her portfolio, which she hadn't opened since her terrible visit to Grayson's. Quickly she organized each piece, trying to put the collection into some semblance of order, and as she did, she realized a sketch was missing. The one with the girl with the face of a wolf. It was the last piece she had sketched before all of this craziness had begun.

Had it fallen out of the portfolio when she dropped it under the tree outside Grayson's? She didn't have time to worry about that now. She slipped on the magic shoes and bolted out the door.

There was no way the bus would deliver her to Russian Hill in enough time, so she grabbed a cab, arriving at the address on the back of Ms. Ivanov's card with five glorious minutes to spare. She might have missed the unassuming building with its pale, ordinary facade had it not been for the granite tile so artistically etched with the name "Ivanov Gallery."

There was a moment, a ghost of a dream, in which Blake envisioned her name engraved outside her very own gallery. Maybe in Paris. Or London. Or New York. The thought of it released a swell of happiness in her stomach, and she found herself smiling. Until she realized that the sign was centered between two unmarked metal doors.

Blake took the one on the right, realizing immediately that she had chosen wrong. This wasn't a gallery. It was an antiques store, a treasure trove of the past, filled with memory holders. Like tiny time machines that had traveled near and far until they had found their way here.

The shop was stacked with mirrors, chairs, armoires, lamps, jewelry, and paintings. A maze of delight for treasure-seeking souls.

Just as Blake spun to leave, she caught a glimpse, a flutter of movement, in a glass case from the corner of her eye.

She turned, traced her hand over the edges. She could feel a vision coming. . . .

"You must be Blake. I'm Ms. Ivanov."

With a gasp, Blake twirled to face a tall, reed-thin woman with a silver silk scarf elegantly wrapped around her head. She wore a pair of fitted jeans with a crisp white button-up blouse that tied in the front. Her makeup was artfully applied, a hint of shadow and lipstick to enhance her beauty instead of cover it.

Blake felt off-balance. She felt that familiar strangeness of waking from the gray space between dreaming and living. She wanted to stay in the dream. To return to the forest. Instead she swayed in place like a tree bending to the whims of the wind.

"Have you been drinking?" the woman asked.

It wasn't a question. It was an accusation that stung.

"What?" And then Blake understood how she must have looked teetering in the in-between place of here and there. She willed herself steady. Too much was riding on this. "No. I don't drink." Seeing Ms. Ivanov was unmoved, she tried again. "I'm sorry . . . I'm here for the interview. I got turned around. The door didn't have a sign."

Eyeing Blake suspiciously, Ms. Ivanov seemed to relax and said, "People always choose the entrance on the right first." There was a trace of an accent trying to stay hidden but noticeable enough to reveal that the woman wasn't from the States.

"Pardon me?"

"The unmarked doors. It is intentional, to see which people will choose. It adds an air of mystery."

Blake nodded eagerly like a newcomer to the world of mystery. Eyes wide, focused. One hand holding her portfolio, the other draped casually at her side. Smile in perfect range of nice but not strange. And a heart that was pleading, *Don't screw this up. Please don't screw this up.*

"Follow me," Ms. Ivanov said.

Blake trailed the woman, not back the way she had entered but through the labyrinth of objects and down a narrow, windowless hall lit by chandeliers made of tiny gold bells. The short journey only took twenty seconds or so, but in that time, Blake suddenly felt as if she might burst with excitement. She tried to imagine what Ms. Ivanov's gallery would look like. Stark with white walls? Gloomy with lighting strategically placed for mood? Mysterious bordering on fantasy?

Ms. Ivanov stopped in front of a white door. Paused. Her hand hovered over the knob for just a blink. Then she opened the door with a grinding screech.

Blake tried to hide her disappointment and utter disenchantment. Her imagination hadn't prepared her for this.

She stepped into a small warehouse with concrete floors and water-stained walls. High windows allowed sunbeams to dapple the otherwise drab space. Blake reached for the right words. Curious? Strange? The kind of place someone gets murdered?

At the center of the chilly room was a paint-splattered table covered with tin cans that were bursting with brushes, pencils and pens. Next to it, an easel already furnished with a blank pad. On both the left and right side were two floor-length mirrors with gilded ornate frames.

"Is this your art studio?" Blake asked, resisting the urge to rub the cold off her arms.

"For the next hour it is your studio."

"Excuse me?"

"I realize this is not what you might be used to," Ms. Ivanov said, "but I like to see artists in a *natural* habitat." The woman's penetrating gaze cut through Blake. "While your portfolio might be a sampling of your art, it isn't the whole story. Is it? Your story is in the process. In the creation, the evolution of the thing. Your very art resides in the heart." With her right hand she was drawing circles over her heart. "Do you understand?"

No, Blake did not understand. But she nodded. To be polite. To be liked. To be accepted.

To get the job. To keep her mind from wandering.

"So," Ms. Ivanov went on, "you will sketch with the pencil I provided, and I will review your portfolio while keeping an eye on your process."

Blood rushed into Blake's cheeks. It wasn't as if she hadn't ever sketched in front of someone—she did it in art class all the time. But that was among fellow artists and students. Here, she felt like a thing on display. The single acrobat in a high-wire act.

"What are the mirrors for?"

The woman deadpanned: "Because all artists must face themselves if they are to have half a chance in this world."

Blake understood now that the mere hour she'd been given to work in didn't matter. Ms. Ivanov's interest in *process* was the point. It didn't matter how much Blake got done. What mattered was the way she approached the work, the way she communicated with the pencil and paper. With herself. If only that hadn't been so especially difficult lately. While Ms. Ivanov retreated to a chair in the corner, Blake made her way to the easel, tugging the stool closer. Forcing herself to focus on the here and now.

"You may begin," Ms. Ivanov said as she unzipped Blake's leather case. The sound of the metal teeth set Blake on edge.

Trying to pretend that Ms. Ivanov's eyes weren't penetrating the back of her skull, Blake picked up the pencil and considered what she might create.

She gripped the pencil tighter, to get the feel of it, to communicate, *We're in this together.*

"Lovely," Ms. Ivanov said under her breath, and Blake could hear the papers rustling as the woman sifted through the sketches.

A smile began at the edges of Blake's mouth. She set the pencil to the paper, already knowing that she was going to create a shaded hand—Ms. Ivanov's hand. There was a complexity to it that she thought the woman would appreciate.

Not feeling entirely confident, and distracted by the mirrors, Blake began. The long, even strokes should have been simple and natural, except that Blake's hand was unsteady in the execution. She took deep breaths, trying to calm her mind and heart. If there was one thing she knew, it was this: To create beauty, one must approach the blank page with humility and love. She needed to become one with the art.

A flicker of white danced at the edge of her vision. She turned to the mirror on her right, where she saw her own reflection, shrinking, vanishing until her form was swallowed up by a dense forest layered in mist. Blake could feel the chill of the floor beneath her feet. The world around her settled into an unnatural silence. *Not again. Please. Not now.* And then the whispers flew.

Whispers echo from the mirror, slow and steady and so garbled Blake can't grasp their meaning. Her hand reaches for the mirror, for the woodland. For the elusive whispers that form two words: Broken promises.

"Blake? Are you all right?"

Coming back to the room, Blake nodded, pulse racing, as she snapped her attention back to the sketch. Stretching her fingers, she tried again. The pencil dropped to the floor.

"I'm sorry," she found herself saying as she retrieved the tool. The words floated across the empty space with no response. Only the sound of rustling papers and a deep regret-filled sigh.

When Blake raised her hand to try again, a sudden sharp pain gripped her from the inside, hot and unforgiving. Her gaze was dragged back to the mirror.

Mist fills the glass. She sees her partial reflection, legs hanging off the stool. The mist parts. Her body comes into view. Her neck. And then her face. But it isn't her face. It's the face of a wolf. The familiar words fill the space: "I've been waiting a long time for you."

Blake swayed on the stool, exerting incredible effort to stay upright. She tilted, righted herself. The room, Ms. Ivanov, this opportunity all fell away into a dizzying void, and it was as though

Blake was nowhere at all. Except sitting with the realization that it was her magic that had been waiting for her. And she—*she* was the wolf!

When Blake's vision cleared, Ms. Ivanov was standing over her.

And words. There were so many words.

"Let me try again," Blake pleaded. Her voice shook. "I . . . I just . . ."

But if I'm the wolf, who are the crows?

Ms. Ivanov looked sincerely disappointed. "I *am* sorry, Blake. You are clearly a gifted artist, but I have others to consider and . . ." She took a breath. "I regretfully must ask you to leave."

The next thing Blake remembered was the abnormally low sky, the sun on her face, and a wistful sea breeze cutting across her skin. While she knew she was here, standing on this square of sidewalk, she felt as if she had left a piece of herself in the studio. Or maybe just the dream of who she could have been.

Blake stared down at her right hand. At the deep lines on her palm, crisscrossing, reaching toward her long fingers. Fingers that couldn't even grip a pencil, let alone create art.

The tremble began in the balls of her feet, working its way up her legs, across her ribs, through that tender place between marrow and bone.

Blake tried to steady herself against the violent tremors snaking through her body as she ripped a piece of paper out of her portfolio. With Ms. Ivanov's pencil still in her hand, she pressed the page against the building.

Her fingers ached with the weight of the instrument as she tried to create a simple daisy. But no matter how hard she tried, she could only make formless shapes that meant nothing, that *were* nothing.

Her breathing increased, rapid short breaths as fresh waves of nausea rolled through her. Each stroke of the pencil was a plea.

There was no denying it. Her art had disappeared. Slowly. Inch by inch, like a candle burning its own life away. Until there was nothing left.

It's not forever, she told herself on the bus ride home as she continued to try to draw even the simplest of shapes. *I'll break the curse. I won't let it have my art forever.*

"Can I see you tonight?" Ian said on the other end of the phone when she got home. "So I can tell you the rest." He'd asked what was wrong, must have heard something in her voice. But she hadn't been able to explain.

The rest of the magic. The rest of his story.

By the time she met him at Dolores Park, the sun was beginning to set, casting the entire city in a golden pink glow. Ian was sitting on the grassy hill with his nose pressed to a book. He was wearing a dark crew-neck sweater and a white collared shirt underneath, making him look a bit like a proper Cambridge student, or what Blake imagined a proper Cambridge student looked like.

When Blake approached, he didn't notice her. He kept his gaze focused on whatever he was reading.

"Hey," she said, planting herself next to him.

Startled, he looked up from the book. Then, with a smile, he reached for her hand, holding it gently and causing her heart to jump. "Is this okay?"

She smiled at the warmth that radiated from him and nodded. "What are you reading?"

"Blake."

For a moment, she didn't follow, and then he held the book up and said, "William Blake. Did you know he was a painter like you?" Ian's expression softened. "Hey, are you okay?"

Blake was exhausted from keeping all her secrets in her heart. She was tired of swallowing the truth and not sharing its burdens. She found herself telling Ian about blowing it at Ms. Ivanov's, about her inability to paint.

It's not forever. I won't let it be forever.

Ian took it all in silently. He allowed the moment to breathe before he said, "Do you think you were just nervous? It sounds really tough having her watch you and the mirrors and such."

Thinking more about it, Blake didn't know if the curse had stolen her art, or if the weight of the magic was just getting in the way, but she *did* know she couldn't tell Ian that part of the story. "I guess it doesn't matter. I didn't get the gig."

Ian squeezed her hand gently. "I'm really sorry. I know what that feels like."

Blake found herself questioning his words. Could he really know what it felt like to watch your dreams go down the tubes?

"I used to play football," Ian said. "Not American—you call it soccer here."

His thumb made small circles across her skin as he spoke. "But I injured my knee in a school match. The docs told me I'd never play again, which meant I had to give up my university scholarship."

Blake's heart swelled an inch and then another, thinking that Ian really did know what a dying dream felt like, and she felt like a jerk for doubting him. "I'm so sorry," she said. "That's awful."

Ian nodded, his gaze catching hers. Then, with a small smile, he said, "So I found another dream."

"What kind of dream?"

"That," he said brightly, "is a tale for another day." He gave her a gentle shoulder bump and said, "You're going to be a great painter. I just know it."

And the way he said it, with so much conviction, made Blake believe him.

"I'm glad you told me," he added. "Everyone should have someone to tell their secrets to, right?"

Blake felt herself being pulled into his orbit again. There was an ease to Ian, a confidence he commanded that made her feel safe. Protected. Wanted. "And you wanted to tell me about the rest of the story about your nan," Blake said, remembering why she was here.

"We can talk about it later if you want."

"No, I really want to hear about it. It'll take my mind off things."

Ian dipped his head and closed the book, positioning himself so he was facing Blake. "I know it sounds wild, but when my nan told me I would journey here and that I would meet a girl with secrets, I thought maybe she was teasing me. But then she told me that the girl had magic at her fingertips, that..." He swallowed and shook his head.

"Go on," Blake urged.

Ian leaned closer. He smelled like the pages of a well-read book. "She said that I needed to tell you that... that magic attracts magic."

His words pierced Blake's core with the precision of a surgeon's knife. She felt a flicker of uncertainty. Guarded yet curious.

"And she said that I'm going to protect you," he added.

"Why would I need protection?" There was no masking the defensiveness in her voice.

"The other day at the palace, you were scared. Some man was following you, Blake . . ." He hesitated before going on. "And if my nan is right and . . . if you really do have magic, then we have more in common than you think."

Blake felt her jaw tighten. She was suddenly aware of the cold draft coming over the hill. "Ian, what are you talking about?"

This time Ian didn't hesitate. He looked her straight in the eye and said, "I come from a long line of magic, too."

Blake wasn't sure she had heard him right. Was it possible? Of course it was. Zora and Phillip had found each other. So had her parents.

Ian's mouth was pressed into a worried line when he told Blake the rest:

"I have no magical abilities myself. Some people in my family can see the future. Some can see the past. My nan saw you years ago."

His words fluttered in the air between them like frenzied moths clinging to the light. In an instant, Blake could feel the invisible thread that joined their lives. *Was that why she had seen his past?*

Maybe he really was here to help her. Maybe it was safe to let him in, even if only an inch.

"I can't tell you everything," she said. There was a *yet* in her words, a promise. A someday. "But it's only fair for you to know that if you help me, you will be in danger."

"Can I show you something?" Ian said. Gone was the confident, self-possessed boy. Now he only looked awkward, unsure, as if he were balancing on a narrow precipice.

"Of course."

Ian looked around, reached into his pocket, and pulled out a burgundy velvet ribbon about ten inches long. "This has been in my family for generations. It doesn't look like much, but if you tie it around your wrist, it makes you warm when you're cold and cool when you're hot." He gave a light shrug. "I guess there are a lot of magical artifacts in the world; many are kept in families for generations. . . ." He continued talking, but all Blake heard was *magical artifacts kept in families.* It hadn't occurred to her, not once, that there were other families like hers, guarding magic and keeping secrets. How much more was there she had yet to discover?

"Blake?"

"Hmm . . . Yes. I'm listening."

"Do you want to try it?"

And before she could respond, Ian had lifted her hand and begun to tie the ribbon around her wrist. As soon as he tied the knot, she no longer felt the cold draft and instead felt bathed in warmth, a cozy sitting-by-the-fire-with-a-hot-chocolate kind of warmth.

"Amazing," she whispered, fingering the ribbon's edge. It was then, at that moment, that Blake wanted to let all her walls down, wanted to tell Ian that the two of them were the same and that her family possessed artifacts, too—one of which was more powerful than the others. So powerful that someone else was trying to find it, maybe willing to kill for it.

Blake untied the ribbon and gave it back to Ian. "Thank you for telling me that, for showing me . . ." She cleared her throat, knowing in the end the best she could give was this: "I can't tell you much about my family's magic, other than that it exists and I'm still trying to figure it all out." Maybe even this admission was more than Remi would approve of, but Remi wasn't here, and Blake was exhausted from carrying so many secrets.

"I know, I get it," Ian said. "And I wouldn't ask you to. But I could better protect you if I knew who that man was or—"

"He's a crow." The words fell from Blake's lips.

Confusion washed over Ian's face. "A what?"

"It's something Rose told me the other night when you dropped me off at the center."

"Your friend who talks to ghosts?"

Nodding, Blake told him about the woman in the green dress and how the man had the same terrifying, sickly look. "And Rose said something about the crows and serpent being here, that I'm in danger. I think they're some sort of secret group."

"But what do they want?"

Blake hesitated, inhaled. Exhaled. And before she could answer, Ian said, "They want the thing you're looking for."

"I think so."

Seemingly unfazed, Ian reached for her other hand, now holding both in his. He paused. "Just because my nan said I'm supposed to help you doesn't mean you'll let me. You decide your future."

Blake swallowed the tightness in her throat. Why did he have to be so earnest, so nice, so open? "I don't want you to get hurt."

With an amused snort, Ian's gaze dropped to the grass momentarily before finding Blake's again. "Ah—so you care about me."

Warmth flooded Blake's cheeks and neck, radiating down her limbs. "Ian, I . . ." He waited, watching her intently as a glint of sun reflected in his hazel eyes. She hadn't even known him for two weeks, and yet she felt as drawn to him as if she had known him a lifetime. Was that the work of magic? Or something else?

Ian's mouth turned up into a warm smile. "I hope you'll let me help. It'll make my nan right about her prediction. She likes to be right."

You decide your future. Blake clung to those words, wanting them to be true. She took a breath and whispered, "Okay."

It was just after dawn when Olivia and Blake arrived at Grace Cathedral.

Blake was glad Remi was busy bringing Cole home that morning, too busy to try to come with her to the cathedral.

Crowds were already gathering in the plaza and swarming up the concrete steps. The church's Gothic facade looked more ominous than usual. Maybe it was the perception of a thickening dark, as if it were nightfall and not dawn. Or maybe it was the weight of the future that Blake carried in every one of her steps.

"So where are we supposed to meet Ian?" Olivia asked as they made their way up the stairs.

"Near the entrance."

"Should I be jealous?"

Blake halted and turned to face her friend. "Huh?"

"You're into him. I can tell."

"I don't really know him," Blake argued.

And yet she did. Know him.

He was the boy who had shown up on the beach that night with salt in his hair and music in his step. Whose arms had protected her from falling into the dark ocean. He was the boy who came from magic, had given her the key to the crown . . . and felt like a secret on the edge of someone's lips.

Olivia hooked an arm in Blake's as the pair climbed the steps. "I thought we swore no more secrets."

"You're right."

"So you *do* like him."

"Oh, I meant you're right about the no more secrets."

Rolling her eyes, Olivia said, "Okay, but don't make me wear some awful maid-of-honor dress."

"You're getting way ahead of yourself," Blake replied. "And how do you know you won't be a matron?"

"Me? Fetching some guy's slippers and making meat loaf? Never!"

The two laughed as Ian came over. He was wearing a pair of dark blue slacks and a white button-up with a thin blue tie. Blake felt a swell of nerves. Not because she wasn't expecting him. But because she wasn't expecting him to look so good in a tie.

He planted a quick hello kiss on her cheek that sent a shiver down her legs. He smiled at Olivia, who merely waved. Blake felt guilty she hadn't told Olivia about Ian's heritage of magic, but it wasn't her secret to tell.

"So, how does this work?" Olivia asked in a hushed voice. "Do we need to walk around looking for the crown?"

"You'll know it when you see it, right?" Ian put in as they entered the cathedral.

Blake felt suddenly small beneath the vaulted ceiling and grand columns. "I don't know," she said. "But I don't think we'll be able to check things out until after his speech."

Olivia said, "We can still—"

"Look around from the pew," Ian interrupted.

Olivia's eyes darted to Ian. "Listen, I know I called you James Bond, but Blake and I are the main detectives here."

Ian gave her a small smile. "Bond is a spy, not a detective."

Blake groaned inside, and as Olivia opened her mouth to (most likely) lay into Ian, she said, "There's a good seat over there. Come on."

The trio shuffled into a pew near the back of the church. Blake wanted to be able to see the entirety of the cathedral, from the altar to the ornate stained-glass windows.

The hours ticked by slowly, and when the bells struck ten, Dr. Martin Luther King Jr. arrived. The crowd went silent as he took the pulpit. His voice was deep, slow, deliberate.

Blake hadn't expected to feel so engrossed, so taken aback by his presence. That's *magic,* she thought. To command a crowd, to stir their hearts and minds, to inspire so many people.

Like everyone else in the crowd, Blake was hypnotized. She thought briefly about her dream to inspire people someday with her paintings and wondered if that would ever happen now. But she wouldn't give up. She would never give up her art. And there was solace in her determination, solace in knowing that she would break the curse.

Ian's hand brushed against hers.

As Dr. King spoke, Blake thought about her mom, about Zora. She looked around the mostly Black audience and felt a small catch in her heart. What was it like not to be able to marry the man you loved because he had a different skin color? What was it like to be treated with disdain, vitriol, even violence? To have to follow a separate set of rules that had been made out of fear and hate? It only made her admire Remi and Cole that much more, their commitment to each other regardless of what society said about who could love whom.

"Are you looking for the clue?" Olivia whispered to her.

Bringing herself back to the reason she was here, Blake nodded as she carefully scanned the church, up and down, side to side. There was nothing. At least nothing out of the ordinary.

King talked about determination, about being your best, no matter who or what you are, that there is worth in everyone no matter if you're a pine tree or a bush, a sun or a star. Blake found herself clinging to his words, to the hope wrapped around them.

I'm an artist. I'll always be an artist.

And also—*I am a daughter, a granddaughter, a niece. And I'll do anything to help my family.*

Bits of sunlight drifted in through the arched stained-glass windows. Blue and pink and gold.

And then the light shifted. A dreamy blaze of lilac beamed across the width of the church like a ghostly finger pointing. Bits of dust twirled in its radiance, the same radiance that had bathed the crowns in Blake's visions. Her eyes followed the wedge of light a few rows up to the other side of the church. Her gaze landed on a woman's lace-veiled head. From this angle Blake could see her profile and the shimmering gold earrings dangling from her ears. Crowns.

Just then the crowd erupted in applause; everyone was on their feet. Olivia was saying something, tugging Blake to stand with her. Ian was squeezing her hand. Cameras flashed. The purple light was thinning like a cloud of mist. Blake climbed onto the pew to catch a glimpse of the older woman now turning and walking down the side aisle. She had dark skin and small, tired eyes, but her perfect posture told another story.

"Blake!" Olivia said, pulling on her skirt hem, urging her to sit down. People were beginning to stare.

"What do you see?" Ian said.

But Blake was already rushing up the side aisle, nearly tripping over the people who were flooding out of the pews. She didn't want to lose sight of the woman.

She hadn't even taken a moment to think about what she was going to say when the woman smiled at her and said, "Blake?" And before Blake could react, the woman's willowy arms were reaching for her, tugging her into a hug. She hadn't realized she was nearly panting, that the feeling of expectation and excitement had flooded her senses.

"Look at you, so grown up and pretty," the woman said as

they were shuffled along with the crowd. "You look just like your picture."

"Picture?" Blake said, trying to play off an already awkward situation, chasing visions that led to people she didn't even know.

"The Christmas photo Remi sent. She always remembers me," the woman said with a smile. "I haven't seen you since you were twelve or so. I'm Gayle. I was a friend of Zora's. We worked together at the club back in the day."

Blake's heart thumped wildly. The crown had led her to this woman who had known her grandmother.

They continued shuffling behind the thick crowd toward the sunlight pouring in from the double doors. "What was she like?" Blake asked, not sure which questions were the right ones, but hoping the magic would reveal why it had brought her here.

Gayle hooked her arm in Blake's like they were old friends. "Oh, she was full of life and spunk, that one." The woman spoke with a faint southern accent. "And her talent was immense. She should have been a Hollywood star. Mm-hmm." Gayle nodded vigorously as if agreeing with herself. "And she was always talking about her girls. How smart and clever and creative they were." She paused, then, with a long sigh, said, "I'm so sorry about your mama. She was a force, let me tell you. She loved the club's dressing room. Was always sticking her fingers into things that didn't belong to her," she added with a snort. "And Zora had a heck of a time trying to get her to sit still."

Blake felt her heart filling up with a sense of belonging, with memories that she couldn't get enough of.

They emerged into the cool morning sun. "I see a bit of Zora in you," Gayle said. "That same spunk. Are you a musician, too?"

"No, but I'm an artist." *Or used to be.*

"Oh, how lovely," Gayle said. "You should come to the big music festival today at Golden Gate Park. It's really for you young ones, but some of my students are performing. You might like it."

"That sounds like fun." But Blake hadn't followed the crown here just to leave empty-handed. "Can I ask you another question? Did my grandma ever mention a mirror?"

"A mirror?"

Gayle's simple response told Blake that the woman knew nothing. But Blake wasn't going to give up that easily. "I know this is going to sound strange, but is there anything you remember about my grandma, something that might have been odd or kind of"—she paused, then went all in—"magical?"

Without hesitation the woman offered, "Her voice was magic, is that what you mean?" And before Blake could answer, Gayle added, "Or do you mean her superstitions?"

"Superstitions?"

"Well, more of a good-luck charm. She always wore a single flower behind her ear—wouldn't go onstage without it."

Blake's field of vision narrowed and all she heard was *flower*. She spoke slowly, carefully. "A white flower with a . . . yellow center?"

Gayle smiled, tugging a pair of gloves from her handbag and slipping them on. "That's the one. She called it a starflower. Said it made her feel like a star."

A river of heat coursed through Blake, pulsing with magic and hope. "Did she say . . . where she got them from?"

With a chuckle, Gayle said, "Why, from her garden, of course."

Blake raced home without even saying good-bye to Ian and Olivia. The entire bus ride was one of nerves and cautious hope.

This is it! Blake thought. *The heart led me to my magic. The crown led me to Gayle and she told me about the flowers, about Zora's garden. It has to be where the mirror is.* But could it be that easy? Would Zora have buried the mirror in the yard? Blake had never seen the white flowers growing, and surely Cole or Remi would have mentioned them when she first told them about the vision of the flowers falling from the sky.

She flew through the house, calling for Cole and Remi as she burst into the garden, scanning, searching for the starflower. She waded through the brambles and blooms, none of which bore the delicate white star shape. Blake slumped against the trunk of the beech tree. *Maybe it's not the right season,* she thought.

"What is all the commotion about?" Remi said at a high pitch as Cole followed behind her.

"It's the flowers," Blake cried, leaping up. She welcomed Cole home and spilled the whole story.

"Let me get this straight," Cole said, "the heart led you to the psychic and the crown led you to Gayle?"

"Pretty much."

"Cole," Remi said. "Do you have a flower like that in the garden?"

Cole shook his head. "I've planted and replanted this garden over the years, and if anything like that was growing here"—he sighed—"it isn't anymore."

"It's called a starflower," Blake put in as if that would somehow cause the flower to materialize from the earth they were standing on.

Remi snapped her fingers. "Wait a second! I kind of remember..." Her frown deepened. "I remember Rose once saying something about my mom bringing in a bouquet of flowers that looked like stars. Rose had never seen them before, and when she asked where they were from, my mom just said that she had picked them up at the market."

Blake's heart began to churn. In that moment she understood that she might never know the wholeness of magic, or its power, its agony, its beauty. She imagined the gentle blooms floating from the sky.

Remi said, "I wish I had Gayle's number so we could call her and ask if she remembers anything else."

"She invited me to a music festival today," Blake said, her voice still high with excitement. "I could ask her. See if she remembers anything else that might help."

"Good," Cole said, rubbing his chin. "In the meantime, we'll do some digging around here . . . literally."

After searching the garden for a little while, Blake called Olivia to apologize for skipping out on her and explained why. "So, can you come to the festival?"

"You're going to kill me, but my mom is sick. I think it's the flu, and I have to run to the store and then make some soup and—"

"It's okay," Blake said. "I still have—"

"Don't say 'Ian.' Bond doesn't compare to me."

Blake smiled. "Never."

"Call me as soon as you talk to Gayle."

Her next call was to Ian, who jumped at the chance to go to an American concert. After she apologized for ditching him and explaining why she had done so, he asked, "So we're going to find Gayle and talk to her about flowers?"

Blake wrapped the phone cord around her finger, hoping against hope that she was on the right track. "Exactly."

When Blake arrived at the de Young Museum in the park, Ian wasn't near the pond at the front of the building where they had agreed to meet. Glancing at her watch, she confirmed that he was already ten minutes late.

In the pond's reflection, the March sky loomed. Like a ghost. Cold and gray and lingering.

A ripple across the water and then . . .

The world is warped and colorless. Blurry at the edges, a ghostly mirage, coming into focus. A soundless city. Lost in its busyness. Buildings that touch the sky. New York, like Blake has seen in pictures and movies. Except this New York is different. Cars unlike anything she has ever seen. The people wearing stiff expressions, staring down at strange gadgets in their hands. The image flickers like an old silent film. Only two teens, a boy and a girl, seem solid. Twins. The girl is wearing a white T-shirt with a picture of Coit Tower. The twins are in perfect focus. Dark hair, wide eyes, weaving through the crowd. Running like whatever they are doing, wherever they are going, matters.

The vision pinwheeled out of focus until it was nothing but an unreachable pinprick of light.

Blake's body tensed with the urge to scream. But the air had left her lungs. Something burned through her, an awareness, a knowing that arose not from her mind but from instinct. No, not instinct—something else that she couldn't describe. It took her a moment to wrap words around the feeling: The awareness came from a moment in time that hadn't even happened yet.

Was that even possible?

Blake struggled against the bone-deep shudder. Against the tension between old magic and new, the past and the present, the curse and freedom.

She had glimpsed the future. Those teens were more than just random kids. She saw it in their eyes, in their stride. She felt it in the invisible yet unmistakable thread that drew her to them.

Martina had been right.

The twins belonged to her.

More than ever, Blake needed answers. She couldn't keep waiting for Ian, so she made her way down a narrow tree-lined path and across the park to the festival. She kept seeing those kids in her mind's eye as she followed the loose beat of the music that felt like it was running wild through the misty woods. She could hear guitars, drums, tambourines, and the soft lilt of some guy's voice singing about clouds and blue skies and Mama's dirt pies. The place was buzzing with energy, raw and unleashed.

Blake felt it in her bones, pulsating in her blood, and it was more than the music and the crowd, it was a sense of something drawing her closer, something she couldn't name.

The tight ball coiled inside her stomach began to relax as she made her way through the festival, where multiple stages were set up, showcasing different bands and artists. Smoke and the scent of spices floated across the air.

"Blake!" Blake spun to find Ian jogging toward her. He wore a pair of Levi's with a slim zip-up jacket. "I'm sorry," he said, catching his breath. "I got stuck in traffic and parking was a nightmare. I... I saw you from a distance and called out, but you must not have heard me."

"Well, you're here now," she said with a smile, and until that moment she didn't realize how grateful she was to have him by her side.

Glancing around, Ian said, "Isn't this wild?"

It would have been so easy for Blake to get lost in the music, in the energy, in Ian's enthusiasm, but she was here for a reason. As if he could read her mind, Ian bowed and said, "Lead the way, my lady."

Together, they weaved through a sea of teens relaxing on blankets, eating and drinking, talking and laughing, enjoying the day as if the sun were shining and nothing could ever be wrong again.

The people danced and sang, swayed to the hurried beat. Some used tented blankets to toss silk and paper flowers into the air. Couples huddled close, banners with hand-painted peace signs flew, trails of bubbles floated into the sky. It was simply incredible. A glimpse of a future she so badly wanted to be a part of.

They searched for the better part of an hour, and Blake started to worry she wouldn't be able to find Gayle in the crowd.

"No sign of her?" Ian said.

Blake shook her head as Ian took her hand and twirled her once, forcing a laugh to bubble up from her chest.

"What was that for?"

"That's my one move."

"Seriously?"

"It's so good, right?"

Blake laughed. "Um . . ."

Ian's hazel eyes drifted across the scene as if he were committing the moment to memory. "I wish we could just stay here, that we didn't have to ever leave." Blake was taken aback by his sincerity, by the sudden loneliness that rolled off him in waves.

"Hey, are you all right?" she asked.

His gaze fixed on her, a penetrating stare that sent shivers down her arms and legs. "I'm really glad I found you."

"And in such a big crowd."

"That isn't what I meant." Blake knew that, didn't she? She could see it in his eyes and smile.

And before she realized, he was pulling her closer, leaning so close his lips swept across hers. She melted into him, pressing into his warmth as if every moment before only existed to lead her to this one. Ian broke free first.

"We should . . ."

"Stay focused," Blake said dizzily.

She couldn't tear her gaze from his. They stood like that in the woods, two souls born into magic. And if that had been all there was between them, it would have been enough.

The music pulsed so loud that the ground vibrated. Then, from the corner of her eye, she caught sight of something sickening and familiar.

A green dress.

Blake rushed toward the woman, spun her around.

The young woman gasped. "What the hell is wrong with you?"

Blake realized her mistake the moment she set her hands on the woman's arm. There were no open wounds. And there was no hum. No throbbing deep in her eardrums.

"I... I'm so sorry," Blake stammered, feeling suddenly ridiculous that she had let her overzealous imagination get the best of her. "I thought you were someone else."

The girl scoffed as Blake spun and slammed into Ian. He caught her, holding her arms gently. "You all right? What just happened?"

"I thought maybe..." Blake reached for an explanation as she pulled free. "I thought she was the woman from my school, but I was wrong."

Ian's head snapped up as he surveyed the crowd. "Do you think she or the man from the palace... do you think they're still following you?"

"I have no idea."

"How about I get us something to drink? Wait here," Ian said as he hurried over to a vendor near one of the stages.

Blake scanned the edge of the park, where the trees were the thickest. She thought she heard someone call her name from inside those woods. When the man's voice sounded again, she found herself drawn to it as if by instinct.

Blake. Blake.

She walked. Then ran. Tripped, stumbled, excused her way through the angry stares and curses. Ian was calling after her, but it was too late. Blake was already lost in the mob, and he was far behind.

This is insanity. I'm running through a rock concert in magic shoes, chasing after an echo. But the adrenaline had gripped her, and it forced her to move, to chase.

Suddenly Blake heard her name everywhere—in the fluttering of birds' wings, in the laughter and music.

The second she entered the thick grove, the world fell silent.

Her heart pounded. She doubled over, hands on her knees to catch her breath. When she stood upright, she saw that she had wandered several yards beyond the edge of the festival, past the crowd that was still visible through the grove. She had begun to head back when the low hum began, rising faster and faster until it was all she could hear. All she could feel.

Her mouth went dry.

Slowly, she turned.

Before her was a copse of dense trees, half-lost in shadow. "I know you're there," Blake said, voice rising.

There was no answer.

A movement in the shadows. Leaves crunched underfoot.

Blake's body went stiff and queasiness overtook her. An intense and unfamiliar buzzing began at her feet and raced up her legs and into her spine.

Glancing around the isolated woods, Blake took a step back.

Blake. Blake. Blake.

The buzzing grew more intense, a feral energy racing through her blood, demanding to be spent. "Who are you?!"

Everything went still. As if the words had sucked Blake into a black hole. There was no music. No bustling crowd. Only the painful throbbing, growing louder and louder. The pressure reached an intensity that made her gasp.

Run, Blake. Run.

And then Ian was there, reaching for her. "Blake!"

She fell back. "They're here! The crows! I have to stop them!" she cried. But the second the words left her mouth, she knew she had missed her opportunity. The humming, the screech . . . they had vanished.

"You're sure?" Ian took a few steps deeper into the forest. He moved smoothly, quietly. His eyes narrowed, roving.

Leaning against a thick trunk, Blake swallowed the frustration and anger. "No . . . I mean, they were here. Or at least a man was, but he's gone now."

"How do you know?"

"Because I can't feel him anymore!" Blake clenched her fists and took a deep breath. "I'm sorry. I . . ."

Taking her hand in his, he said softly, "Hey, it's okay."

Blake nodded, wishing she understood who was calling her and why they sounded so desperate. She looked up at Ian, wanting nothing more in that moment than to be a normal teen.

"We should keep looking for Gayle," she said.

But after two more hours and no Gayle, Blake went home empty-handed. Except for a glimpse of the future in a reflection.

And in Ian's kiss.

The next morning, Blake sat out on the back porch alone with some tea and a sleeve of cookies.. She had happily slept in. She had gotten a call last night that school had been canceled for the next few days—something about a leaky pipe and the building's poor infrastructure.

Yay for floods, she thought, wondering why the house was so quiet. *Maybe Remi and Cole went out to run an errand,* she thought, munching on some cornflakes, turning everything over in her mind and gazing across the garden.

"Where are you?" she whispered, thinking about the mirror.

Then, out of the blue, she found herself smiling as she imagined Ian dancing at the concert. As she imagined the two of them walking hand in hand. Kissing.

Magic attracts magic.

Blake had become lost in her imagination, in the possibilities of Ian, of his family's magic, when a spark of light glinted off the silver teapot. She cast her gaze to the reflection, where a cloud of thin mist had formed. Pulling her closer and closer . . .

The willow tree stands in the shadows—a golden light begins to pulse at the center of the trunk, splitting it open to reveal a wolf, dark and lean, stalking low to the ground as if it's on the hunt.

The ground trembles, shakes violently. The wolf begins to dig and dig, its claws ripping the earth to shreds as something emerges. A tower growing up toward the sky. A single crow circles the top of it.

Caw. Caw. Caw.

With a growl, the wolf leaps into the air and snatches the bird from the sky.

And then Rose's voice: The crows are here. Here. Here.

Blake sucked in a sharp breath as the vision vanished. "That was Coit Tower," she whispered. Just like the girl's T-shirt. *Is it another clue leading me somewhere?* Lost in her thoughts, she barely noticed when . . .

Keys jangled.

Footsteps sounded.

The back door opened.

The garden drifted into the shadows as Remi walked toward Blake, arms out, face drawn, tears rolling. Blake's expression hardened. She knew this feeling of dread igniting in her stomach. She had lived this memory one other time, and before Remi spoke Blake knew.

Someone had died.

27

It was exactly nine a.m.

Blake remembered because the old grandfather clock in the hall was chiming.

One. Two. Three.

And Blake was counting out each second because she couldn't bear to hear the words that were falling from Remi's lips: *Rose is dead.*

The news of a loved one's death is cruel....

Last night.

Unbearable . . .

In her sleep.

And always inevitable.

The moment shrank down to a small half-done painting in Blake's mind: gray-streaked sky, withered blooms. And Remi. Wrinkled clothes, dark, empty eyes. Maybe in another life Remi would not have known tragedy, loss, or the curse. Maybe in another life she would have a carefully cultivated calm that could stand up to the storms.

Later, Blake wouldn't remember if she fell into Remi's arms or if it was the other way around. But she would remember her aunt's trembles, her convulsing chest as the tears flowed.

Blake was stiff, cold, an iron wall. She remembered Rose's voice echoing across her vision only moments ago. *Here. Here. Here.*

"I need to see her," Blake finally said. "I need to see Rose."

"Honey," Remi uttered shakily, "I don't think that's a good idea."

I wasn't there. I promised I would be there. I promised to get her ready for George.

Blake advanced.

"Please," Remi cried, gripping Blake's arm like she was afraid to let her go. Streaks of black mascara trailed down her cheeks. "She's already . . ." She was searching for the right word, as if any would be right. As if anything would ever be right again. Finally she said, "Gone."

She's already gone.

Which meant that Remi had been at the center, alone with Rose's dead body. She hadn't called Blake right away. She had stolen the good-bye.

"How long have you known?" Blake said, trying to keep her voice even.

There was a brief hesitation. Then: "They called before dawn. I didn't want to wake you. To put you through that."

Hours. It had been hours since Rose had left this world.

Love is an excuse for doing bad things to people, Blake thought.

I love you, so I was protecting you from the truth.

I love you, so I hid your magic from you.

Blake couldn't be there anymore. She couldn't listen to the reasons and excuses and empty words. So she ran. Remi called after her.

But her feet kept moving. Until she got to the front door and realized she was still in her flannel pajamas. Thinking quickly, she grabbed her purse and Cole's long coat from the rack by the door, tugged it on, and stepped into the cold.

Blake didn't register the rush of icy, merciless air in her ears. She didn't acknowledge the nearly empty bus or her shivering hands as she dug in her bag for coins. She didn't care that strangers' eyes were on her, casting their ill-conceived judgments of a girl in her pajamas. All she could think about was the unrelenting grip of the curse.

Please, no.

She clung to these two words. A prayer. A hope. A plea. Because the idea of the curse touching Rose was too painful to bear. She was an innocent.

An innocent who loved me. And Remi. And Mom.

When Blake finally stumbled into the center, thunder rumbled, low and menacing.

She slowed her steps as she drew closer to Rose's room. It wasn't real. None of this was real. She would walk through the door on silent feet and Rose would perk up, greet her with a smile, and pay Blake some compliment she had pulled out of the air.

Blake paused near Rose's door, suddenly aware that maybe she couldn't do this alone. She hadn't expected to feel so afraid or to feel the chill so strongly, the loneliness so acutely.

Tears pricked her eyes. Rose's room looked exactly the same as it always did. Blake's artwork lined the walls. George's photos still graced the dresser, and a lavender-and-cinnamon scent lingered.

With the magic wrapped tightly around her feet, Blake took careful, measured steps toward the bed.

Rose was gone.

And now so is Zora.

Blake took a deep breath, slowly stretched her chilled fingers toward the edge of the pillow where Rose had slept. She reached for her magic, willing it to rise to the surface, to show her the past. To show her Rose's last moments. Tears ran down her face as she grasped the pillow more tightly. Just then the world began to split down the center of the room like ice, a crack, slow and deliberate, that revealed an image: this very room covered in a quiet darkness.

A shard of moonlight. Thick shadows. The lean figure of a man draws itself toward the bed. He favors his right leg, as if he has an injury. Blake wishes she could glimpse his face, but she can only see the back of him and his long black coat.

"Is that you, George?" Rose's voice is weak, tired.

The man is quiet at first. But still he paces toward Rose. Her face is lost to the dark.

"George?"

"Yes," the man says, but he isn't George. He is at the edge of the bed. Hovering.

Blake feels herself reaching into the vision, trying to claw her way into its reality. There is no space for air. Only terror.

The man reaches for a pillow. His arm catches in the moonlight. He has a tattoo on his wrist, but his sleeve is pulled down over most of it. All Blake can see are the birdlike claws. And then he is pressing the pillow down . . . over Rose's face.

"No!"

Blake's legs buckled. She collapsed as her scream ripped her back to the present moment. To the empty room, where a woman didn't just die. She was murdered.

Waves of shock rolled through Blake with violent force as she struggled to catch her breath. To process what she had seen.

Nurse Betty ran in, horror-stricken. "What's happened? Why are you on the floor?"

Blake, cold and run through with the sharp knife of a memory that she would never be able to unsee, looked up to meet Betty's eyes as she forced herself to her feet. Rose had been killed under the noses of every employee here. How could something like this happen? How could some stranger just walk in off the street in the middle of the night and kill a resident with not a single person being the wiser? But those weren't the questions Blake asked. Instead, she said, "When exactly did she die?"

Betty's expression softened into one of cautious concern. "Dear, she passed in her sleep sometime in the night. Peacefully."

"Peacefully?" Blake clenched her fists. "You let this happen. You let someone hurt her!" She hadn't meant to give so much away, but her body was revolting against the ugly, undeniable truth.

Rose had been murdered.

The interval between heartbeats was getting smaller and smaller. The world felt like it was closing in.

You'll know them by their claws.

Was that what Rose had been trying to tell her in the vision? That a crow had murdered her?

Betty drew closer, arms extended as if she might embrace Blake. She didn't. "No one hurt her," she said, worry creeping into her voice. "It was just her time to go."

"When?" Blake managed. "What time?"

"I can't be sure, but I found her a little after five this morning. I called Remi right away."

Blake didn't know why she was asking these questions. They wouldn't bring Rose back and they certainly wouldn't catch her killer. But Blake needed something tangible, a beginning thread, in order to stitch together some sort of understanding.

A thread . . .

The tattoo. On the murderer's wrist.

Adrenaline coursed through her. Dark suspicions pierced her mind. One after the other. After the other. The claws on the murderer's wrist. Black and sharp.

“Are you okay?” Betty asked.

No. I am not okay. I might never be okay again. Blake needed to be alone and that meant she had to show some semblance of rational behavior. “I’m sorry—I just... can I just have a minute?”

Betty hesitated, pressed her lips together. Blake worried she was going to linger, that she didn’t trust a hysterical girl to be alone.

“I’ll just be down the hall,” she finally said.

The second she was gone the tremors took hold of Blake. Uncontrollable shivers warning her that the truth would hurt, that there were scarier things than the curse.

There were humans.

Blake picked her way through the room, touching anything and everything, trying to connect to another vision, to find some clue that might help her identify the murderer, but then what? It wasn’t like she could go to the police with the truth: *Yes, Officer, I used my magic to see the killer in the act.*

Blake knew what she had to do but the thought of it made her sick.

“Rose,” she whispered, wiping a tear. “I’m so sorry. I should never have asked you for help, for...”

Blake froze.

Zora had chosen Rose. She had used her to warn Blake that someone was coming, someone who wanted to take her magic. And that meant Rose was killed for one reason and one reason only—to keep her quiet.

What don't the crows want me to know?

Blake sucked in air through her mouth and released it through her nose. If she was going to remember, she had to be calm, had to create a safe place for the memory. Then slowly, she reached back with her mind, searching for the last words Rose ever spoke to her: *You'll know them by their claws.*

28

Blake wandered the city aimlessly, mindlessly. Everything was dull edges and gloomy shadows.

Making her way home, she found herself outside the church. It was the memory of a ritual, of her parents lighting candles at altars for the sick, for the dying, for the guarded wishes they held deep in their hearts, that had guided her here.

A few moments later she was inside, standing before a small side altar. Candlelight cast flickering shadows across the stone walls. With a trembling hand she lit a candle for Rose.

"I'm so sorry," she whispered, stepping back. Although she was sure that no number of flames or prayers would ever diminish her guilt.

Collapsing onto a small bench, she stared at the dozens of tiny flickering candles. She felt disembodied, a ghost, outside herself, staring at her soaked form. A girl slumped in a worn seat, swallowed by an oversize coat, searching for answers only the dead seemed to have.

With her head down, hands folded in her lap, she whispered, "Why didn't you tell me, Dad? If I'd had my magic, I could have . . . I might have . . ." She paused, eyes roving, mind spinning. Heart straining. *I might have broken the curse by now. I might not have lost my art or Rose or . . . you and Mom.*

I might be able to read all these confusing symbols. I might be stronger.

Then, as if her father were sitting next to her, responding to her blame, she added, "Don't you see? It was for nothing. You left me powerless for too long."

She imagined him telling her, *I promised to protect you.*

"Except that you didn't," she muttered.

Blake thought about the dream echoes, and the mirror's whisper at Ms. Ivanov's gallery. *Broken promises.*

Those were the same words Remi had used. And how many times had Blake broken her own promises? To Olivia: *No more secrets.* To Rose: *I'll be there to get you ready for George.* To Remi and Cole: *I'll be honest with you.*

Maybe it was the stillness of the moment or the traumatic aftermath of witnessing Rose's murder, but Blake felt a surge of something, a fluttering in her chest, just below the surface.

It was the same feeling she had had when she was ten and her art teacher told her that her potential was unrealized. That her ability to create unforgettable art was inside, waiting to be discovered. It was up to her and her alone to excavate its power.

Unrealized.

Was that the peculiar stirring she felt? While her magic had expanded from bits and pieces to something substantial, Blake couldn't help but feel like there was more. That the full power of her magic was simmering just below the surface. Like a frozen pond that just needed to thaw. *Or a volcano that needed to erupt,* she thought.

Her mind drifted back to Rose, to any clue she could remember that might help identify the crows. Rose had said that there were three of them. Blake had had three terrifying encounters, including the one in the park, the one with the woman in the green dress, and the one with the man at the palace.

Then she thought about what Cole had said at the start of all this: *There were others who knew about the mirror and the shoes. They wanted their powers.*

But if that were true, why not steal the shoes right off my feet? Blake wondered.

No, the crows had a bigger connection to all of this, to Rose's murder, to the mirror. Somehow, she knew it was all linked.

And then she remembered: Zora had gotten a letter demanding that she give the shoes up. It had to be from the crows! But that was over thirty years ago. Could the same people who had been after Zora's magical artifacts then be after them now?

The letter.

Blake hadn't seen it in the stack she'd gotten from Remi. She needed to touch it, to see if there was a memory attached to it that might give her the answers that the dead were keeping from her.

Remi was sitting on the sofa by the fireplace, an afghan wrapped around her feet, while the flames crackled effortlessly. She was staring at one of Cole's crossword books, tapping her mouth with a pencil.

Blake stood near the doorway for a moment, collecting herself. Remi's head snapped up. She studied Blake for a moment longer than was comfortable, as if she was about to speak but was choosing her words carefully and couldn't come up with any. "What happened to Rose wasn't a result of the curse," Remi finally said, but Blake wasn't sure her aunt believed that.

"I know," Blake agreed, hoping her confidence didn't lead to: *How do you know?* Thankfully, Remi blew right past her response and added, "She lived a long life."

Blake nodded, biting back the words that so desperately wanted to claw their way out of her throat. *Rose was murdered.*

Blake wanted so badly to tell her aunt, to unload all the lies. But what good would it do? Remi would only freak out, call the cops, likely shut down all of Blake's searching, and Blake had come too far, uncovered too much, to turn back now.

She took a small breath; anything more felt like it might rupture her chest.

Cole came into the room just as Remi stood and walked across it. She pulled Blake into a gentle embrace. Her words came slowly as she tugged Blake closer. "I should have told you so long ago about the mirror and the curse. I have spent too much time trying to protect you from all the bad things, and I don't just mean the curse . . . I mean life. The parts of life that we have no control over."

"It's okay," Blake whispered, breathing in the goodness that was her aunt.

Remi stepped back. Tears pooled in her dark eyes as Cole set a trembling hand on Blake's shoulders. "We were so afraid of something happening to you after your mom and..."

Remi wiped a tear with the back of her hand. "And I couldn't bear it if... I felt that my fear had choked you when you deserved to bloom."

Blake was already shaking her head. "No. You guys wanted me to be safe. You were trying to keep me safe." There was good reason for their overprotectiveness, for Blake's father's desire to protect her, too. Maybe even for Zora's. And yet none of their efforts had changed anything other than to build a world of lies, to smother magic, and to bury a secret that had the potential to free the family from more tragedy.

Remi reached out and cupped Blake's chin. "No more trying to build a moat around you. Or keeping you in the dark. Do you hear me?"

Blake peeled off Cole's coat and sat on the sofa, rubbing her hands in front of the fire. If there was ever a time to ask about the crows, it was now. "What about the letter you mentioned before? The scary one Zora and Phillip got about giving up the shoes and the mirror? I didn't see it in the pile you gave me. Do you have it?"

Remi walked over to the fireplace and rested her elbow on the mantel as she faced Blake. "I do."

"I think..." Blake proceeded cautiously. "I think they might still want the magic."

"Blake—"

"Rose had said Zora came to visit her, that she could hear her and... and she said that the crows are here," Blake admitted. "And if I can touch the letter, maybe I can see who they really are."

Remi paused. Then, seeming to decide something, she nodded to Cole, who marched out of the room and returned with the red envelope, which he then passed on to Remi. Its watermark sent a tremor through Blake. A beady-eyed crow gripping a two-headed snake in its mouth.

"Why wasn't this with the rest of the letters?"

"I had already told you about it," Remi explained, taking on that familiar mama-bear stance. "It seemed unnecessary... and okay, a little worrisome. Besides, I don't like this one touching my parents' words." She sighed, holding the envelope out to Blake—an olive branch. "But I said we'd work together."

Blake took the letter from her aunt and sat on the sofa. The room folded in around her.

Her vision telescoped so that all she could see was the crow.

The crows with the serpent. They are coming.

Blake's eyes locked on the talons. Black and curled like gnarled roots. Exactly the same as the ones poking out from the murderer's sleeve.

You'll know them by their claws.

Blake struggled to draw even breaths as she tugged the paper from the envelope, unfolded it, and read the carelessly handwritten words aloud:

"'You both will suffer grave consequences if you don't turn over the mirror and shoes in your possession. Bring the objects to the Ursuline Convent at midnight. Choose your fate wisely.'"

Then her gaze dropped to the bottom of the page, to the single printed sentence: *Principium et finis.*

Blake tried to jog her memory of the class she had taken last year for all of three weeks before she transferred out. "It's Latin."

"It means 'the beginning of the end,'" Cole supplied.

"The end?" Blake said. "What's the end?" She had the same feeling that she had when waking from a dream. That blink of a moment when you're floating between spaces and forget where you are. Forget who you are.

"Do you sense anything?" Remi prodded softly.

Blake opened herself up to the memories that she hoped still clung to the paper.

Show me who you are, she repeated silently. At first there was nothing, not even a whisper of a memory. Biting back frustration, Blake redoubled her efforts, clearing her mind of all thoughts, centering her magic with single-minded determination. Then slowly she connected to a source of energy that felt like it was in her control. *Like threading a needle,* she thought.

Tiny black spots danced in her vision. A dipping sensation like riding a swing up, up, up before soaring down.

Men's voices race past Blake, so close it feels like the men are sitting next to her. The cacophony of their chatter rises like a bitter wind, high-pitched and low-hummed, one voice folding over the next in a maddening rhythm.

As the voices sweep past, she reaches out with her mind and takes hold of them.

"She won't give the mirror or the shoes up," one says.

"Then we'll take them," another, more threatening voice adds, "off her dead body if we have to."

"I didn't sign up for murder."

"You signed up for loyalty without question. And if I ask for your blood or anyone else's, you will give it."

Blake blinks herself back to a physical awareness. The shadows have vanished.

But the living room has narrowed to a tunnel. There, at the end, is a flicker of light. Voices echo down the narrow passage.

Blake hears a cat screech in the distance. And then a woman's voice. "The window, Phillip."

A flurry of motion. Rapid footsteps. The echoes of a pounding heart. Blake's fingers suddenly curl around a shape, a cool metal thing. And there is something else in her grasp. The shoes, pressed against her chest. She would know their feel anywhere. And yet she knows that if she glances down, she'll only be holding the letter.

At the end of the tunnel a blanket of mist forms, slow at first and then so thick all Blake can see is white. The next words . . . they don't penetrate her ears. She doesn't hear them as much as feel them, sliding through her blood, weaving between her ribs and into her heart. Like a serpent.

"Choose your fate wisely."

And like a candle being blown out, the tunnel is gone.

Blake didn't remember how long she sat there in the faint sunlight breaking through the clouds. She didn't remember how long she stared at the letter that held two memories: the crows' and her grandparents'. She didn't remember diverting her gaze to the red shoes so effortlessly wrapped around her feet, as if they were made for her.

Remi and Cole remained silent as ghosts. It was Blake who spoke first, revealing every detail of what she had heard and seen. "I . . . I could feel the mirror. I could *feel* what Zora felt."

The power of her magic pulsated deep in her bones.

"Tell us everything you saw," Remi said.

And so Blake did.

Cole took hold of the fire poker and jabbed at the wood in the fireplace while Remi said, "I know you're wondering the same things I have wondered a million times. Who are these people, and where are they now?"

"But why would they be here? We don't have the mirror." Blake groaned. "And why would they care so much about shoes that they might not even be able to use? It doesn't make any sense."

Remi went over to the side table, tugged open the drawer, and riffled through it.

"What are you looking for?" Blake asked.

"A damn cigarette, but I threw them all out after . . ."

Cole was at her side in an instant as she closed her eyes and inhaled deeply. "I can feel the mirror," Remi said quietly, laying a hand on her stomach. "I can't explain it. But it's like a faraway storm getting closer and closer."

Blake trusted her aunt's intuition. And for a second she let herself believe that there were no lies between them, that Rose hadn't been murdered. "We will break this curse," she said, and just as the words left her mouth, she could see the fear mount in Remi's eyes.

But there was something else, too. A hard, determined focus that hadn't been there a moment ago.

"I had another vision," Blake said. "Of Coit Tower."

"I wonder why . . ." Cole said mostly to himself.

To identify the crows.

"I don't know," Blake admitted. "Maybe I'm still getting clues because we still haven't found the mirror? I'm heading there tomorrow."

"We'll go with you," Remi said, then immediately sucked in a breath and pulled a face. "Except, Cole, you have that follow-up test at the hospital."

"It can wait," he said.

"No way," Blake put in, enjoying her role as protective parent for once.

"She's right," Remi said. "And we have Rose's celebration of life tomorrow night."

"Then we'll go to the tower the day after," Cole suggested.

No, no, no. Rose had been murdered because Blake had been getting too close. That much was clear. She needed to figure out what the magic was trying to tell her and she needed to do it before anyone else got hurt.

"The day after tomorrow," Blake agreed, but as soon as she uttered the words, she knew it was a half-truth. She'd head to the tower tomorrow without them—during the day, so there would be a lot of people around. Maybe she'd bring Olivia and Ian. She'd come right home afterward, and if she had to, she'd return with Remi and Cole the next day. She just knew that she couldn't wait.

Remi looked at the fire, gazing into the flickering flames for a long moment. "When will this be over?"

Soon, Blake wanted to say. She could feel it in her gut, in her spirit. She was getting close to the crows *and* the mirror.

Guilt flared through her, but when she thought about all the lies that she had already told, the guilt was swallowed by her knowledge that she had lied only to keep Remi safe. But that was a lie, too, or might as well have been. Nothing would keep her aunt safe from the curse. And Blake was still boiling a pot of deceit in the name of love. Just like her father.

Still all she could do was make a silent promise: *I'm the wolf, and I'm going to destroy the crows.*

That night Olivia slipped into Blake's room. She swiftly closed the space between them and pulled Blake into a hug. "I'm so sorry."

Blake fought the tears. Not just for losing Rose but for the way in which she lost her, the way in which she was partly responsible for her death.

When Blake pulled back, Olivia said, "What is it? What's wrong?"

"I'm not sure you really want to know," she managed. "It's worse than you could imagine."

"Which is why you have to tell me. Now."

Blake took a deep breath and went over to her desk, where Olivia had stacked her sketches neatly. With her back to Olivia, she let the awful words spill from her mouth.

Silence filled the room. A gasp. And then Olivia was at her side, forcing her to look her in the eye. "You're sure?"

"It's the same people who sent Zora the letter demanding she give up the shoes and the mirror."

"But why kill Rose if they want something you have? Or at least they think you have."

"Because she was getting close to telling me who they are," Blake said, struggling to keep her voice even, struggling to accept that any of this was real. "Which means they were watching or listening." Tears streaked down her cheeks as the realization took hold of her. "The bastards were listening to our conversations." There was a small tickle at the back of her mind. "But that doesn't make sense. . . ."

"What doesn't?"

Blake told Olivia about the painful throbbing in her ears, the pitch and hum and static whenever the stalkers were around. "I never felt that when I was with Rose, though. Maybe they were too far away?"

And before Blake could respond, Olivia was already discounting her theory. "Then they wouldn't have been able to hear you."

Just then the cat wandered in, swishing his tail back and forth languidly as he studied Blake with sleepy eyes.

Blake told Olivia what happened when she touched the letter.

"Imagine if you could do that with the mirror," Olivia said. "If you could feel it in your hands . . . imagine what else your magic could do."

That night Blake fell into a deep sleep. Where she dreamed.

A door.

At the end of a long, narrow hall.

Before her hands touch the brass knob, she feels the cold.

From behind, footsteps. More than one or two or three.

She throws open the door, plunges ahead, and slams it in the dark.

Instinct drives her forward, through the haze. One step. And another. A melody echoes from all sides. Similar to carnival music but slow, very slow.

Through the mist, she sees she's in a forest clearing. There is a single row of white tents. Their tattered folds flutter in the breeze. Her gaze follows their peaks to a mirror roughly twenty feet away, ornately framed and at least twice her height. Before the looking glass is a small, round table where a wooden box fashioned with a crank rests. Her dad used to call the toy "diablo en la caja"—devil in the box.

One step and then another.

Like a ghost, she makes no prints in the dirt. Picking up her pace, she rushes past the tents, where she sees the symbols: the seeing heart, the crown bathed in lavender light, the tower, and in the last tent... the ocean. A fish rolls out of the breakers. Rainbow colored, its scales like glitter, its eyes wide and golden. A creature from a fairy tale. And then another and another, multiplying with each crash of the waves. All dead on arrival.

She flies past them all.

The music grows louder.

El Diablo's crank turns and turns.

Three paces away she halts. There is no reflection. Only a bright red glimmer, like a distant star. A chill rolls off the glass.

The box's crank turns slower and slower. It stops.

There is a single moment of breath, a silence that's glaring, and still...

The box pops open and a murder of black birds erupts, vanishing into the sky soundless as butterflies. The mist blinds her.

Blake hears the beating of wings before she sees the razor-edged claws closing in. The birds, so much larger than she imagined, come at her with a vengeance.

Caw. Caw. Caw.

She collapses onto the ground, throwing her arms up over her head. Claws tear her clothing, rip her flesh.

Bit by bit.

It is her father's voice that penetrates the violence, like an ax casting its final blow. "Dejalo libre." Set it free.

There is a shred of sky that Blake clings to.

Heat courses through her body. She feels the magic blooming in her blood, spilling out and onto the ground in waves of heat and power.

Her mouth is open before the shriek rips through the air. "NO!"

The mirror's shards fly. The glass bites into wings, breasts, and skulls. The birds drop out of the sky, bloodied and trembling.

She gets to her feet, surveying the death toll as the remnants of her power, barely contained, whisper, "Finally."

Blake woke in a cold sweat.

She felt like she was unraveling, bits and pieces of her floating away. Scraps of dreams and visions and memories taunted her. It was three a.m. Everywhere she looked she saw the wings. They were in the shadows, in the corners, in the waning light of the moon.

The tower and the rainbow fish. More symbols. They reminded her that she wasn't done yet; this quest wasn't over.

For a moment, Blake felt her blood pulsing beneath her skin, a raw energy waiting to be unleashed. Something was opening inside her—a door, a bloom, a raw and unchecked power she knew nothing about. It was like trying to see the whole of the ocean through a two-inch gap.

Blake closed her eyes and brought the dream's final image to her mind's eye. The crows—broken and bloodied at her feet.

The air felt unnaturally still as she repeated her father's words: *Set it free.*

Slowly, a memory surfaced. The night of the binding, she had woken up again. Two shadow figures stood in her doorway, her dad and Abuela. Blake leaned into the memory. Someone had said those same words, hadn't they? *Set it free.*

It was a question, asked by her father. "Can she ever set it free?"

It. The magic.

Abuela let out a gentle noise. She said, "The fullness of her power will..."

And then the memory was gone.

The fullness of her power will what?

Angry, frustrated tears stung Blake's eyes, but she wouldn't let them fall. She hugged her knees to her chest and stared out at the wintry sky, making promises to herself.

I'll find the mirror.

I'll set the girl free.

I'll break the curse.

I'll destroy the crows.

When she woke again, the phone was ringing.

Bleary-eyed, Blake peered over her comforter. Wasn't someone going to answer that?

The phone chirped incessantly, forcing her out of bed. She stumbled into the hall, where she picked up the receiver from the table. "Hello?"

"Blake?"

"Yes."

"It's Ms. Ivanov from the gallery. I wasn't sure I would catch you. Isn't it a school day?"

Blake had to focus on forcing air into her lungs. "Oh . . . hi, Ms. Ivanov. Yes, but there was a flood at school." For a blink, she had the ridiculous thought that the woman was calling to ask for her pencil back.

"Well, then, how serendipitous that we connected. I know this may be out of the blue," Ms. Ivanov said, "but I haven't been able to stop thinking about a sketch in your portfolio."

Blake's heart thrashed wildly.

Ms. Ivanov went on: "The unforgettable one of the wispy tree and the girl lying on one of the branches. I believe it's called *The Dreamer*?"

Immediately the image of the sketch came to life in Blake's mind. It was one of her first tree drawings. "Oh, well... thanks," Blake managed.

"I'd like to purchase it."

Heat spread across Blake's chest, instant and unrelenting. "Really?"

A small chuckle. "Yes."

"Okay, um... how much?"

"I believe *you* set the price." Then, as if Ms. Ivanov sensed Blake's shock, she added, "If I were selling it in my gallery, I wouldn't let it go for less than five hundred dollars."

Five hundred dollars! And then the dreams began: *I could fly to Paris for the summer, or London!* She imagined celebrating with Remi and Cole once all this curse business was over. They'd go to the best restaurant in the city. Maybe even have some champagne. "Yes!" Blake blurted. And it wasn't just the money, it was the idea that someone as accomplished as Ms. Ivanov appreciated her art, wanted to hang it in her house, on an actual wall, for who knew how many eyes to see.

"It's agreed, then," Ms. Ivanov said. "Can you drop it off next week? I'll be out of town until then."

Blake nodded, then said, "Of course. Yes. Thank you . . . thank you so much."

"And, Blake?"

"Yes?"

"Never let your heart go for less than it's worth."

After setting the receiver back on the cradle, Blake stood in the hall, stunned, wondering, even smiling. Buoyed by the change in tide that a single phone call could make. Today everything would change. Blake had already planned to meet Olivia at Coit Tower that afternoon, and now she had something tangible that she should look for there: the rainbow fish.

Quickly, she called Ian, hoping he would answer.

"I'll pick you up," he said once she'd told him where she was headed.

"It's okay," she replied too fast, wishing she could take back her tone, which said, *I can't explain you to my family. Not yet.* Then to smooth things over, she added, "How about we meet for a soda at one and then we can go together?"

Blake soared through the next few hours, her spirits elevated by a single phone call. *How quickly the tide can change,* she thought as she spat toothpaste into the sink. *How quickly luck can knock on your door,* she thought as she dressed in a pair of black pedal pushers and a yellow sweater.

How glorious life can become when you let it, when you're happy, she thought as she told Cole all about her art sale, disappointed that she couldn't tell Remi, who was at the market.

"I'm proud of you," he said, beaming. "I always knew you were incredibly talented, but now maybe . . . now you'll believe me?"

Blake threw her arms around his neck, nearly knocking him over.

"Sky's the limit, kiddo," he said.

Blake wanted to keep this feeling, to hold it close, to preserve it forever. She realized that she wanted not only to create art, she wanted to share it. She wanted to offer her heart for all its worth. And that meant that there could be zero space for failure. She *would* break this curse.

With a piece of toast hanging from her mouth, Blake had barely shouldered her satchel and reached for the front door when Remi came in, two paper sacks in her arms.

"I'm going to Liv's," Blake said. "But Cole has something to tell you."

"Sounds ominous," Remi teased. "Fine. Don't forget dinner at six tonight."

Right. The celebration of Rose's life. There would be Rose's favorite foods, photos, trinkets, and stories. So many stories.

"I wouldn't miss it," Blake said.

Remi set the sacks on a nearby credenza and gently took hold of Blake's elbow. "Listen, Cole and I won't give up. He's still researching the flowers, and we're going to stop by Gayle's on the way to the hospital to see if she remembers anything else. And Coit Tower tomorrow."

A dozen scenarios played out in Blake's mind, all leading back to the truth. So many truths tucked into dark corners, changing into secrets. If Zora hadn't hidden the mirror, if Blake's father hadn't bound her magic, if promises hadn't been broken, how different their lives might be. And yet Blake was guilty of the very thing that brought them all to this moment.

She had lied, kept secrets. She had broken promises.

Remi's gaze fell to the red shoes, then she raised her eyes back up. "My mom once told me that magic is mightiest when it's tied to other magic. I think people are the same. We will face this. Together."

Her aunt was right. United, they would be mightier. Not just in dealing with their grief, but in putting the pieces of information together that might reveal the whereabouts of the mirror.

Blake knew that she needed her aunt and uncle. She needed their love and strength, their knowledge and brainpower. But most of all, she needed not to be the carrier of secrets like those who had come before her.

It was that exact moment when she decided. Tonight, everything would be different. She was tired of keeping Cole and Remi in the dark, trying to keep them safe. As if being in the dark is ever safe.

After she found whatever she was supposed to find at the tower, she would tell Remi and Cole the whole truth. And the three of them would put the pieces together.

Blake swallowed. "Tonight," she said, "we can try to figure things out." *I'll tell you about the stalkers, and Rose's murder. And whatever I find out today. I hope you don't hate me for keeping so much from you.*

Blake was already down the steps, walking down the sidewalk, when she felt a warm draft touch her cheek. She turned. Remi stood on the doorstep, smiling.

Touching her face, Blake returned the smile and said softly, "I love you, too."

30

"So, we're looking for a rainbow fish?" Ian asked, rolling his straw back and forth across the table.

"A glittering one," Blake said, glad the café wasn't busy. "And I think it might be at Coit Tower."

"A glittering fish and a tower." He smiled. "Sounds like an adventure."

"And I have to tell you something else," Blake added. "Because you should know about the danger."

"Tell me." His voice was warm, gentle.

And then the bottled anger bolted from the cage, fresh and painful. She told him Rose had died.

Ian's expression went from one of interest to one of absolute remorse. Reaching across the table, he took her hand in his. "Blake, I'm so sorry."

Blake didn't want to stay locked in a moment of pity, so she plowed ahead, worried that if she didn't get the words out now she might never do so. "Actually, she didn't just die, Ian. She was killed. I . . . I saw it."

Ian regarded her like he was trying to decide what to ask next. Or maybe he was assessing how much trouble she was worth. "You were . . . there?"

"Not exactly." Blake explained that she had started having visions a few weeks ago, but there was nothing practiced or controlled or predictable about any of it. "Except that when I touch things, I can sometimes see a memory."

Ian's reply was a whisper. "I'm so sorry you had to see something like that." He took a slow, careful breath. "Did you get a good look at them?"

"Only the back of... him." Blake shook her head. "Like I said, I can't really control what I see, but I know she was killed, Ian." Her eyes met his. Ian's had shifted from hazel to a distant gray. "You believe me, right?"

Ian swallowed, then nodded. "That's the nature of magic," he said. "My nan said that everyone in our family had to train and practice to control even a quarter of their power."

Blake couldn't even imagine what she would give for that kind of training.

"We should call the police," Ian said.

"And tell them what? That I had a vision? I saw a shadowy guy with a tattoo?"

"Whoa. Hang on," Ian said. "He had a tattoo?"

"I saw claws sticking out from under his sleeve," Blake said. "On his wrist."

Ian's eyes looked suddenly unfocused as he took a deep breath. "Why would anyone hurt Rose?"

"I think she was going to tell me how to identify the crows, the people stalking me."

"How would she even know about them?" Ian asked. "Wait. Does this have anything to do with her talking to ghosts?"

Blake hesitated, wondering how much she should divulge, but

she had already told Ian so much, and maybe he really could help her. She said, "She could hear my grandmother's ghost sometimes. Zora was the one who was trying to warn me."

If Ian was surprised, he didn't show it. But Blake could see the wheels turning in his head. "Why do you think these people are after you?" he asked.

"I should have told you how bad this was. . . . I'm sorry. It wasn't fair to drag you into all this."

"Hey," Ian said, tracing his thumb over her hand. "I'm *supposed* to be here, remember?"

"You said I have a choice, and that means you do, too," Blake said. "I wouldn't blame you for walking away."

"You know I can't. . . . I won't do that," he offered. "But maybe I could be more help if I knew why these people are after you." There was an undercurrent of anger in his voice that Blake hadn't heard before.

Blake leaned closer across the table. "Remember when you told me about your family's artifacts? Well, my family has some, too, and I think . . . the clues are leading me to one, to something that was lost a long time ago."

Ian sucked in a sharp breath as the server set their bill on the table. "Is that what you saw in the ocean that night?" he asked. "A clue?"

Blake was nodding before the words came out. "I'm close, Ian. I know I'm going to find the crows. I can feel it and I've had . . ."

"What?"

"A dream. Where I destroy them."

Ian sat back, frowning. Blake could see the doubt in his expression, and she didn't blame him. How could a teen girl go up against some threatening secret organization? She had asked the same question. It wasn't like her magic involved physical power.

They made their way out to the car, and as he opened the door for her, he took hold of her arm and tugged her back, forcing her to look him in the eye. "Blake . . ." he began, his voice hovering.

"What's wrong?"

Ian pulled her into a hug, holding her tightly. When he pulled back, he kissed her briefly, softly. A muscle in his jaw twitched. Then his expression changed. And he retreated. Not all at once, but in increments, as if he was struggling to decide which way to go.

It took a moment, several moments, for Blake to respond. To the desire, to what felt like rejection. She took a wide step back and cleared her throat.

He raked his fingers through his dark hair.

Blake managed to look up and meet the intensity of his gaze. There was a war going on behind those eyes, emotions battling, but what were they battling for? "I promise," he said. "I'm going to protect you."

The thought formed before Blake could stop it. *But you have no magic. And there are three of them.* The thought of Ian getting hurt made her stomach clench into knots. "I don't want anything to happen to you."

"Don't worry about me." Ian turned away so Blake could only see his profile. "Who else knows about Rose?"

She took a deep breath and said, "Olivia." Then added, "And maybe you're right. Maybe I need to call the police."

"At least tell them you suspect foul play," he suggested. "Maybe they can interview the nurses or see if anyone saw the man with the tattoo." Ian ran a hand over his face. "Look, whatever you're ultimately looking for—and you don't have to tell me what exactly it is—we're going to find it."

Blake studied Ian, tried to imagine him as the boy on the dock as he stared down at the ground. "I had a vision of you."

Ian's head snapped up.

"You were a little boy on a dock near a shimmering lake."

A look of disbelief hung in his eyes. And when he finally spoke, he said, "I spent my summers at a lake with my family. How could you have seen that? It was so long ago."

"Like I said, I don't really have control over any of this," Blake admitted, not ready to tell him that the vision had come to her when she hugged him at the Palace of Fine Arts. She worried that he might never touch her again if he thought she could get into his memories like that.

For a split second Ian wore an odd expression of regret that made Blake's heart sink. "You okay?" she asked.

"Come on," he said, flashing a determined smile. "We have a clue to look for."

Blake had hiked the steps leading to Coit Tower dozens of times, but on this afternoon, the climb was different. She was journeying toward the unknown, wondering what might be waiting for her at the top.

The lot at the museum was already full, so they had no choice but to park at the bottom near Filbert and take the hidden steps. Thick foliage draped over steep stair railings, creating a jungle-like effect that obscured the houses that Blake and Ian passed, with the exception of a glimpsed rooftop here and there.

The view from the top of the tower was unparalleled, but gray clouds were amassing and soon the skyline and water were likely to be shrouded in fog.

Blake and Ian waited for Olivia on the tower's first floor. All the while Blake kept her ears attuned for the familiar hum so she would know if the crows were nearby.

As people milled about, Blake studied the frescoes and murals on the walls, quickly losing track of Ian. He'd probably gone to the restroom, she thought as her eyes took in the artwork.

The paintings reached from floor to ceiling, bright vivid colors depicting San Francisco in the 1930s with themes ranging from agriculture and labor to urban and rural life. But the faces were all the same: somber and faraway. She searched each mural for the rainbow fish, but was never able to find it.

Blake hadn't realized how much time had passed until Ian came up from behind her. "It's kind of hot in here. Can we go outside?" he said.

"Of course. Are you okay?"

"Fit as a fiddle," Ian said brightly. "I just needed some fresh air. Hey, check it out." Blake followed his gaze to a man sitting at an easel at the edge of the parking lot.

They headed over.

Blake could smell the acrylic paint before they reached the

small, elderly man, who wore a fedora and had slumped shoulders. He sat on a crooked wooden stool next to a folding table that held his supplies of brushes, tubes of paint, pencils, and paper. There was an extra stool next to a sign that read "Let Me Create a Perfect Cartoonized Version of You."

There were samples hanging on a second easel. But at the moment the man wasn't drawing cartoons. His weathered hands were busy creating the tower, a perfect likeness of it. "Hello," he said, never taking his eyes from his work. "Would you like a cartoon?"

"That's really pretty." Blake felt a longing in her chest that made it hard for her to breathe. *Do you have any glittering fish drawings?*

"She's an artist, too," Ian said, smiling.

"What do you paint?" the man asked.

"Different things." Blake wished Ian had never said a word.

"Things?" The man laughed lightly. "Art is never things."

Blake knew her answer had been a lousy one, so she tried again. "I paint whatever my heart wants."

The man stopped and turned to her for the first time. He tipped his hat back so she could see the deep wrinkles around his eyes. "Would you like to try?"

Blake froze. "Oh. No. I . . . I'm not really . . . *able to.*"

The man was already on his feet, clearing the cartoons off the second easel and clipping a blank sheet of sketch paper to it.

"Really..." Blake tried again, her voice noticeably shaking. "I don't really have time."

Silently, Ian placed his hand on the small of her back, then said in a low voice, "Maybe *this* is the tower you were supposed to find."

Blake was nodding. "Okay," she said. "But will you keep an eye out for Olivia?"

"You bet."

The man gestured for her to sit. "We artists must stick together."

Blake planted herself on the stool, staring at the blank sheet of paper. With a deep breath, she picked up a pencil on the easel and pressed it against the paper. Her fingers quivered as she curled her toes inside the shoes, wishing silently. But not for the art, for her magic. She could feel that the two were inextricably linked. As if her ability to create was buried somewhere underneath all the magic, trying to break free. And if she could just connect...

The pencil swept across the page. Lines, nothing coherent, and as she sketched, she felt a slow and steady pulse begin to beat beneath her skin. A hum that called to her. Like a distant song.

With each stroke, Blake felt further from the world. It was only her and the pencil scratching against the paper. Faster. Harder.

Her vision blurred, but her hand kept moving. An unnamable power rising. Rising.

And then she felt a terrifying growl climbing up her throat.

A sharp pain caused her fingers to cramp, and the pencil fell to the ground, breaking the spell.

Blake reached for her throat. What the hell was *that*?

Heart pounding, her eyes fixed on the drawing: a single black crow, flying toward a wolf. Sharp talons spread like knives. And the tower, in the background, a tower just like the one standing in front of her.

"Amazing," Ian said.

The man was nodding, holding his hat in his hand. "You are very talented, young lady."

Trembling, Blake stood, staring at the sketch as if the crow and the wolf were going to leap off the page. It wasn't her best drawing, she knew that, but it was something, a beginning. And more than that, she had felt her magic stirring, trying to speak to her.

Blake unclipped the sketch and offered the man some money, but he refused. "May I keep the drawing instead?" he asked.

She agreed. Then, looking at her watch, she twisted her mouth nervously. It was already two o'clock.

Blake felt suddenly chilled, and turned to Ian. "I'm worried about Olivia."

"Want to keep looking for her?"

"I just need to find a pay phone so I can call her." *Maybe her mom started feeling sick again,* Blake thought.

Back in the car, the radio was playing the Zombies' "She's Not There." Ian tapped his thumbs on the wheel as they turned down Broadway looking for a pay phone. Blake kept thinking about the wolf and the crow and wondered why her magic would have brought her to the tower to draw them. She had already figured out her connection to the wolf at Ms. Ivnanov's. And was there some significance to the tower T-shirt her daughter had been wearing in the vision? Blake shook the thought away. Right now, she had to focus—she would put the tower behind her and look for the rainbow fish somewhere else. A long line of unmoving cars filled one side of the street. There were two police officers up ahead directing each car to turn around.

"There must have been some kind of accident," Ian said.

Blake's entire body went cold.

The car came to a stop as Ian rolled down his window to talk to the waiting officer. "You'll have to U-turn it, son. Road's closed."

"What happened?" Ian's voice was even, controlled.

"Car accident."

"Is everyone okay?" Blake's heart was in her throat.

"Can't give you those details, miss." The officer pounded his fist on the roof of the car. "You can make the turn right up there," he said.

Ian inched the car forward and began to make the turn when

Blake hollered, "Wait!" Before Ian could brake or even shout her name, she had jumped out and was climbing onto the roof of the car.

"Miss!" the officer called.

From her vantage point Blake could see beyond the cop cars and the ambulance. She scanned the accident scene, looking for Olivia's white Buick. And when she saw the two vehicles that had crashed, a Ford pickup and a black sports car, relief flooded her body.

Olivia was safe. Everything was okay.

Blake was back in the car and Ian was already turning around before the cop could shout another warning.

"Next time you throw yourself out of the car, make sure the driver has come to a full stop!" Blake could hear the panic in Ian's voice.

"I had to know it wasn't Olivia," Blake argued. That the curse hadn't found her, too.

Ian ran a hand through his hair. "You'll feel better when you call her."

He turned down the next street, and it was another two miles before Blake located a phone booth in the distance. "Up there," she said. Just as she glanced out the passenger window, she saw a guy walking down the sidewalk. He was carrying a white paper shopping bag with a store name printed boldly across it—"Johnny's Records"—but it was the symbol beneath the name that stole Blake's breath.

A rainbow fish.

"Ian!" She pointed to the bag.

A couple of seconds passed before the realization touched his eyes. "My God, I'm a prat!"

"A what?"

"An idiot," Ian groaned. "I know that store. It's a few blocks from where I live just west of Ashbury. I've bought records there, Blake!"

"Should I stop him?"

"You think the next clue is in his bag?"

That was the right question, because as soon as those words left Ian's mouth, Blake knew it was too random, too dicey to send her a message this way. She had been guided to big places: the festival, the cathedral, the tower. Not to chance encounters with strangers. "We need to go to the store," she said.

A few minutes later, Ian and Blake had made a complete loop back toward Golden Gate Park. On the east side of it, they turned onto Haight Street just as the clouds thickened and threw down sheets of rain. Thunder rumbled in the distance. There was no parking in front of the store, so Ian let Blake out and told her he'd meet her inside.

Holding her purse over her head for cover, she hopped out of the car and ran toward the store's door, which had a glittering rainbow fish painted on the glass.

Inside, the place smelled like smoke and leather. Unfamiliar rock music blared from several speakers, nearly drowning out the sound of the now-pounding rain. Blake was the only customer in the dusty little shop, which organized its records in rows of bins. The walls were decorated haphazardly with album covers from Elvis and the Beatles to the Supremes and the Beach Boys, and plenty of others that were entirely unfamiliar to Blake.

Wiping the drops of rain off her face, she inched down the first row, knocking into a milk crate she hadn't seen.

A young guy popped out from behind a box a few feet away, startling her. And maybe himself. He gripped his chest and let out a quick breath. "I didn't hear you come in. Welcome to Johnny's." He wore a pair of jeans that looked too big for him and a T-shirt with green and yellow stripes. His hair was long and straggly, but his smile was inviting.

"I . . . I saw a shopping bag with a rainbow-colored fish on it," Blake said.

"Oh yeah," the guy said, still smiling. "It's our new logo, to kind of double advertise. Pretty cool, right?"

"Double advertise?"

"The shop and the band," he said. "I'm Johnny. This is my store. I'm also the lead singer in the Scales—maybe you've heard of us?"

Scales? Could the fish she had seen in her visions really have been pointing her to some new rock band? Not wanting to be rude, Blake said, "Sounds familiar."

"We just cut our first album," Johnny said excitedly. "Want to see it?"

Blake followed him down another row of bins, where he riffled through covers, then stopped and tugged an album free. "It's fifty percent off today. Last one. It must be your lucky day." His eyes flicked to the front window. “Man, that’s a wicked rain,” he said as he handed Blake the album.

There it was.

On the plain white cover—the same glittering fish she had seen in her visions. She traced her fingers over the image painted in metallic strokes that glimmered under the lights. Her pulse quickened.

“We write all our own songs,” Johnny went on. He was pointing as Blake turned over the cover to look at the song titles printed there. “I named them all,” he said. “‘Hate,’ ‘Ashes,’ ‘Bury’—get it? It’s our love letter to the city. Haight-Ashbury.”

Blake’s gut was a tight fist, clenching tighter and tighter. “What’s the fish trying to tell me?” she whispered.

Johnny cocked an eyebrow. “Huh?”

“Nothing,” she said shakily. “I’ll take it.”

“Really? Cool. I’ve got a lyrics sheet in the back that goes with it.”

Blake nodded politely as Johnny took off toward the rear of the small shop and disappeared through a door. She held the record close to her chest, torn between absolute euphoria and trepidation because she had found the fish, right here in this little record store, an unlikely place in unlikely circumstances. But what did it mean? What secrets did this album carry?

From the corner of her eye, Blake saw the front door open. Ian.

Except that it wasn't him.

A shorter-than-average man wearing a gray fedora stepped inside. He looked to be in his thirties, broad shouldered and thick waisted. Or maybe it was the thin tie that made his waistline look bigger.

She looked past the man now, searching for Ian. Where was he? Had he gotten stuck in the storm somewhere? She turned her attention back to the album, eager to pay for it and get out of this place so she could listen to the songs. There has to be a clue in the lyrics.

The smell of cigarettes found her before the guy stepped up to the bin next to her. Not paying her any attention, he began to sift through the albums.

Just as Blake averted her gaze, she saw it. There on his wrist was the crow. And not just its claws, but the entire bird, angled, angry, and clutching a two-headed snake in its beak. The same symbol from the demand letter.

Blake held back a gasp as her mind hurriedly replayed Rose's murder. The killer had been tall, lean. Nothing like this . . .

"Have you been looking for me?" he asked, keeping his eyes on the records.

There was no space in Blake's head for thinking, or in her heart for feeling anything other than terror and dread.

She twirled away, but before she could take a single step, the guy grabbed her from behind and placed one hand over her mouth while pinning her arms in place with the other.

"You're afraid," he said. "That's good."

Fear choked her as she twisted and writhed, trying to break free, but she was no match for the man's immense strength.

"There are more of us than you know," he whispered. His voice was so close to her ear that she could smell his sour breath. "A whole murder of us."

His thick chest was pressed against her back, allowing her to feel the chuckle rising there. This sick bastard was enjoying this. The man's hands clamped down harder, stealing every one of Blake's hard-earned breaths.

An intense buzzing rushed through Blake's body.

The music resounded with a painful, maddening rhythm. And all Blake could hear was *murder. Murder. Murder.*

The door flew open.

Ian.

He was running toward her. "Let her go!"

The guy jerked Blake back, away from Ian's reach. "I don't take orders from you."

Ian slowed his advance. His right hand was extended as he inched closer. He kept his left hand in his pants pocket. "You don't want to do this. Just let her go."

"See?" the guy said. "That's the problem. Bad advice. Everyone's always doling it out for free. But I want something of value." He tightened his grip on Blake.

The buzzing inside Blake grew more powerful. A feral energy began racing through her blood, coiling in her with a charged energy like wings beating against a cage.

The guy grunted, pressing his mouth closer to Blake's neck. "Your boyfriend doesn't look like someone you should trust."

Ian's face was solid granite, but his eyes... They told another story. Cold, calculating, angry. His hand flew from his pocket. Something whizzed through the air, a blade.

The guy screamed, releasing his hold on Blake. She ducked and pivoted out of his reach, watching in horror as he jerked the pocketknife out of his shoulder with a grunt.

There was a moment of rage, a flash of fists and jaws.

A sharp pain ripped through Blake's head. Everything was a blur. The man collapsed onto the ground. His head hit the floor with a loud thunk. Right next to the album she had dropped. Its pristine white jacket was now splattered with blood. Operating by pure instinct and adrenaline, she retrieved the record and stuffed it into her satchel just as Johnny came out looking dumbfounded. "Hey! What's going on here?"

Ian grabbed Blake's hand and dragged her out.

They bolted down the sidewalk. Rain pelted their every step.

A block later, Ian slowed his pace, glanced over his shoulder to make sure they weren't being followed, and pulled her under a small overhang. "Are you okay?" he panted. Blake couldn't read his eyes—was it fear she saw there? Dread? Rage? "Bloody Christ," he said. "Did you get hit? You're bleeding."

Blake didn't remember being hit, and at the moment she had enough adrenaline pumping through her blood that she didn't care. "I'm fine."

"I should have aimed higher," Ian spat.

"We need to get out of here!" Blake cried.

"The car is parked near the store, but I live just around the block," he said, tugging off his jacket and placing it over Blake's head. "We can figure everything out there."

Blake was already nodding when Ian took her hand, and together, they stepped back into the storm.

33

Ian's apartment was small, a tucked-away box perched on the first floor of a respectable-looking but damp building that smelled like it was growing mold beneath the floorboards.

The only furniture included a tattered sofa, a coffee table strewn with newspapers, Ian's guitar, and a console beneath the large bay window that bathed the room in a distant gray light. A tiny one-countertop kitchen peeked through an arch, and to the right was a narrow hall with a closed door at the end. The apartment looked like it couldn't decide if it was being moved into or out of, but one thing was certain—it didn't have the feeling of being lived in.

About the only sign of commitment was a small oval mirror and the black-and-white framed poster, both gracing an otherwise empty wall. Inside the frame was an image of a posed soccer team huddled on the field, hoisting a single player on their shoulders. The king was holding the prized trophy, a cup. In the crowd behind them, someone waved a sign with a logo of a bird perched inside a circle.

"That's the Royston Town Football Club," Ian said, like someone reaching for normal. "My favorite team."

Blake knew another message was hidden in those few words: *The team I dreamed of playing for.*

Studying Ian now, she realized he was unmarked. "You weren't hit?"

Ian shook his head.

"Where did you learn to throw a knife like that?" Blake's voice was more accusing than she intended.

"I spent a lot of time in summer camps," Ian said distractedly. "They taught us about knives and knots . . . and survival. You need some ice."

Blake reached up and touched her chin with a wince as Ian crossed to the kitchen, where he pulled an ice tray out of the freezer.

She went over to the mirror hanging on the wall and peered at the damage to her face. The cut was no bigger than an inch, but she could already see the strawberry-size lump growing beneath her skin.

Ian returned with ice wrapped in a towel. "I really hope I didn't do that to you."

"I got in the middle of the scuffle. I'm sure it wasn't you." Blake pressed the cloth to the wound, keeping her gaze on Ian. He looked lost, unfocused, torn between impossible choices. "You okay?" she asked softly.

"How about some tea?"

Ian began to turn, when Blake grabbed hold of his arm and said, "You're trembling."

He briefly lifted his hand as if he might move the stray curl out of Blake's face, or perhaps gently stroke her chin, but whatever he had intended to do, he changed his mind and dropped his hand quickly to his side. "I'm fine," he said, pulling free and returning to the kitchen.

Blake couldn't help but wonder if he was angry with her for putting him in that violent situation. He had agreed to help her blindly, to follow his nan's vision, but that didn't mean he was willing to risk his own safety for hers.

She suddenly felt like a stranger here. As if she had walked onto the stage of a play that she had no part in. A long and dark chill coursed through her, and she felt the need to do something, anything to keep from standing still.

Setting her purse on the sofa, she retrieved the album while Ian banged around the kitchen. The blood that was smeared across the rainbow fish turned her stomach as she walked to the credenza near the window. The rain had slowed to a gentle *tap tap tap*, trickling down the glass in tiny rivulets.

Blake lifted the record player's boxy lid, and just as she was about to remove the album from its cover, she spied something sticking out from a stack of records, something sickeningly familiar.

Fingers trembling, she tugged her sketch free. The one she had lost at Grayson's.

The Wolf. Her mouth went dry.

There was a moment, several breaths, and what felt like a thousand heartbeats during which Blake tried to make room for an explanation of why Ian had this sketch.

Just then the teakettle screamed, startling her.

She took a step back, thinking her legs would buckle as a realization slammed into her with such force that she nearly gasped.

Ian had been at Grayson's that night. It was Ian's eyes she had felt watching her.

Holding tight to the sheet, she tried to reach for a memory that might give her some answers, but Ian's footsteps told her he had already returned.

She spun to find him standing there. "Didn't mean to startle you." He was holding two teacups, one white, one pale green. "Blake? Is something wrong?"

Her pulse fluttered dangerously.

Ian's gaze followed hers to the sketch. She was waiting, hoping for the impossible, hoping for a believable tale. "I can explain," he said.

"Can you?" Blake finally inhaled.

Ian set the cups on the table.

"Do you care about me?" he asked.

She hadn't expected that.

"How did you get this?" Blake was still gripping the sketch, warring with all the lies. Layer upon layer of lies that had tipped the scales so far from the truth that she wasn't sure what was real anymore.

"We have something special, Blake, and . . . and before I tell you what I have to tell you, I need you to remember that."

She pleaded silently for all of what was happening now to be wrong, for Ian to be able to tell a story she could digest, one that would rewind time back to two minutes ago when they were . . .

something other than this. "You were there that night," Blake said, holding back the tremor in her voice. "You were . . . watching me."

"I was protecting you." He inched closer, watchful, like someone carefully approaching a viper.

Blake felt suddenly locked in the moment, torn between the fear rising inside her and Ian's claims of protection. Ian. The boy who had saved her from leaping off the pier, the boy who came from a family of magic, too. The boy who had saved her life just moments ago at the record store. He was here, standing right in front of her, and either lies or the truth were on the tip of his tongue.

"Please hear me out," he pleaded. "I have answers to all your questions." His eyes took on a deeper green tone, dark and endless. He inched closer.

Tipped his head lower.

And before she could blink, his lips met hers. His touch was both cool and fiery. Blake felt dizzy, lost in a place between everything and nothing.

There was no space between them, no air. Blake was spinning, lost, falling into a tight corner of Ian's memory that wanted to stay in the dark. Her body responded, pressing into him, shutting down the part of her mind that was screaming *No!*

But she needed to see. . . .

She deepened the kiss, searching his mind. And then she found what she was looking for.

Ian stands in this very spot. The cold sun is at his back, casting long shadows across the room. There is someone else here. Talking to Ian, nodding, listening. Blake expands the scene, desperate for another view....

There he is. The violent man from Johnny's Records.

Reality punched Blake in the gut, and in the span of a single breath, she broke free, shoving Ian back.

"I'm sorry," Ian groaned, clenching his jaw. He threaded his fingers through his hair. "I shouldn't have... It wasn't supposed to be like this."

A sense of dread fell over Blake. Tears stung her eyes. Inching back, she choked out, "You're one of them!"

Ian's face went pale.

She realized her mistake too late. Her accusation had given too much away. She darted for the door. Ian's hand shot out, taking hold of her. "You can't go," he said, his voice dark and distant. "Not with those shoes on your feet."

And with those words the facade crumbled.

Blake grabbed Ian's wrist. There was no crow tattoo.

"I didn't kill Rose," he said calmly.

"You're one of them." Blake's stomach roiled, and the shadows began to crawl as she made space in her mind for a horrific thought: *Ian is a crow. Ian is a crow!*

She jerked free and turned to go, only for him to block her path.

"Please, Blake. Trying to run will only make things worse."

Blake clenched her fists. "You knew that man in the record store."

"We'll get to that. But first . . ." He crossed the room and chained the door. "You need to hear me out."

Blake was unpracticed in this dance, but there was something bubbling inside her, an ancestral whisper guiding her. *Give nothing away.* Not even a flinch to tell him that the idea of his betrayal made her sick to her stomach. But she needed to know what he knew.

Blake couldn't find the words, couldn't bring herself to even try to pretend.

"Truth?" Ian said as the rain increased, leaving behind a gloom too heavy for even the sun to conquer.

"If you can manage," Blake spat.

"Please," Ian said, gesturing to the sofa. "Have a seat."

Blake swallowed her reluctance, forcing herself to sit and be an audience for someone she had cared about who now filled her only with hatred and horror.

"I didn't want it to be like this," Ian said, pacing before her. It didn't take long for him to spin a ridiculous tale about his boyhood in England, of the nanny, *not* nan, who raised him after his parents died when he was only eight, the nanny who filled his head with fantastical stories of magical and powerful objects. "Then one day, two years ago, the woman who raised me, Margaret, she vanished," he said. "The last I heard she was with some family, a man and a woman, but the trail ended there."

Blake's forehead bunched into a tight frown. *How could some nanny know anything about my family? About our secrets?* Her blood pulsed with panic and disbelief. But she had to focus, to concentrate on Ian's words, to show her interest. To keep him calm. Then what? Those two words raced to the beat of her heart.

Then what. Then what. Then what.

Ian continued: "It was a really tough time. Remember when I told you I wanted to be a pro football player? How I got injured?"

"What does that have to do with—"

"I needed Margaret to tell me where to find the magic. I thought maybe it could help me."

"My shoes..." Blake faltered, regained her composure. "They can't help you, Ian."

His cold eyes pinned Blake to the sofa. "Maybe not to play football, but like I said, I replaced that dream with a bigger one."

It hurt like hell to talk to Ian, to look at him. But all Blake cared about now was getting to the truth. All of it. "Then why do you want the shoes?"

"It's not just me, Blake. There are others now."

Blake gripped the edge of the sofa. "The crows."

"We prefer Corvus," Ian said proudly. "It's Latin for crow.

Seeing that the Order of the Corvus and I had the same goal, which was to track down magical artifacts, they recruited me. And then there was the mascot of my favorite football team."

Blake must have looked like she wasn't following because Ian clarified: "The crow, Blake. The order's mascot is a crow. It was a sign. I was meant to join the Corvus."

Magical artifacts? Was that how he had ended up with the ribbon?

"Why, Ian?" Blake felt like she was dragging the words from her mouth one at a time. "Just for . . . magic?"

Ian's expression tightened. "Do you really think it's fair that some people get magic and others don't? That my parents died, that I got injured so I could never do the one thing I'd wanted to do my whole life?" He shook his head. "Magic makes for an uneven playing field, Blake. The Corvus welcomed me with open arms, and it was time I took some power back."

She realized how different two paths could be. *I got Remi and Cole. Ian got the Corvus.* "Who are they?"

Ian hesitated, then, after a long inhalation, he said, "We have operated in secret for over two centuries, originating when saints, mystics, sorcerers, and healers began to rise up with their tales of miracles and magic. It disrupted the balance of things, the structures that had been in place since the beginning." His voice rose with an eagerness that Blake wanted to suffocate.

"So, your mission is to destroy magical artifacts?" Blake said, realizing with a sinking feeling how wrong she and her family had been to believe someone wanted only to take the objects' power. "Then why not just steal my shoes?" she asked. "Why go to all this trouble?"

Ian nearly smiled, tucking the expression away at the last moment. "We want more than the shoes, Blake. And what better way to get my hands on the mirror than to be part of the very search to find it?"

Blake was shaking now. "Except I don't know where it is!"

"I understand." Ian's voice was calm. "But there are other things I want."

A thick silence hung in the air.

Ian said, "One is to determine who's been following you."

"What?" Blake balked. What kind of game was Ian playing? "The crows are following me."

"The man from the Palace doesn't work for us. And the woman from the school? Impossible. No women are permitted to become members of Corvus. So, who are they?"

"I have no idea," Blake hissed. Then, feeling emboldened by

her anger, she added, "But the better question is who was the guy from Johnny's?"

"Ned? He doesn't know how to follow directions."

"Which were?"

"He was supposed to scare you. Make you think he was following you," he said, pacing. "He was never supposed to touch you."

"Why now? Why today?"

"Your visions were bringing you too close to my true purpose, and given what happened at the tower—"

Blake felt as if someone had set a match to every nerve in her body.

"You mean the drawing I made?" She suddenly realized that her magic had been warning her, telling her that she was standing right next to the crow, and she hadn't seen it. Rose's warning from Blake's vision of the tower flew back to her: *The crows are here. Here. Here.* She had meant the crows would be at the tower!

Ian ran a hand through his hair. "Let's just say it was proof that I had to expedite the plan. Well, that coupled with you seeing Rose's murder and the man with the tattoo. I knew it was only a matter of time before you had a vision of who I was and why I'm really here. It was too risky. When you said you'd seen me as a kid on the dock, that's when I knew I had made the right decision to accelerate things. So here we are."

He stopped, turned his eyes on Blake. "I care about you. Please, try to see things my way. Look at all the damage magic can do. You've said so yourself. Let me help you. I can destroy the mirror, and you will never have to worry again about magic."

His twisted logic almost made sense, or maybe Blake's heart just needed it to.

"You're a liar and a thief," Blake said, each word puncturing her own heart.

Ian looked wounded, but how could he have thought this would turn out any differently?

Blake glanced down at the shoes, realizing the Ian she knew was a figment of her imagination, a character he played to get exactly what he wanted. There was no nan, no line of magic—only the dotted one he had followed here. He had ingratiated himself with her, gotten her to trust him, to invite him into her life and into her quest. Inhaling slowly, she forced out, "You said... destroying the magical artifacts is only part of what Corvus does."

"Blake, listen." He sat on the sofa next to her. His nearness made her skin crawl, but she couldn't recoil and risk provoking him. She squeezed her hands together until the bones ached. "You can get rid of your magic for good," he said. "Don't you want to live a normal life?"

"Get rid of the shoes, you mean."

"That's a given. What I'm talking about is so much bigger." Ian's voice was high and animated. "We have new ways, scientific ways, of extracting all this unnatural power from you. It's mostly painless, and I would be there for you, helping you through all of it." There was a cold pause before he added, "And you could be a great artist, famous. I could make sure that happened."

The shock of his words cut Blake to her core. *Unnatural? Extract?* And was he really using her art to lure her into his twisted scheme? *My God, he is insane.* What he failed to realize was that Blake's magic and her art were inextricably linked. But how could she explain that to someone who had so little regard for the truth of magic? It took everything in her to keep her distress from showing. She had to appear logical, reasonable, and above all else interested in Ian's sick and twisted ideas.

A dozen scenarios, all revolting, played out in Blake's mind as she tried to process each piece of the truth. Ian was a traitor. The crows stole magic, from things and people. God, how many people had been through the extraction? And then there was the last bit Blake still didn't know. "I . . . I can't even think about any of that until I know who killed Rose."

"I'm not a murderer."

"But someone in your order is." Blake dropped her head and

closed her eyes. There, in her mind's eyes, she saw the ugly truth. Ian had been the one to drop her off at the center. She had been stupid enough to tell him she was going there for a message, and to tell him what the message said afterward. He was the reason Rose had died, and that made him a murderer even if he wasn't the one who had stolen her last breath. "You pulled the fire alarm."

Ian said nothing.

A slow buzzing radiated through Blake's body, traveled up her legs, across her chest, and toward her spine. It pulsed with terror and desire and power. "So, this is the real you," she said. "The real Ian." Not the masked liar.

Ian reached out and took hold of her hand. "Please, Blake. We can be happy. We can be together."

"I will never choose you," she growled, shoving his hand away. She could no longer put on an act. She knew now that Ian had no intention of letting her leave, or letting her keep her magic.

The sky had darkened to a black canvas.

"Maybe not," he said scornfully. "But I have a job to do, and nothing is going to get in the way of that." His expression hardened. He stood and leaned against the wall. "The others are going to arrive soon. You can either go willingly or fight a war. Either way, you'll never win."

The feral energy was racing through her now, quick and furious.

"Give me the shoes, Blake." His voice was so even, so calculating and controlled, like someone who was barely keeping himself from an outburst of violence. It scared her worse than if he had been screaming at her.

She forced herself to look into his eyes. The magic pulsed in her legs, coiling tight. The walls were closing in. "I can't do that," she managed.

Ian dropped his head with an expression that was a mixture of regret and sorrow. When he looked back up, his eyes held nothing but chilled desire. "Then I'll have to take them from you."

He came at her, all hands and greed.

Everything shrank down to a single action, a single thought as natural as breathing. Her dad's voice echoed all around her.

Set the magic free.

The power rose in her dizzyingly fast. Instinctively, Blake threw her arms out to defend herself. But before they connected with him, Ian was suddenly knocked off his feet, like an invisible hand had plucked him from the earth and catapulted him into the air. He slammed against the wall with a loud thump, knocking the football poster down. Glass shattered. His body slumped to the floor.

The space was nothing but breath and pulse. Hurried and expectant. Chest heaving, Blake stood over Ian's weakening form. His forehead had a nasty gash, but the bastard was breathing.

Someone began to pound on the door.

Blake rushed to the window. The lock had been painted over, making the window unopenable.

"Ian?" a man's voice called out. "All okay in there?"

Blake reached for the heat simmering in her core. For the magic that came from a primal place, a place of longing and pain, a place of loss and betrayal and endless lies.

The lights flickered once, then plunged the apartment into utter darkness.

Pressing her hand against the chilled glass, she let the magic rise. And rise . . .

The window split like ice and then it shattered.

Gasping for air, Blake launched herself through the opening in what felt like a single motion. She was running.

Running. Running.

And then came a new voice, very deep and rough as granite. "Blake!"

Blake didn't stop. Didn't turn.

Quick, furious gasps . . . legs churning . . . faster, faster through the dark.

"BLAKE!"

This time a familiar voice. Something inside Blake gave way. A great rush of shock. The magic bristled, barely contained. She halted. Right there under the faded glow of a streetlamp. She spun.

The relief came first, slow and steady and overwhelming, waves of it, accosting her senses.

"Olivia?" Blake's voice came out raspy. "What are you . . ." The reality of the last few moments flew at her with a vengeance, reigniting her flight response. "We have to go! Ian . . . he . . ."

"I know," Olivia said, arms outstretched as if she were ready to catch Blake if she fell. "We've been looking for you."

We?

Just then a figure emerged from the shadows. A tall, lanky man not much older than Cole. "Where is Ian?" he said with a British accent.

"Who are you?" Blake said.

A flicker of surprise registered in his blue eyes. Then he cast his gaze over Blake's shoulder before returning his attention to her. "We can explain everything, but we need to get off the street."

"You can trust him," Olivia said gently. "He saved my life. And there is so much to tell you, but right now we have to go."

Blake felt the urge to run again, to burn all the poison that was Ian from her lungs and mind and heart. He wanted the shoes and the mirror, and the very magic pulsing in her veins. Magic that could destroy and hurt. The image of Ian being thrust across the room was burned like the sun against her eyes. She had trusted him, let him into her life. Everything he had told her was a lie. But Olivia wasn't Ian.

"I hurt him, Liv," Blake admitted as Olivia rubbed her shoulder and said, "That's good. Now come on."

Half a minute later, the trio made the quick trip down the block, back to the record shop, which, quiet and empty, showed no signs of what had happened in it earlier. Blake stared at the rainbow fish gleaming on the door, her heart racing. Then Olivia led her across the street, up a short flight of steps, and into a warm, welcoming home that smelled of eucalyptus and peppermint. Olivia took Blake through the dim entry into a rose-colored sitting room where a fire was dying in the stone hearth. The girls sat on a sofa near the dwindling flames as the man closed the drapes.

"What's going on, Liv?" Blake said shakily.

Just then, two women walked in. The first was a short, elderly woman carrying with her the scent of fresh-brewed coffee. The other looked a few years older than Remi, judging by the faint wrinkles sprouting around her blue eyes. "My dear," she said, "what an ordeal you must have been through."

Blake's hands were clenched at her sides, but her voice was steady and measured. Her head throbbed. "Who are you?"

"I'm Judith," the younger woman said. "We're . . . family."

"And I'm her brother, Henry," the man put in. "This is our mother, Margaret."

Margaret's hands trembled as she cast her gaze to the plush rug. "I was Ian's nanny."

The last I heard she was with some family, a man and a woman, but the trail ended there.

So Ian had spoken some truths, Blake thought.

"You left him," Blake said, before she realized her tone sounded accusing.

Margaret shook her head. "He changed after the injury, pushed me away. I asked him to come with me to the US, but he refused. He said he was going to find even more powerful magic than mine."

Huh. In the end Ian had abandoned her, Blake thought, finally allowing the gravity of the last fifteen minutes to sink in a bit further. Margaret, Ian's nanny, was part of Blake's family?

As if anticipating Blake's next question, Margaret said, "I'm your grandmother's cousin, but I never knew her." For the first time the woman smiled, making her small, round eyes nearly disappear. "Although I have read about her incredible musical talents."

Blake folded herself into the moment, tight and guarded, but as Judith and Henry told their story, she found herself unfolding. Yielding to their words, to the inescapable truth that bad luck had plagued their lives just as it had plagued Blake's. They used words like *descendants, broken promises, tragedy,* and *old magic*. A few minutes later Blake learned that the three of them had come all the way from England in search of the mirror.

"To break the curse," Blake said, remembering the question she had put to Remi about other family members being affected by the curse.

"A curse perpetuated by broken promises," Henry said.

Judith sighed. "We had no idea that Ian was dangerous. That he had become a part of the Order of the Corvus."

"You know about the society," Blake said, more as a statement than a question.

Henry added a few pieces of kindling to the waning fire. "We have been trying to reach you for weeks."

"But something was blocking us," Judith said.

Blake stared into the flames, lifting her gaze as the realization hit. "You . . . were the woman at my school. You were frightening and . . . and you," she said, turning her attention to Henry. "You were the man at the Palace of Fine Arts." She gave the siblings a long, hard look. "But wait . . . you didn't look like you do now. You looked scary."

Judith pulled up a chair and eased herself into it like someone preparing for a long read. "Magic is a capricious beast, Blake."

"It felt as if the magic was putting a veil over your eyes," Henry ruminated.

A long exhale from Olivia and then, in a stunned voice: "It was the protection spell," she said. "It must have kept you from seeing what was real or something."

The words echoed a truth that settled like a stone in Blake's chest. She reached back, back to the night her magic was bound. Back to the warning her grandmother had given.

In binding her magic, she will be shielded from any powerful magic in her path. She will not recognize it. Instead she will fear it.

But that fear hasn't protected me, Blake thought bitterly. *It has only tangled the threads of truth.*

Everyone's eyes were pinned to Blake, and when she finally spoke, she repeated her abuela's words. She groaned in frustration. "I must only be able to feel Remi's magic because it isn't very powerful."

"Then this spell . . ." Margaret rasped before choking out a couple of rattling coughs. Judith began to rise, but Margaret held her hand out to stop her. "Can't an old woman cough?" she grumbled. "I'm fine. We must continue." Her milky eyes shifted to Blake. "This spell must no longer hold power over you if you see us for what we are."

Instinctively, Blake knew Margaret was right about the binding spell being broken. And undoing her abuela's work had nothing to do with removing the St. Christopher medal and everything to do with the magic Blake was born with, blood magic. Magic that, no matter what, would rise, spread, and adapt. She found herself nodding.

"I felt it at Ian's," Blake said. "I lifted my hands, and without my touching him, he was thrown against a wall. It was like . . . like the magic knew I needed it to survive."

Stroking his whiskery chin, Henry said, "Magic is often responsive. To hate, to fear, to love . . ." He trailed off.

"To danger," Blake added.

"And where is the skuzz bucket now?" Olivia said, speaking of Ian. "I hope your magic pummeled him."

"He was unconscious when I ran." Blake shared what Ian had told her, including his "extraction" ideas. For a few long seconds, no one spoke.

"Do you think he has already reported to Corvus?" Judith asked Henry.

"He'll likely nurse his wounds awhile," Margaret chimed in. "That boy is too arrogant and too proud to admit failure. No," she said with a shake of her head, "Ian will concoct another plan, one in which he doesn't play the fool."

I'm *the fool,* Blake thought. *I was so stupid to ever trust him. To not* see *the truth right in front of me.* Layer upon layer of anger buried the painful sense of betrayal shredding her insides. Deep down, she knew she would have to deal with whatever backup plans Ian was making, but right now, she needed more answers. She turned to Olivia. "You said Henry saved your life."

Olivia tipped her face toward the fire. "I had just gotten to the tower when I saw Ian talking to some slimy older guy," she said. "Ian didn't look like himself. He looked mad and it gave me bad vibes, so I followed them to the back of the tower and eavesdropped. I couldn't believe it, Blake. They were talking about the mirror!"

"Then what happened?" Blake prodded, not sure she wanted to know.

"When Ian caught me spying," Olivia said, "he looked petrifying. I took off to find you, to tell you the guy is a fraud, but his slimy friend caught me." She wrapped her arms around herself and shook her head. "I knew I shouldn't have worn heels."

Given what happened at the tower. So that was what Ian had meant.

Olivia went on: "Anyhow, I kicked the guy in the nuts right before he knocked me out."

"He knocked you out?!" Blake was on her feet now.

"It's just a bump," Olivia said casually.

"We've checked her out," Judith added, as if that made any of this okay.

"And think of the stories I can tell my grandchildren." A smile played on Olivia's lips, but Blake saw a flicker of leftover fear there that no smile was big enough to hide.

"It's just lucky I found her," Henry said. "The Corvus are pitiless monsters, hiding behind a false mission of goodness and truth."

Blake resisted the urge to throw her arms around Henry's neck and thank him profusely for saving her best friend's life. Instead, she said, "It was you. . . . I heard you calling my name at the palace and in the park."

Henry nodded. "When I saw you with Ian, he looked familiar. I thought perhaps I was mistaken, but Margaret had a boyhood photo of him and the likeness was too striking to ignore. When you didn't respond, I followed you to the tower to make sure you would be safe."

Margaret was still wringing her hands. Her face was twisted into a pained expression. "It's my fault. I should never have told Ian of the magic. But he was such a sad and lost boy. His father was always working, leaving me to raise the poor child. I was only trying to give him hope."

"You mean his dad is alive?" Blake said. "He told me both his parents were dead."

Margaret pressed her lips together in a tight line. "His father died last year. Ian didn't attend the funeral."

Judith put an arm around her mother's shoulders. "You couldn't have known Corvus would recruit him, that he was capable of such deception."

"Or that he would follow our trail to you, Blake," Henry said, so low Blake had to strain to hear him. "We are immensely sorry for that."

There would be time for apologies later. So many apologies for lies, secrets, stupid choices. "You said you came all the way from England," Blake said. "How did you know I was here in San Francisco?"

"Old family records," Judith said. "And when we arrived, it wasn't hard to locate and follow the trail of magic. That's how we found you outside just now. Henry sensed you were nearby."

Magic attracts magic.

"Is that your power?" Blake asked. "Tracking?"

"Among other things," Henry said.

Judith folded her arms across her chest. "We both have the power of disguise."

"Like Zora," Blake whispered as she leaned closer to the hearth. Looking back to Judith and Henry, she said, "You mentioned that you couldn't communicate with me, but why not go to Remi or Cole?"

Margaret sighed, sinking into the sofa next to Olivia. "We weren't sure you knew of the mirror or the curse, and the last thing we wanted to do was invite bad luck into your lives, or to instill this dreadful fear . . . so we waited."

"And we watched," Judith said.

"It wasn't until today," Henry offered, "that we realized you were looking for the mirror."

A pause.

Olivia exhaled, stood, and looked Blake in the eye. "I told them."

"It's remarkable that your visions were trying to lead you to it," Margaret said.

Blake shook her head. "But they didn't. The heart led me to the truth about my magic. The crown led me to Gayle and the flowers, but that was a dead end. And the tower . . ." She described how her ability to create art felt like it was returning, thawing after a freeze. That she had painted the wolf and the crow, as well as her dreams and her belief that she herself was the wolf. "I think my magic was trying to warn me, to tell me Ian was the crow. But I didn't see it . . . not until it was too late."

"Or maybe your heart just didn't want to see it," Olivia said softly.

"But what about the fish?" Blake wondered aloud. "Why would that lead me to danger?" She explained what had happened at Johnny's Records.

"The fish," Judith said, "maybe it was leading you here to Haight-Ashbury, to us. Don't you see? You thought the visions, the symbols, were all about the mirror when really they were all different pieces of information or warnings."

Blake stared down at the woven rug. She watched as the geometric designs blurred in and out of focus. She considered, rejected, then reconsidered. Far-fetched ideas raced through her, trying to fill in the blanks. Trying to connect the dots.

"Why does magic have to be so unclear, so fragmented?" she asked.

"Because your magic is unpracticed," Margaret put in.

Just then a rapid two-pulse breath swept across Blake's cheek. Her hand went to her face. Another breath and another and another.

Something was wrong with Remi.

Heat rippled the air around Blake.

And then the sickening realization. She had left her purse at Ian's. Inside was her identification with her address.

Ian will concoct another plan, one where he doesn't play the fool.

Blake bolted for the door, knowing before she reached it, knowing with anguished certainty that she was already too late.

There was no air.

No sky or moon or city. Only blurred lights whizzing past the car window as Henry raced over the hills.

Inside Blake, the magic swelled. Barely leashed. Like it wanted to claw its way out.

Finally, Oakwood Street.

The house, its windows brightly lit, gave Blake hope that she was wrong. That Remi was only asking her to hurry home so she didn't miss Rose's celebration. But the moment Blake crossed the threshold, that hope died. Only devastation welcomed her.

In the living room, chairs were turned over, lamps tipped onto their sides, framed photos of Rose smashed, and glass strewn everywhere. And then there was the blood—drops of it mixed with the shock and despair heavy in the air.

A guttural sob escaped Olivia. But Henry... he was tiptoeing through the wreckage like a trained soldier preparing to meet the enemy face-to-face. "We need to call the police," he was saying. "Don't touch anything." But Blake had stopped listening. She knew this was beyond the authorities' grasp. This was a game of cat and mouse. She had hurt Ian and now he wanted to hurt her.

She knew better than to call out for her aunt and uncle. They weren't here. She had felt the void of their absence the moment she entered the house.

Desperate as she was for clues, Blake's hands were reaching, touching, sensing, searching for a memory, but finding only the deep, shadowy waters of her dreams. She tried again. She searched for a slant of sunlight, for the taste of sugar, for warmth against her flesh, but she was spent, emptied. Dreamless.

She crossed to the dining room. The scene here was the same, in shambles. Plates and glasses were shattered. The crystal vase of pink roses was tipped over, dripping water over the edge of the table into a puddle on the floor.

The scene carried with it the certainty of suffering, of loss, of death.

"My God!" Olivia cried.

Blake followed her gaze to the corner, to where a trail of ashes swirled around the copper urn. Rose's urn. Was nothing sacred?

A book lay in the mess. The same one Ian had been reading the day she met him at Dolores Park. There was a piece of paper poking out.

Sickened, Blake forced herself to go over and take hold of the letter, quickly reading it out loud.

"'When you have the mirror, find me.'"

Blake's eyes alighted on the pages where the letter had been stashed. Ian had underlined the first stanza of a poem titled "Poison Tree":

I was angry with my friend;
I told my wrath, my wrath did end.
I was angry with my foe;
I told it not, my wrath did grow.

The world echoed with silence.

Blake fell, got up, fell again.

Olivia was there, hooking her arms under Blake's, dragging her to her feet.

Until there is nothing left.

Sometimes that's all there is. *Nothing.*

But Blake held to a scrap, to the last promise she could keep. Even if her family was gone, even if Rose was dead, she could still find the mirror and break the curse.

Rage and despair and horror throbbed in her muscles and blood and bones. There was no space to think, to wonder. Only instinct and rage fueled her now.

Drove her to put one foot in front of the other.

"Blake," Olivia cried, "where are you going?"

"Stay here!" Blake ordered as she hurried to the backyard. The garden lights were lit; the once bright and vibrant garden was the place intended for Rose's ashes.

"I know you're here," she whispered as she scanned every inch of the garden. Walked each winding path. Got on her hands and knees, groping at the limbs and tangled branches of ground cover plants, at the shrubs, and blooms. She would rip this garden to shreds, uproot every living thing until she found the flowers she knew were here, somewhere.

The starflowers—they were the last clue she could follow, the last clue to lead to what she needed to find.

Blake let her eyes go just out of focus, until the only thing in her line of sight was the grand beech tree.

Nimbly, she hoisted herself into the tree, climbed its long, thick limbs. Higher and higher until there was nowhere left to climb. She cast her gaze across the yard, across the garden Cole had tended so lovingly, across to the tulips Remi had planted that would bloom in the coming weeks.

Wiping away hot tears, she drew her magic to the surface, hoping it would connect her to her ancestors, to their strength. To a memory this tree had to have witnessed.

A slow and steady vibration began beneath the branch, channeling into Blake. She could feel its energy waking to the full power of her magic.

And then, slowly, the garden and all its colors began to slide away like paint dripping down a canvas. Red was gray, and blue and black and pink were white.

Blake blinked, sucked in a sharp breath that burned her lungs. But the world was still nothing more than black and white.

Leaning against the branch, Blake cast her gaze across the colorless garden. What once had pulsed with life and color was now nothing more than gray, gray, and more gray. On her next sweep, Blake let her eyes slide over the garden more slowly. Over the wide blooms, and luscious petals, across the juniper and the lilacs. Until she hit a snag.

There, beneath the stone bench, a vibrant circle of gold flowers, the only color in the garden, shimmering as if the moon had cast a spotlight on the blooms.

Blake was on the ground in seconds. Reaching beneath the bench, she saw that at the center of the flowers was a single white bloom. She plucked it from the earth and brought it out into the light. The starflower, a cluster of tiny delicate petals just like in her dreams. Quickly, Blake fetched a hand shovel from Cole's greenhouse and began digging. Deeper and deeper, plunging the little shovel into the earth.

Clink.

Blake felt the blood leave her face.

She rammed the shovel into the ground again.

Clink.

Throwing the tool over her shoulder, she tunneled into the soil with her bare hands. And then she felt something cold, solid, and pulsing with magic. Heat ran through her fingers and up her arm like a bolt of electricity, nearly causing Blake to let go.

With a deep breath, she gripped harder and tugged the mirror free. Then, wiping the glass with her sleeve, she held it up to one of the yard lights. The frame was an intricate filigree of burnished gold.

Barely breathing, Blake traced her fingers over it, searching for a memory. The image crept over her slowly and in glorious color. A verdant forest, dense with shade. And in a golden shaft of sunlight was a coffin made of glass, splintered with tiny fissures, like a prism or a diamond. There was no mistaking the girl inside, the same one Blake had seen in her visions. But now she was resting peacefully on a bed of lavender velvet, and in her hair was a delicate crown made of the starflowers.

It's you, Blake thought just as a small boy emerged from the woods. He draped his body over the coffin, heaving with misery.

Blake found herself reaching for him, but the image spiraled out of her reach, vanishing into the dark.

Now the mirror pulsed with light.

Blake peered into the glass, expecting to see her own reflection. But the only thing she saw was an image of the girl's gaze staring up at her. The girl blinked, eyes widening as she searched Blake's face.

Heat coursed through the mirror.

"Tell me how to set you free," Blake said.

Silence hung there in the air.

Then, as if coming to a horrific realization, the girl shook her head back and forth, back and forth. Tears trailed down her cheeks. She opened her mouth.

There was no sound.

Only a silent scream.

The End

EPILOGUE

SEPTEMBER 16, 1968
VASSAR COLLEGE

This marks my nine hundredth journal entry. It's ironic for someone who once hated words, but now they are a sort of escape, a way to make sense of a crazy world that seems to be filled with greater and greater dangers. Sometimes I think the darkness is so thick, there will never be light again. Martin Luther King Jr. was assassinated in April, followed by Robert Kennedy in June. Our country is at war. There are civil-rights and human-rights demonstrations every day, violence is escalating, and . . . I am no closer to finding out what happened to Remi or Cole than I was a few years ago.

still cling to the hope that they are alive, but after all this time, I think maybe it's a foolish dream.

Still, I'll never give up. I see now that the fish led me to Judith and Henry, a family I didn't know I would need until I lost Remi and Cole. But the magic knew. It always knows.

With Judith's and Henry's help, I've spent years along with Margaret looking for Ian, searching for stories about accounts of magic, or the Order of the Corvus, but every lead has just been a dead end. I sometimes wonder why Ian never came back to the city to retrieve his precious prize. Maybe he thought this was a greater way to punish me. ~~*Or maybe he knew I might kill him.*~~

I didn't sleep last night. Actually, I don't sleep much most nights. I end up lying awake thinking of the horrors from more than three years ago. I relive the nightmare over and over and over, trying to find something I could have done differently, trying to find a clue I missed even after we combed through the house. The police gave up searching for Remi and Cole after only one month: an unsolved missing persons case, they called it. Olivia called it preposterous. She's the only family I have left, at least from before the curse. And while she's in school at Wellesley, we talk every week and exchange letters. Lately, she hasn't brought up the magic or the memories, and to be honest, I'm kind of glad. I already have enough reminders of them.

I see now that the only reason I found the starflower, and the mirror, was because I had finally come into my full magic. I could see what Cole and Remi and no one else could see. In the end, finding the mirror was about discovering my power, about calling the magic up, giving it breath and life.

There was a time when I didn't look into the mirror anymore. Each time I did, the girl only screamed as if she didn't remember all the times before, and it seemed cruel to keep putting her through that pain, especially because I don't know how to set her free. I've never seen what the mirror can do, or the powers Remi talked about.

Blake set the pen on the desk and looked up at the page pinned to her wall. She had torn it from Ian's book and kept it close as a reminder. Now she took it down, studying the words.

I was angry with my friend;
I told my wrath, my wrath did end.
I was angry with my foe;
I told it not, my wrath did grow.

And I watered it in fears,
Night and morning with my tears;
And I sunned it with smiles,
And with soft deceitful wiles.

Every day, Blake dragged her pen under the most importan words.

And it grew both day and night,
Till it bore an apple bright;
And my foe beheld it shine,
And he knew that it was mine,

And into my garden stole,
When the night had veil'd the pole:
In the morning glad I see
My foe outstretched beneath the tree.

This was her promise to Ian.

She set the poem aside and gazed at the wall of small paintings.

Each was part of a trail of healing and memories: the tree, the seeing heart, the tower, the starflowers, and the faces of Remi and Cole and Rose. Ms. Ivanov's was the first gallery to carry Blake's artwork, but the faces? Those were priceless, never to be sold.

Blake's gaze fell to the picture of her mom, the same one Rose had given her for her eighteenth birthday. The St. Christopher necklace her dad had given her hung over the frame. She couldn't bring herself to wear it, but she kept it close, as a reminder of his love. With her free hand, she traced the frame's edges as a small smile tugged at her lips.

And then came the waft of air, sweeping past her cheek, light as a barely-there breath.

Blake froze. Everything went still.

A moment passed. And then another. Tears filled her eyes.

There it was again. A single gentle caress. *I love you.*

Blake touched her cheek softly, pressing her fingers into the warmth, into the unmistakable message.

Remi was alive.

ACKNOWLEDGMENTS

Every book changes you as a writer in some way. This book pushed me into new territory, into places I wasn't sure I could go in both mind and heart; I was surprised at every turn, and I have so many people to thank for the journey.

I'm a believer in magic, and my agent, Holly Root, has it in spades. I am so appreciative of your unwavering belief in me and the stories I want to tell.

Kieran Scott: Who could have known that a trip for beignets in the Big Easy could have been so serendipitous? An enormous thank-you for your infectious excitement for this project and for asking me to join you and the team on this wild ride. To my luminous editor, Britt Rubiano, thank you for your creativity, your wit, and your endless positivity.

There are so many unsung heroes in the bookmaking process, and the team that made this one happen from words to cover and beyond is exceptional in every way. Heartfelt thanks to Sara Liebling, Marci Senders, Jonathan Bartlett, Guy Cunningham Martin Karlow, Meredith Jones, and Dan Kaufman. And to Seale Ballenger—you carry grace by the armful.

To the "Mirror ladies" Julie Dao, Dhonielle Clayton, and L. L. McKinney: Your talent and creativity are inspiring!

Every writer needs early readers, to tell us when we've hit the mark and when we've gone over the edge. Janet Fox, thanks fo giving both in equal measure. For AMC—there are no words fo your brilliance. For Sarah Simpson-Weiss—you keep me afloat Thanks for bringing the life jacket every single day with kindnes and humor.

For my family: There are no words for how much I love you and how much I appreciate the very air you breathe. Thank you fo putting up with me and the repeated message, "I've got an idea. For Mom, you loved every iteration of this book, and saw the magi before I did.

And to readers, librarians, teachers, and creators: Thank you Thank you. Thank you. Without your support we would all be los in a story-less world.

AGNES'S FAMILY

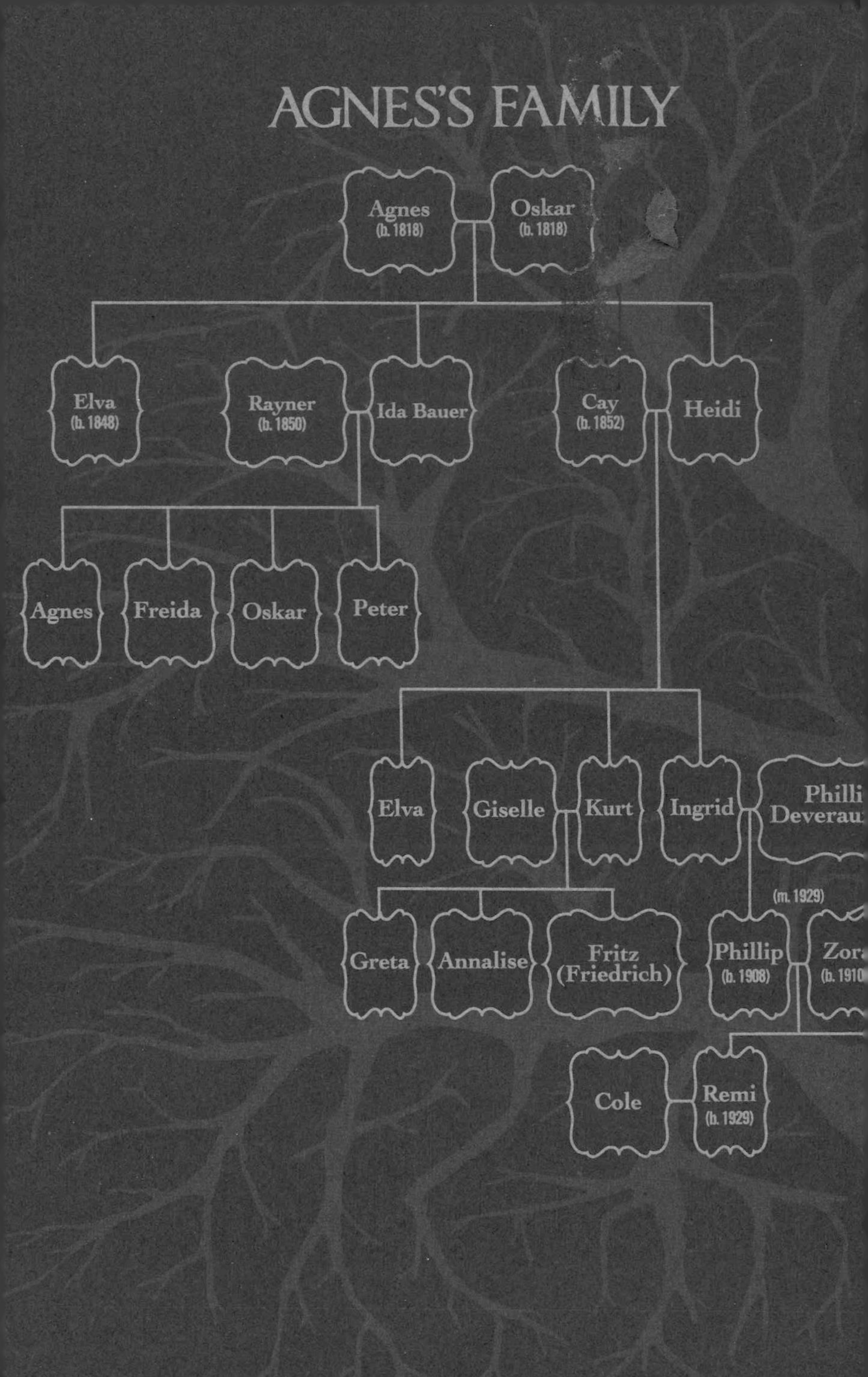